THE PRIEST AND THE FRIAR . . .

"What will you be doing when we get among the Flavian worlds?"

"Why, Father," stammered the friar, "I hardly know. This is my first mission. I suppose I will have to begin proselytizing on my own, among the poor."

"On your own? In the most corrupt sector we have ever come across? You were shocked by what you saw on Gravitas, and that was just a training school for priests. Have you ever seen men fight to the death for the amusement of cheering crowds?"

The friar shuddered.

"You will be hard enough put to find salvation for our own soul in all that, much less redeem the sinners. I shall pray for you, Friar. No wonder the Franciscan casualty rates are so high.

"Mark this, my boy: A ruling class that lives by exploitation lives in terror. If they think there is new thought stirring among the masses they will react with hysterical brutality. Save your gentle preaching for the nice planets. The brutal empires, such as we are headed for, require quick surgery at the top."

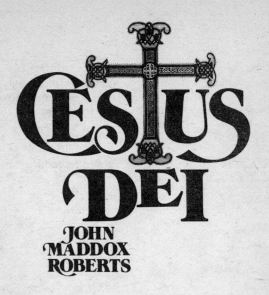

CESTUS DEI

JOHN MADDOX ROBERTS

A JIM BAEN PRESENTATION

TOR

A TOM DOHERTY ASSOCIATES BOOK

A TOR Book

Published by:
Tom Doherty Associates, Inc.
8-10 West 36th Street,
New York, New York 10018

First TOR printing, June 1983

ISBN: 48-584-0

Cover art by Kevin Eugene Johnson

Acknowledgements:
Part of this novel was published separately, in substan-
tially different form as *The Strayed Sheep of Charun,*
copyright © 1977 by John Maddox Roberts.

Printed in the United States of America

Distributed by:
Pinnacle Books
1430 Broadway
New York, New York 10018

I

Archbishop Hilarion occupied his rightful seat in the Great Hall of United Faiths with the stoicism of many years of experience. On the floor, a minor imam of some obscure Islamic sect was droning a speech welcoming the new representative from Shriva, which, despite its name, was a planet settled entirely by Mormons. The archbishop yawned expertly, without moving a muscle of his face.

The real business of the day would not begin for some hours. It would be the knotty question of which among the great faiths had right of control over the Magsaysay System, a complex of more than two hundred rich planets settled two millennia before by colonists of every faith known to mankind. The debate had been raging for fifty years and was at last heading toward some sort of resolution, a resolution toward which Hilarion had been planning for the quarter century since his predecessor had passed the problem on

to him. Hilarion looked forward to an eminently
satisfactory conclusion. It was with some compla-
cency that the archbishop surveyed his colleagues of
the United Faiths, the most powerful assembly of
humanity since the Great Decadence.

The first impression a visitor or pilgrim had of the
Great Hall was of size, the second of color. The oval
amphitheater of seats ascended one hundred meters
to the edge of the Dome of Tcherbadayev, the faerie
structure that symbolized peace and a sort of quali-
fied brotherhood to all, or nearly all, of rediscovered
humanity. Within this huge covered cup sat the
concentrated sanctity of this world, which still held
all the holiest places of the human race. The saffron
robes of the Buddhist monks glowed brightly among
the emerald turbans of the Imams of the Medina
Caliphate. The breastplates of the priests of the Third
Temple glittered in sharp contrast to the somber colors of the various orders of the Re-established Church
of Rome. The habits of a dozen minor faiths added a
rainbow sprinkling to the whole. The ascetics of the
loose Hindu Oneness added no color. They wore only
loincloths, and those only out of deference to the sen-
sibilities of the other faiths. The Hindus displayed
solely the warm tones of brown flesh, the common
denominator of earthborn humanity these days. Only
out among the stars were to be found the variety of
racial traits that had once been a part of the wealth
of humanity.

It was unusual for Archbishop Hilarion to occupy
his seat so early in the day, and the seats around him
buzzed with discreet speculation as to what business
the eminent Vatican authority on strayed sheep affairs had with the Inner Council today. That business
resided in the bishop's briefcase. It was not one of the
great problems of his office, like the Magsaysay con-
troversy, but it concerned strayed sheep and the

salvation of some millions of souls. The archbishop had been known to keep an episcopal synod in session for three weeks until they agreed to release a huge sum from Vatican funds to help bring back into the fold the Christian inhabitants of the planet Courvoisier, some twelve in number, on the far side of the Judaic Sector.

A barefoot Franciscan friar in a gray habit approached the archbishop's seat, bent, and spoke. Wordlessly, the archbishop stood, smoothed his white Dominican habit, picked up his briefcase, and followed the friar from the Great Hall. The voice of the imam droned on.

In the chamber of the Inner Council, the five humans deemed holiest by the vast majority of rediscovered humanity sat watching the white-robed archbishop as he arranged his papers. Around the semicircular table, the archbishop glanced at the five most powerful beings in the rediscovered galaxy, whom he had to sway to accomplish his purposes. At one end of the table sat Krishna Anantanarayanan, crosslegged in a white loincloth, who had not spoken more than five times in all the years that the archbishop had been addressing this august body. Next to him was the grand imam, the Voice of the Prophet, in his green turban and red-dyed beard. On his left was Pope Innocent LXXII, whose following was numerically the largest, although the wealth and power of the Church of Rome were equaled by the others. The senior high priest of the Third Temple, head of the Great Sanhedrin, sat toying with a scroll. Next to the high priest sat the lama of Sinkiang, spiritual head of the Buddhists. The lama's temporal power was not great, but his wisdom and experience made his advice to the council invaluable. The archbishop rattled his papers and cleared his throat.

"If it please Your Sanctities," he began, "my business this day concerns the newly rediscovered Flavian System, adjacent to XV Sector. The rediscovery of this system was reported to Your Sanctities some seven years ago, following an expedition by scoutships of the Church Militant. These ships effected the rediscovery while following hints given by a captured pirate, and aided by some badly deteriorated chart thimbles found in a pre-Decadence storeroom of the Vatican Library. The Franciscans sent a team of missionary friars to one of the outer worlds of the Flavians on a reconnaissance, and their report was submitted to me last week."

"I recall the expedition's report." The grand imam's voice was impatient. "The sector was settled entirely by Christians. Why should the matter be brought to the attention of the council?"

"I shall come to that presently, Your Sanctity," said Hilarion. "First, let me provide an outline of the situation; then you may decide for yourselves whether a Declaration of Council is called for." The imam, grumbling, settled back in his chair. He didn't like this infidel priest, and he didn't like the way the archbishop had of involving the whole UF in matters that were essentially the concern of the Vatican.

"The Flavian System," began the archbishop, "was settled in the first part of the third millennium by colonists from Italy, Yugoslavia, Greece, the Balkans, and southern Russia, at a time when these were valid political entities. At the time of settlement, these pioneers belonged either to the Roman Catholic or United Eastern Churches, but all became united under the Church of Rome toward the end of the third millennium. Their tithe records continue until the first quarter of the fourth millennium, when all records are lost in the general chaos of the Great Decadence. The Franciscan report on the progress of

these worlds, if you wish to call it progress, is as
follows: The Flavian System, which once contained
more than one hundred worlds, is now reduced to
some two score. All planetary bodies requiring advanced technology to inhabit and exploit have been
long since abandoned. A few of the system's planets
retain a minimum of technology, which they use to
ruthlessly exploit the more primitive worlds. Principal among these is Charun, which lives so thoroughly on banditry that there is no work for its people
to do, and they live lives of pampered poverty, with
bread and circuses giving the fulfillment once provided by faith."

"Yes, yes," said the high priest, "but this is an old
story, and far from the worst the Decadence has to
offer. Why, I remember when the world of Ben Aaron
was rediscovered . . . well, we dealt with the problem.
What has your Flavian System to offer that is so
unique? It sounds like a classic case of the Punic
Syndrome, eh?" The high priest's bantering tone was
intended to needle the archbishop, but Hilarion was
too old a statesman to rise to it.

"As you say, Your Sanctity, the symptoms of the
Punic Sickness are present here: a moneyed aristocracy who must amuse an all-pervasive mob, slave
raiding on a large scale, gladiatorial combats and
other abominations, reversion to paganism, emperor
worship, widespread piracy. . . ."

"That is all very terrible, and we hear of such
cases about three times a week," said the Pope.
"Now, what is it that concerns the council?"

"I was just coming to that, Your Holiness," said
Hilarion. "It seems that some of these worlds are
engaged in the creation of the soulless."

For several moments there was silence around the
table. Android constructs were an affront to all the
faiths. The high priest was first to speak.

"My apologies for my former levity, Archbishop, this is indeed serious. Your Holiness, do you wish to petition for a Declaration of Council sanctioning a holy war? If so, the Sanhedrin will be willing to support you with certain of the Hosts of the Lord."

"My thanks for your support, Most High," said the Pope diplomatically, "but perhaps if the archbishop will enlighten us further, forty or so worlds seem hardly of sufficient importance to justify a full cleansing, soulless constructs or no."

"To be sure," continued the archbishop, "a full-scale crusade will not be necessary. Most of the traffic in the soulless originates from a planet called Cadmus. The strongest measures are called for against this particular world, but the rest are, for the most part, guilty of no more than grievous error. There are a handful of oppressors and many victims."

"Burn it," growled the imam. "Creation of the soulless is a usurpation of divine function. All who practice are to be struck down and their world cleansed with fire and steel!"

"This matter will be handled by the Church Militant, not the Legions of the Faithful. The Church of Rome has its own views concerning culpability and guilt. All that is necessary is a Declaration of Council supporting the right of the Church of Rome to take whatever action, military or otherwise, is deemed fit by representatives sent to study the situation." The Pope's voice was flat and steely. The lama spoke for the first time:

"Bishop, you have mentioned that slavery is practiced in these worlds on a large scale. Why is this necessary when soulless constructs are available?"

"Technology has declined on these planets, Your Serenity, and genetic engineering is no exception. The laboratories for producing the more complex types of

construct have long since shut down. All that are left
are those turning out the simple and simple-minded
type that are good for nothing but fighting. Their only
qualities are obedience and animal ferocity. Human
slaves are far more versatile and useful."

"Archbishop, did you not mention 'reversion to
paganism'?" The high priest's voice was mildly
reproving.

"I did, Your Sanctity." Hilarion's face was composed, but his teeth were inwardly gritted. It was
precisely this point he had hoped to avoid.

"There is in this report, no doubt, some estimate of
the percentage of pagans to practicing Christians?"

"Paganism runs some 99 plus percent."

"Then," said the imam, "there can be no action by
the Church Militant without a formal request from
the ruling person or body of any given world or
system. Were you trying to sneak something past us,
Archbishop?"

"I am ready to present all the facts at my disposal,
Your Sanctities, but it seemed that the matter of the
soulless demanded first priority."

"And as such," said the high priest, "it serves as
an excellent screen whereby you may dodge the question of whether the Church of Rome truly has first
right over these planets. If there has been a 99 per
cent reversion to paganism, then any faith could
equally well claim missionary right. In the matter of
the soulless, of course, we will be willing to sanction
any military solution that you should deem necessary.
For the rest, your missionaries must persuade your
strayed sheep as best they may."

Pope Innocent LXXII, 943rd Supreme Pontiff of the
Church of Rome since St. Peter, sighed wearily as she
removed her tiara. She contemplated the great triple
crown with displeasure. You'd think they would have

devised something lighter in nearly four thousand years, she thought. Within the frame of her white coif and wimple, her face was unlined and serene, but that was the result of rejuvenation treatment. She was 150 years old, and at times like this she felt every minute of her age. Idly, she wondered what a Carmelite music teacher from New Orleans was doing with the Fisherman's ring on her hand.

"That was ill done, Hilarion. Now they'll all be sending missionaries and looking for a chance to send in troops. This new imam's the most rabid since Achmet IV. Three years in the Caliphate and two medium-sized holy wars to his credit. He knows the Temple and the Vatican won't stand for much more of his high-handed tactics. The situation is stable now, but anything could upset it. You shouldn't have provoked him over a matter as trivial as the Flavians."

"The facts were impossible to hide, Your Holiness. The imam was so enraged about the soulless that he completely missed the vital factor, but Ben Asher is too old at this game. I shall take steps immediately to send an agent to the Flavians."

"No doubt you have such an agent in mind. A Jesuit?"

"Father Miles of Durga. Your Holiness will no doubt recall the name? He was instrumental in settling the affair on Tombstone."

"The name is familiar to me. Has he not a rather peculiar background?"

"It is a man's convictions that determine a man's merit as a servant of the Church. Many of us are of peculiar backgrounds."

"Still, perhaps the situation in the Flavians is too delicate to turn over to one of the Jesuit commandos." The Pope favored the Franciscans and was decidedly cool toward the headlong tactics of the Jesuits.

"Your Holiness has no more faithful or zealous

servants than the Society."

"Perhaps too zealous. There has been much protest within the UF concerning activities directed from Loyola. Within the Church itself there's a great deal of grumbling, not all of it unjustified."

"There is always jealousy over organizations that enjoy distinction and favor. As for the UF, the loudest complaints are always from the Caliphate and the Temple. A rival's success is always annoying."

"Nevertheless, the Society takes too much on itself these days. The trend has been worsening ever since the Second Reformation. Policy originates from the Vatican, not from Loyola. Someday soon there must be a reckoning between the Society and the Papacy."

"Until that time, Your Holiness, they are useful servants."

"You had better begin to take a greater interest in these matters, Hilarion." There was something in the Pope's tone that brought the Archbishop up short. When he spoke, it was with carefully guarded inflection.

"How so, Your Holiness?"

"The matter of the Magsaysay System will soon be concluded. My advisers inform me that you have contrived a diplomatic coup of some magnitude. There will be a reward for such service. No doubt you will find a red hat becoming."

"Your Holiness honors me far beyond my merits," said the archbishop, inwardly exulting.

"Spare us your false modesty, Archbishop. I will speak further. I have worn the Ring for almost fifty years. I cannot wear it forever. Within the next twenty to thirty years, I must retire. If you serve me well in that time, I will support you for elevation to the Papacy. It will be up to the College, of course, but if I lay the groundwork your chances will be far greater than those of any other cardinal."

"Your Holiness, I am overwhelmed." The archbishop's shock was sincere.

"This is not a decision lightly made. I was looking toward this day since you graduated from the seminary. Such are the duties of this office. Go now, see to this matter of the Flavians. And take closer note of the doings of the Jesuits."

Hilarion was slightly dazed as he walked back to the Great Hall. To think that he had what amounted to a guarantee of the Papacy! And he had always felt that he was manipulating the Pope to his will. He was beginning to repent of his arrogance. Over his soul there settled an unaccustomed mantle: humility. His thoughts were interrupted by the young Franciscan friar who had summoned him to the Inner Council chamber.

"Your Excellency, I've served here at the UF for my full year, now. Am I permitted to rejoin my order?"

Archbishop Hilarion studied the young man who had been his page for the past year. The young man had the air of almost preternatural patience and serenity that characterized the Franciscan friars.

"Well, Friar Jeremiah, have you decided that the life of a diplomat is not for you?"

"I agreed to give it a year, sir, but my place is out working among the strayed." He gestured toward the great Dome of Tcherbadayev, through which the great stars and the tiny ones glittered, clear in the Antarctic sky.

"A pity," said the Archbishop. "You have the patience requisite for these dealings. Well, then, you are dismissed as soon as you have carried out one last duty for me. Come to my office this evening after vespers. I shall have a set of orders for you to deliver to Father Miles of Durga on the planet of Gravitas in the Loyola System. When you have delivered these orders, you may go where you will."

"I thank Your Excellency most profoundly. I shall always value the apprenticeship I have served here." The friar bowed, hands buried in the long, wide sleeves of his habit.

"I shall miss you, Friar Jeremiah."

II

Parma Sicarius's world was a world of grass. In fact, Thrax possessed nothing in abundance except grass. From the fifty-foot bamboo of the tropics to the wiry thin growth of the mountains, the most advanced vegetable growth native to Thrax was some sort of grass. The planet possessed virtually no metals or mineral wealth of any kind, and the water supply was too unreliable to permit agriculture. The seas and rivers held fish only in sufficient quantities to support very small fishing communities. As a consequence, Thrax was a pastoral world, peopled by nomadic tribes who moved their herds from one pasture to another as season and water supply dictated.

Parma was herding the tribe's remaining masses of sheepox toward the End of Green Fair, where some of the animals would be traded to offworld merchants and to other tribes. It had been a bad year, and Parma viewed the coming Fair with a mixture of anticipation

and trepidation. First had come the failure of the
tribe's springs. Sources of water that had never failed
in all the generations that the tribe had used them
were dry this year. Then a disease had killed most of
the beasts spared by the drought. Finally, when word
of the weakness of the tribe had spread, the raiders
came. Parma's tribe, the Sicarii, were fighting men as
good as any, but the vulture tribes of the mountains,
who lived solely by plunder, had banded together for
the kill. Still, the Sicarii gave as good as they got, and
they retained the nucleus of a new herd. If the next
few years brought sufficient water, the tribe's fortunes could be restored. If not, then the Sicarii would
be swallowed up by the vast, windy plains as count-
less other tribes had been swallowed.

Parma tried to forget these somber facts, and concentrated instead on the excitement of the coming
fair. They came twice a year, at End of Green and End
of Dry, when the tribes congregated near the southern and northern pastures, respectively. There they
were met by offworld merchants in their fabulous
shuttle platforms, which carried off the wool and
meat of the sheepoxen and sometimes the live
animals. Occasionally, especially in bad years such
as this, they also bore away children sold as slaves.

He had been lucky. He had survived the elements
and the raiders for seventeen years. He had the lean,
rawhide build that comes of a strenuous life and a
diet consisting almost entirely of meat. Over his
saddlebow was thonged a small round shield, and he
carried a long, slender lance in his right hand. In a
scabbard of hide at his belt was a knife, its broad,
curved blade as long as his forearm from elbow to
knuckles. The knife blade and the lance point were of
keen offworld steel, nearly indestructible. The only
other piece of metal he owned was a small eating and
general-purpose knife. Every member of the tribe had

one of these knives and carried it thrust into boot, belt, or topknot.

Once at the fairgrounds, after camping in the Sicarii traditional campground, Parma sought out the contest rings. The young men of all the tribes contended for prizes and honor at feats of strength and arms. Perhaps a good showing there would win him a wife.

At the rings, Parma sighted some mountain and plains tribesmen, hereditary enemies of the Sicarii, men whom Parma would have attacked on sight in any place other than the sacred precincts of the fairgrounds. A scar-faced mountaineer in the hard leather armor of his region crowded Parma unabashedly, though each would have happily slit the other's throat a few miles away. There were wrestling matches, sword battles, knife fights, boxing tournaments, and mounted duels with blunt lances. Fights were decided when a man was thrown in wrestling, knocked unconscious in boxing, unhorsed in the mounted combats, or when first blood was drawn in the blade fights. Parma entered his name in the blade battles, knowing that the parents of his future bride would be much influenced if he distinguished himself. In his tribe Parma was the swiftest handler of knife and buckler, and he had four enemy thumbs to his credit from skirmishes in defense of his tribe's herds.

On the evening of the third day of the fair, Parma's father beckoned him over to the chief's tent. Parma grinned broadly, knowing that this must surely mean that a match had been made for him. He had fought five matches, battling men armed like the Sicarii with knife and buckler or with the sword such as the mountaineers favored. He had won them all, and was unscratched, and he had seen many older men, with the three-forked beards of fathers with marriageable daughters, conferring among themselves as they gestured in his direction.

As he stooped to enter the chief's tent, Parma caught the somber expression on his father's face, and when he had passed once sunward around the tent and seated himself moonward of the entrance, he saw that the chief would not meet his eyes and that there was a stranger from offworld seated between the two senior tribesmen.

Offworlders tended to look much alike to Parma, and this one was typical of the breed. He looked plump and overfed, pale from months spent aboard ship. What little hair he had was cropped short, and he wore tunic and trousers of a bright metallic cloth. Holstered at his belt was an object that Parma knew to be a weapon. The tribesman had seen offworld merchants use them to speed the slaughter of sheepoxen they had bought. It was, thought Parma, just the kind of unmanly weapon such soft men would favor.

Parma could not understand the meaning of all this. Nobody seemed willing to start conversation, so Parma broke the silence.

"Good grass to this abode. Why am I called here?"

"My son," began his father, "this honored stranger has come to us with an unusual offer: He has seen you fight, and so impressed is he with your prowess that he wishes to buy you."

Parma was stunned, looking from his father to the chief in bewilderment. The chief added hastily:

"Of course, we explained to him that you are a free man of the tribe, and not ours to sell, even had we wished. We offered a number of the children, who are likely to starve anyway, but it seems that this man only buys fighting men, though for what purpose, I can't guess. He has offered the price of five thousand sheepoxen." The eyes of both men were pleading, but they were too proud to beg Parma's assent, even though it would mean the salvation of the tribe.

Parma was stunned yet again. Five thousand! That was enough to replenish the herds, provide dowries for all the unmarried girls, and keep all the children for the future strength of the tribe. At one stroke, the security of the tribe would be assured for the next ten years. Parma's answer was swift and firm.

"Make it five thousand for the tribe, plus one thousand for my father, and blades for a hundred knives, and points for a hundred lances."

"Done," said the stranger.

The gratitude of the older men was unspoken but sincere. Parma was not unhappy with the bargain. He was so used to thinking in terms of the tribe above all other values that his own liberty seemed a paltry price to pay for what he had gained. Returning to his tent, he gathered his few belongings, disposing of those he thought would be superfluous. His horses, saddle, lance, and rope he gave to his younger brothers and cousins. He paid homage to his mother's thighbone in the tribal shrine tent, burned sweet herbs to the tribe's gods, kissed his father, and sought out the man who had bought him. He found the merchant by one of the fearsome floating platforms, laden with hides and wool, sheepoxen, joints of meat, child slaves, and a small group of grown warriors, looking fatalistic but unbowed. The merchant looked at Parma, consulted a list in his hand, and said:

"Well, you're the last, then. Hop aboard and we'll be off."

Parma climbed onto the platform without the slightest hesitation. These offworld devices were pure sorcery to him, but he had no apprehension concerning what was to happen. Whether he was to be skinned alive or crowned Emperor was immaterial. The important thing was that he had saved the tribe, and he was anxious to get away before this man thought to go back on the bargain.

Soon, a buzzing noise began, and a dome that had been invisible became opaque, enclosing the whole platform. The man who had paid for him approached Parma, carrying a thin ring of glistening metal, which he proceeded to clasp around Parma's neck.

"You are now my property, my boy, and this ring is in token of that fact. It is in contact, in a way you could never understand, with this little black box at my belt. It will tell me if you are sick or well, if you are lying, and, most important, if you are attempting escape or suicide. My name is Zoltan Kreuzer, slave merchant. I allow you to keep your knives because, if you should attempt violence against me or anybody else without my permission, the ring that you now wear will render you instantly unconscious. Behave, and you will live well; fail to behave, and you shall regret it."

Without further words, the slaver passed on to another man in the little dejected group on the platform.

The journey passed in a daze for Parma. He and the other slaves from Thrax had been heavily drugged to ease the shock of traveling from a bronze-age society to a star-spanning empire. The pastoral life of Thrax already seemed far past and vague to Parma. The sheer abundance of metal in sight at all times would have been enough to drive him into shock in ordinary conditions. By the time that a landfall was reached, the resilience of youth had taken the upper hand, and Parma was beginning to anticipate the life to come with some eagerness.

"What world do we land on?" asked Parma, in his uncertain Esperanto, of a crewman of the huge merchant vessel.

"This is the city of Ludus, in Charun — the end of the line for such as you. From here you will emerge as a rich man, or as a corpse. Most probably as a corpse." The crewman leered as he conducted his charges down the ship's loading ramp and into great, teardrop-shaped land transports. These machines took the slaves to a vast, domed stadium, empty of spectators, where they were surrounded by men in black tunics holding bright red rods in black-gloved hands.

At a table sat Zoltan Kreuzer and another man. This new man drew Parma's attention. Kreuzer was a soft little man, and so, in different degree, had been the crewmen aboard the great ship. Even the black-tuniced men, who were obviously guards, seemed pathetically soft, slow, and clumsy, compared to the rapier men of Thrax. This new man was something different. True, he was not of the rawhide and whip-cord leanness of the Thraxians, but instead a short, burly, bullet-headed man, broad of shoulder and waist, and projecting an air of iron-hard toughness that seemed bred of some life totally divorced from the wild freedom of the plains. His short-cropped hair and scarred face had the economy that was displayed in every movement of his body. Parma had only heard of cities, great insect-warrens where men lived in un-thinkably crowded conditions, but this man looked like what such a life might produce: a brutal, flexible, steely man who faced no enemies among the ele-ments, but who had fought his fellow men from the cradle upward, with no help from tribe or clan.

The slaves were herded onto a track that circled the inside of the stadium and told to run. They were encouraged by the red rods of the overseers, which, when applied to backsides, stung like hot coals.

While the slaves ran, Kreuzer and the other man observed them and a set of screens and dials on a panel before them, where data from the slaves' neck rings were recorded. As one man after another dropped out, the bullet-headed man made notes with a stylus on a small pad thonged to his belt.

"These aren't as good as your last group from Thrax."

"It's been a bad year on the North Continent, where I do my dealing. None of these can be said to be in the best of shape, but feed and train them well, and they will repay you many times their purchase price. One of them is special. You see the one with light brown hair in a topknot?"

"Yes, he'll be dropping from the run soon. He's a plainsman, through and through: Look at those great ugly riding calluses on his inner thighs. Such men are not accustomed to using their feet."

"This man, though, is of a tribe called Sicarii, a very small tribe of the southeastern section of the North Continent. The Sicarii prize their horses greatly, and take great pains to spare them when conditions are desperate. They dismount and run beside their horses, and hold running to be the manliest of accomplishments, next to fighting. Their endurance is the endurance of a fine running beast in good training. Observe this young man."

Indeed, after five laps of the stadium, several of the slaves were reaching the end of their endurance. After ten, only a handful were still running at all. After twenty, only Parma and three mountaineers were still maintaining the steady, mile-eating trot of experienced hunters. When fifty laps were passed, even the watchers were fatigued. One by one, the mountaineers dropped out. Only Parma and one of the mountain men remained. The stocky man was staring at his screens and dials in astonishment. He could see that the mountaineer was running at the end of his strength, only courage keeping him on his feet, but Parma's readings showed respiration and heartbeat running only a little above normal, the acid buildup in his muscles kept to a minimal level by a system superlatively adapted to prolonged exercise. In the end, the trainers called a halt to prevent the mountain man from killing himself. Parma took the towel that was handed to him and wiped off the sheen of sweat that covered his body, wondering what test was next, utterly unaware that the thirty miles he had run was a record for the stadium. The powerful little man approached, accompanied by Kreuzer. He studied Parma's sinewy form with some intensity, and Parma studied him in turn, coming to the conclusion that this was not a man he would care to look at over the edge of a shield.

"Listen well, barbarian," said the dangerous figure, "I am your new owner. My name is Marius, and I am a trainer of fighting men. If you heed me well, and give me no trouble, I will make you rich, famous, and free. If you defy me, you will suffer in ways you cannot even comprehend as yet. What are your weapons?"

"He uses the short curved sword and buckler, Marius," said Kreuzer, "the best I've ever seen. He's a natural for the Classical Forms in Augusta. Such cunning knifework is seen only once in a generation, if that often. He's worth a fortune."

"And I've no doubt that's what you'll want for him," said Marius. "But there are good fighters in plenty. The question is: Can he kill?"

"The chief of his tribe assured me that he has killed four men in skirmishes with raiding parties from rival tribes."

"Well, that will have to do for the present. Send the lot to my school. We'll settle the price this evening."

III

The Loyola System, headquarters of the Society of Jesus, consisted of three inhabitable planets. Loyola, Pietas, and Gravitas. On Loyola was carried out the administration of the Society, its great seminary and schools, and its military training depots. On Pietas, novices went through their year of meditation prior to entering the seminary. Pietas was a world bleak and colorless, its soil producing no life form more advanced than an edible but tasteless tuber, on which novices lived during their isolation, with no company save their own thoughts.

Gravitas was a world unique in its geological makeup. It had an eccentric core of great density, which orbited the axis of the planet within the molten center of magma, in a direction opposite to the rotation of the planet. The result was a fluctuating gravity. Gravitas made one full rotation in its year, which was the equivalent of four hundred Earth days. At the equator, on the day that the core was directly at the opposite side of the planet, the gravity was 10 per cent higher than Earth normal. Two hundred days later, when the core was directly below, the gravity had more than doubled. On Gravitas the graduates of the seminary of Loyola underwent their advanced physical and psychological training prior to ordination and assignment to a commission in the Church Militant. Each man and woman had spent a full Gravitas year enduring the terrible gravity and undergoing a fearsome set of physical and mental exercises before being deemed fit to begin the five years of military service that were required for advancement to any of the posts in the missionary, education, intelligence, and diplomatic branches. Those of superior military aptitude went on to higher rank in the Church Militant, which was officered largely by Jesuits. Members of all the branches could secure appointments in the administration of the order.

Father Miles of Durga was conducting a class in conversion psychology, outdoors, as was always the case on Gravitas, in the broiling sun of the long day or the bitter cold of night. The students lay on their backs with their heads propped up on stones so that they could see their teacher. They were always supine when not exercising, to avoid strain on the heart. Men wore tight trusses and a sort of corset against hernia and back injury. Women wore the corsets with the addition of rigid breastplates. No other clothing was worn by undergraduates, no matter what the weather. Constant medical examinations guarded against blood clots, varicose veins, and all the other maladies that chronically afflicted humanity when exposed to excessive gravity.

". . .thus it is always desirable to arrange festivals of the Church so that they fall as near as possible to the pagan festivals that they are supplanting. Men will always react more strongly to a change in their festivals than to a change in the reason for celebrating them. In addition, it provides a sense of familiarity and continuity that cushions the shock of conversion during the crucial first-generation period. Class dismissed. Report to Father Nkosi for unarmed combat."

Miles had timed the class to end at the arrival of the Franciscan friar, whom he had watched approaching for some time. The friar's gray habit stood out in sharp contrast to the seminude bodies of the students and the black habits of the instructors. The friar was making heavy going in the intense gravity, which was nearing maximum.

Brother Jeremiah was wondering if Hell was like this. He had been on Gravitas for five hours, and his back felt as if it were about to break. His feet felt worse, if possible. The stony ground of Gravitas stabbed sharply into his undefended soles. He was also wishing he had not turned down the offer, at the spaceport, of one of the absurd-looking trusses. He was beginning to suffer a most abominable aching in his groin, as his testicles and all his internal organs were now twice their normal weight. He tried not to think of his woes, and instead turned his thoughts to the astonishing world on which he found himself. He had been walking for hours since leaving the spaceport and had always been in the midst of hundreds of classes of students. Like most members of other orders, Jeremiah had thought of the Jesuits as a very small, secret organization. It was difficult to believe that this multitude was only a small part of one year's turnout from the seminary of Loyola. He was at first deeply disturbed at the near nudity of the students of both sexes, but he quickly discovered that the gravity here killed lascivious thoughts as effectively as emasculation.

There was something both inspiring and repellent in this masochistic planet. From the moment of his arrival he had felt these conflicting sensations. The obvious dedication of both students and instructors gave him a sense of the resurgent spirit of the Church, but here the intensity was almost fanatic. The disciplinary exercises of the students were preparing them for life service on worlds where conditions were barely tolerable for human life, but sometimes they seemed to approach pointless suffering.

In some places students stood at rigid attention, arms raised to shoulder level, and stayed in that position for hours. Jeremiah passed a hill where students were carrying stones from a pile at its foot and depositing them downhill and tossing them on another heap at the bottom. It seemed mortification of the flesh carried to the extreme. Most disturbing of all were the fields where students were practicing fighting, both armed and unarmed. In one field, Jeremiah watched in astonishment as a tiny, black-robed nun felled three attacking male students in quick succession with a six-foot wooden staff. Bloodied and bruised, they retired to their places in class and three more tried their luck, with no more success. Elsewhere, men and women were fighting in groups in what seemed deadly earnest. Calloused feet and hands smacked into bodies with sickening sounds, and people were tripped or thrown to fall with stunning force in the doubled gravity. But always they rose and returned to their endless exercises, seemingly indestructible and immune to discouragement.

Jeremiah was not sure what to make of it, and his mind was whirling. He had never seen physical violence before, except in holos. He wondered what this infernal scene had to do with Christian spirit. At last, he found the class he had been looking for, under a queer rock formation called the Horns of Hattin, al-

though few remembered whence the name had come.
Father Miles himself was a priest much like any
other. His skin was paler than had been produced on
Earth for centuries, and his blue eyes were a trait
now rare on the mother planet, though common
enough out among the stars. His face was lean and
ascetic, his body difficult to judge in his voluminous
black robe. His hair was close-cropped, with temples
and nape shaved in the Jesuit fashion. His hands were
small and almost delicate.

"Peace to you, Friar. So, the Vatican remembers
me?"

"And to you, Father. These orders come from Archbishop Hilarion, Papal nuncio to the United Faiths."

"Thank you for your trouble, Friar. Please lie down
while I read; sitting will strain your heart as much as
standing." The friar complied without demur, wondering how the priest bore the gravity so effortlessly.
Maybe the stories about the Jesuits being something
superhuman were true.

The orders were in a golden tube, sealed at one end
with a plastic substance resembling ancient sealing
wax and bearing the stamp of the Office of Strayed
Sheep Affairs. Miles pulled at the seal and it came
loose, attached to a scarlet ribbon, which was in turn
wrapped around a roll of parchment. Had any hand
but Miles' loosened the seal, the contents of the tube
would have been consumed instantly, leaving no
trace. Miles took in the orders in a few seconds.
Buried in a mass of verbiage, they informed him that
he was directed and required to remove himself to the
Flavian System, now a part of XV Sector, taking with
him whatever personnel he thought necessary, to
study the situation currently pertaining and take
whatever action he deemed discreet, prudent, and
necessary. The order tube and seal would assure him

free transport on any Church vessel and secure co-operation from Church authorities.

"I haven't had a *carte blanche* like this in years," remarked the priest. "Do you know anything about the situation in the Flavian worlds, Friar?"

"Just rumors, Father. They were rediscovered a few years ago, and some friars of my order were sent to make a reconnaissance. They found an advanced stage of moral and religious decay. That's all I know."

"Well, no sense in wasting time. Is there any business keeping you here, Friar?"

"No, I wish to return to the spaceport. I've been directed by my order to make my way to the Flavians and establish a mission among the poor. But first, if I may rest a little . . ."

The Jesuit laughed unexpectedly. "If I let you walk back you'd spend a month in the hospital before you ever saw the Flavians. I'll have a bouncer sent to pick us up."

Jeremiah could have wept with gratitude.

The Papal titheship *Peter's Pence* was a great golden sphere, marked here and there with the silver crossed keys of the Vatican. Jeremiah stared unabashedly, for space travel was still new to him. Born and raised on Earth, educated in the Franciscan monastery in Brisbane, his first space voyage had been in the great passenger liner that had taken him to Loyola, where he had caught the supply packet to Gravitas. Now, on the shuttle from the Loyola spaceport to the titheship, which was headed for XV Sector, the realization that he was actually in space was beginning to dawn on him.

On Loyola, Father Miles had left him briefly to report to his superiors and to pick up the reports on the Flavian System, and had returned in a cassock clean of the grime of Gravitas, with a wide pouch at his belt and a six-foot staff of knotty wood. The priest seemed to deem this sufficient traveling equipment. The friar marveled that an important functionary of the Society of Jesus should be ready to travel to the ends of the rediscovered galaxy at a moment's notice with so little impedimenta. True, Jeremiah's own effects were even more austere, consisting solely of his rough gray habit and a scrip that was now nearly empty save for a small book, but that was only to be expected of a member of a mendicant order. He had expected a Jesuit to travel in some state.

Once aboard the titheship, they were ushered into the presence of the captain, a hard-faced Benedictine monk in a brown habit and an archaic billed cap. He waived formalities and came straight to the point.

"Peace to you, Brothers, and where are you bound?"

"To XV Sector, and once there to wherever we may find a fleet of the Church Militant, to convey us to the newly rediscovered Flavian planets." The Jesuit's voice was carefully modulated, free of irritants.

"No problem there. We rendezvous with our convoy as soon as we reach XV Sector. But that near the edge, there is always danger of piracy. I need not tell you that there is no more tempting target than a titheship. Fifty disappeared last year. Brother Arthur will show you to your cells. Meals are twice a day, before matins and after vespers. This is a monastery ship, and you will observe all prayer calls while aboard: lauds, nones, matins, vespers, all the rest."

"We always do," said the Jesuit.

"Mass is celebrated in the chapel three times daily. When you have been shown your cells, Brother Arthur will conduct you to the dining hall, where you may eat."

"I am not hungry," said Jeremiah, still suffering from the effects of his trip to Gravitas.

"I would suggest you eat anyway," said the monk, "since this evening we begin three days of fasting prior to celebrating the Feast of the Epiphany."

Once settled into their cells, life fell into the comforting and familiar round of fasting and prayer for Brother Jeremiah. It reminded him of his life in the monastery in Brisbane. It was disconcerting to celebrate Epiphany so soon after he had celebrated it on Earth, but one thing men had been unable to accomplish since reaching the stars was coordinating the calendars of the various planets, satellites, both natural and artificial, and ships inhabited by men throughout the rediscovered galaxy. Easter, Ramadan, Chanukah, and all the other festivals and observances of mankind were scheduled to fit whatever time system was adopted.

Sometimes Jeremiah watched Father Miles as he went through his various rituals and his physical and spiritual exercises, so different from the simple meditation and prayer of a Franciscan. The priest could sit in the doorway of his cell for hours, pressing his palms rigidly against the doorframe. Sometimes he would stand on his head, or stare at a nearly invisible dust mote as it made its intricate progress among its fellow motes in a Brownian movement around the cell. These exercises seemed to Jeremiah to smack of paganism, or at least heresy. He could not fit the strange activities of the Jesuit into the framework of his own concept of Christianity. Occasionally, Jeremiah would engage the priest in conversation, and the Jesuit was always ready to talk. The friar remembered that the Jesuits were often members of secret societies within the Society, dating from the Great Decadence and the suppression of the Jesuits of those days. Greatly daring, the friar broached the subject.

"Father, forgive my boldness, but, do you belong to

one of the . . . brotherhoods?"

"Why, yes," said the Jesuit. "I am an initiate of the Third Rank in the Brotherhood Cestus Dei."

The friar was stunned. The Brotherhood Cestus Dei, vulgarly called "God's Brass Knucks," had been one of the military brotherhoods responsible for bringing about the great Second Reformation in the days of Pope Leo XCV. Picked from among the most capable and fanatical of the Jesuit and Dominican orders, they had been employed as secret agents and even, it was said, assassins, in the holy work of the Great Cleansing. There were rumors that the Brotherhood was still alive and functioning, but Jeremiah had always dismissed these as idle. He had been sure that the Brotherhood was now defunct, if indeed it had ever existed at all. And now here was this Jesuit priest calmly asserting that he was an initiate of the fearsome Brotherhood!

"Truly, sir? I'd thought the Brotherhood a legend! Why do you so honor me with your confidence?" The young friar's voice was puzzled, but the priest chuckled shortly.

"Heavens, boy, there's no secret any more, not these past two hundred years. Nearly all of us belong to one or more of the brotherhoods these days. In Cestus Dei we just emphasize the physical side of training a bit more than in the rest of the Society."

Jeremiah shuddered as he remembered what he had seen on Gravitas, and wondered what kind of training could emphasize physical discipline more.

"But," continued the priest, "I know we are a feared, sinister group. Well, that's the price of being too secretive. In the early days, secretiveness was necessary for survival. If it had been suspected that the Society of Jesus was fostering subversive groups within its midst, the Society would have been stamped out for good. Now, young friar," said the priest, changing the subject with bewildering rapidity, "what will you be doing when we get among the Flavian worlds?"

"Why, Father," stammered the friar, "I hardly know. This is my first mission. I suppose I will have to begin proselytizing on my own, among the poor."

"On your own? In what by all reports is one of the most corrupt sectors we have ever come across? You were shocked by what you saw on Gravitas, and that was just a training school for priests."

"To be sure, Father, I am inexperienced, but I find that sophistication comes with travel."

"True enough," snorted the priest, "but your order doesn't give you sufficient preparation. Have you ever seen men fight to the death for the amusement of cheering crowds?"

The friar shuddered. "I have not seen such, as you well know, but these practices have been stopped before."

"Yes, but your job is not to stop the practice, but to convert the crowd, every last man, yes, and the fighters too. That is the kind of thing you will be up against in the Flavians. You will be exposed to every kind of evil and corruption of which the human soul is capable, and that is every kind, else it would not have been necessary to find the words to describe them. You will be hard enough put to find salvation for your own soul in all that, much less redeem the sinners."

"I confess, Father, I shudder at the task."

"Stay by me, son, at least for a while. You can learn a great deal, and be of assistance to me at the same time."

"I thank you for the offer, Father, but I must go on my own way, and I cannot find it in my heart to agree with Jesuit methods. My way will be hard, but I shall pray for guidance."

"I shall pray for you too, Friar. No wonder the

casualty figures are so high among the Franciscans. Mark this, my boy: A ruling class that lives by exploitation of the less fortunate lives in perpetual terror. If they think that there is new thought stirring among those masses, then they will react with hysterical brutality. Save your gentle preaching for the nice planets, son, where men live at peace and preferably in small, self-sufficient communities. The brutal empires, such as we are headed for, require quick surgery at the top.''

IV

Parma's training in the School of Marius began in earnest. After a brisk run, the trainees were taken to the mess hall and fed a large breakfast. Parma became familiar with foods he had never encountered before: eggs, bread, unfamiliar forms of meat and milk that certainly never came from a sheepox or mare. He found it all delicious and had trouble getting used to the idea that there was no shortage of food and that he could have as much as he wanted at every meal. After the austere life of the Thraxian plains, this seemed as alien as any other factor of his new life.

After breakfast, the trainees were led to a small stadium and shown the various styles of combat for which they would be training while at the school. The head trainer, a shaven-headed man with very dark skin, addressed them as a group of armed and armored men filed into the little arena.

"Here at the School of Marius, we specialize in the Classical Forms. This means, basically, that you will train with the large shield and long sword or the small shield and dagger. Other weapons may be used according to personal taste, such as the ax, mace, and lance. In addition, some of you may be selected to train with the net and trident. Your trainers you will know by the red wands they carry." The trainer brandished his own. "You will obey instantly any order given by a trainer or you will suffer." He beckoned, and two of the fighters stepped forward. "The first demonstration will be Light against Heavy. This is one of the two most popular types of contest. When your turn comes to fight, you'll look as good as these men."

Indeed, the fighters were a gorgeous sight. Their bodies were tanned, sleek, oiled, and incredibly fit, each muscle standing in stark relief, as if carved from granite. The Heavy wore a huge, elaborate helmet with a wide brim and a high, square crest sprouting a blaze of red plumes. His face was obscured by a visor bearing intricately fretted eyeholes. His right arm was covered by a sleeve of interlinked metal rings, and his left leg was covered from the top of the knee to the ankle by a metal greave. He wore no armor on his body, only a wide belt supporting a short scarlet kilt with a gold fringe. All the metal he wore was plated with gold. On his left arm he carried a large rectangular shield curved almost into a half cylinder. The Light wore a similar helmet, but of smaller and lighter proportions, with a small crest and no plumes. His right arm bore a series of overlapping metal bands from wrist to elbow, and he wore greaves on both legs, with the addition of thigh plates. His shield was small and round, and his short sword curved like Parma's own, but with the addition of a chased cupguard. The Light's metal was silver, his kilt green.

After they had sparred for several minutes, Parma

began to see the sense of their equipment. The Heavy fought a static fight, keeping his big shield rigid in front of his body, left foot advanced, sword drawn well back behind the right edge of his shield. He made his thrusts and cuts very cautiously, usually in opposition to a blow from the Light, and these strikes he made with lightning speed, withdrawing instantly behind his shield.

The Light's fight was a dynamic one. Keeping his shield high to protect his chest, leaning far forward to keep his exposed belly out of range, he skimmed in to engage his opponent and leaped nimbly back, wielding his short sword in brief jabs and cuts, sometimes under his shield, sometimes to the right edge, and occasionally over it. In his attacks, he often advanced his right leg in front of his left, unlike the Heavy, and more than once the long blade rang on the Light's greaves. All the Light could see of his opponent were his helmet and his left leg from the knee down. By attacking constantly, changing his line of attack swiftly from one side to the other, he hoped to tire his enemy's shield arm, causing him to expose himself for a crucial instant. When the Heavy's sword arm appeared, it was protected by its mail sleeve and, in any case, his blows were always timed to come between two movements of the Light's attack, making a time hit on his sword arm impossible. The Heavy hoarded his strength, moving his shield as little as possible, turning his whole body to meet his enemy's changing line of attack, knowing that his shoulder and arm would tire much more quickly from shifting the heavy shield than his legs would in moving his entire weight. His tactic was to let the Light tire himself out with the sheer fury of his unrelenting attack, then to make his strike when the Light's legs became rubbery and his attacks began to lose their fine co-ordination.

It was a battle of endurance as much as of skill.

The nature of their armor, limbs protected and vitals exposed, guaranteed that, in a real fight, there would be few crippling injuries. Wounds would be, for the most part, either superficial or fatal. After about a quarter hour, the trainer blew a small whistle and the two combatants retired to sit on a bench at the edge of the arena, sweating profusely, and their places were taken by another pair.

These two were entirely different. One wore a small, close-fitting helmet of almost spherical form, with a low comb and round, staring eyeholes. His shield was long and oval, slightly concave, and he wore the usual mailed sleeve. On his left shin was strapped a small, light greave, and he held a short, straight, double-edged sword with an openwork basket hilt. All his metal was a glossy black, and his kilt was of some bright, shimmery silver fabric. His opponent was the most bizarre fighter yet. He held a slim, three-pronged spear in one hand and a folded net in the other. Except for the inevitable armored sleeve he was nearly naked, wearing only a belt of metal scales with a groincup of elaborately decorated and enameled steel. He was the only fighter who fought bareheaded, and his face was devil-may-care, handsome, and sardonic, with a jauntily broken nose and a wide, quirky mouth. His hair was abundant and curly, confined by a silver fillet.

"This is the other type of fight most popular these days, the fight of sword and shield against net and trident. Netmen always fight swordsmen, never other netmen. The others will sometimes be matched against men armed in the same fashion. Only netmen can afford to be friendly with one another around here." There was cynical laughter from the men on the bench.

The trainer blew his whistle again and the two fighters commenced their battle. Both moved constantly in an unending broken step, from one side to the other, leaping back and darting forward in an almost dancelike rhythm of bewildering complexity. The netman darted his trident and essayed several casts of his net, but his opponent's armor and helmet offered no corners on which the meshes could snag. After each cast, the netman quickly drew the net back in with a cord connected to his wrist, always keeping the swordsman at a distance with his trident. The swordsman, in turn, was trying to cut the net, the cord, or the shaft of the trident, since he was getting no chance to attack his opponent bodily. That would only come if the netman tired first.

At last, he had his chance. The netman jabbed his trident at the staring eyeholes of the helmet before him, simultaneously making a high cast of the bunched net. The swordsman ducked under the trident and charged in low, letting the net fly over his head, drawing back his blunted weapon for the thrust to the belly that would signify a fatal stroke and the end of the match. Abruptly, though, the netman danced back, pulling hard on the connecting rope. The net reversed direction, blossomed open, and neatly enveloped the swordsman from behind, catching him bent over and off balance. The trainer's whistle sounded again, and the netman stooped to help his erstwhile opponent extricate himself from the entangling meshes.

Parma found these fights quite thrilling, and was eager to try his own skill against one of these peculiar warriors. He still was not quite sure what this was all about, but it looked enjoyable. From the stadium they were taken to a great enclosed exercise yard where they were led through a series of exercises that left even the fittest of them sweating and gasping. This was followed by another visit to the mess hall, after which they returned to the exercise yard, where they were given oversized and overweight weapons to drill with. A trainer handed Parma a huge two-handed sword, and he practiced cuts and blocks with it all afternoon, until his arms and back screamed with fatigue.

At the evening meal, Parma ate such a gargantuan amount that his neighbors stared pop-eyed, wondering where he found room in his lean frame to store it all. After supper, he was conducted to a hospital, where he was examined and tested, injected with antibodies, given a thorough medicinal bath, had his teeth inspected, repaired, and cleaned, and then was led to a small room where he was directed to lie on a table surrounded by strange machines. He should have been terrified, but a tranquilizing drug had been administered with his food. A light over the table blinked rhythmically in his eyes, and the next he knew he was back in his quarters, and the light of morning shone through the window.

He felt better than ever in his life, and he nearly flew to his feet with an excess of energy. There was a full-length mirror next to the door of his cell, and he wandered over to it. He had never seen such a mirror before, only the little ones hawked by the traders at the fairs, and it was strange to see his whole body reflected. When Parma reached the mirror, he gasped. His body was so clean that his skin seemed to glow. He was perfectly pink-white, with all trace of suntan removed, along with all his scars. The lump on his side where a broken rib had mended improperly was gone, as were the great unsightly riding calluses on his inner thighs and buttocks. His hair was glossy and free of dirt and vermin, his teeth startling white. But the greatest shock was that every vestige of body hair had been removed.

The effect was statuelike and oddly sexless, and Parma wasn't sure that he liked it, but he could not deny that he felt wonderful. He began to think that perhaps he would enjoy his new life. He had always thought of the dwellers in village and city with some contempt, but they certainly lived well, and they seemed to prize the manly virtues of strength and skill at arms. He put on his loincloth, which had been cleaned to astonishing whiteness, as had his sheeppox cloak, which he did not need here. Even his belt and sheaths had been oiled and polished, as had his boots. When he went out for the morning run, he felt as if he could run all day.

The days soon fell into a familiar pattern: exercises without weapons and lectures on technique in the mornings, then the midday meal, and after that drill with various weapons, at first overweight ones to build up muscle and endurance, then real but blunted weapons in set fights with other students in which every move was planned, and at last free fights in which he could test his skill against the others. After the evening meal, their time was their own, and they were permitted to wander freely about the city in which the school was situated. As long as they were back in their cells by lights-out, they were not harassed. The rings around their necks prevented them from escaping or doing mischief to themselves or to anybody else. The drugs they were constantly administered kept fats from building up in their bodies and encouraged the growth of muscle tissue. There were also drugs to combat depression and apathy, but none to discourage the desirable qualities of pugnacity, alertness, and hatred.

Parma quickly learned what was in store for him from the netman he had seen fight on his first day: Victorio, who took a liking to the young Thraxian. "First," Victorio had said, "you'll be sent to a small contest where you'll fight other unknowns, sandwiched between the big acts. Then, if you do well, you'll be picked for solo fights in the big games, maybe even the consul's games. You'll probably be killed before that, though. Most men are."

"But why are these fights held?" asked Parma.

"Just for entertainment, I suppose. On Charun and the major worlds, the people do no work, and all the warfare is performed mainly by constructs, so there's little enough excitement in their lives. If you ask me, I think the consul keeps these games going to keep people's minds off the extravagances of the court."

Parma wasn't especially surprised or shocked. He knew that people who didn't belong to his tribe were a little strange, and that offworlders were so incomprehensible as to be outside his reasoning altogether. He didn't think of their practices as evil, since morality was something he could only apply to his own tribe. As for the prospect of being killed, that did not disturb him in the least. The life of a fighting man was an honorable one, and the only thing he had really worried about on being sold was that he might be forced to do degrading labor, which meant any kind of work other than the tending of animals. Had that happened, he would have lost all self-respect and will to live. He was not sure about killing men, though. He had only done that to protect the tribe's herds, which was praiseworthy. Afterward, there had been the wizard to perform the rites that protected him from the vengeful spirits of the slain. But then, maybe these offworlders didn't have spirits.

Parma blotted his sweaty face with a towel. He had just finished an hour's drill with Victorio, learning to use his knife and buckler against the net and trident. Without the reach of a sword, he was at a severe disadvantage. His body was covered with welts from the metal pellets that weighted the net. Of six matches he had won only one.

"You're learning, Parma," said Victorio. "Still, the knife is no weapon against the net. Better learn the sword."

"The knife's my weapon," said Parma with a grin. "I'll just learn to be faster." Suddenly, his attention was drawn by a new group of fighters entering the practice area. He stared with wonder, doubting his eyes. They were women!

"Victorio, do women really train here along with men?"

"Of course. Women fighters are rather a specialized taste, but they are very popular with a certain element of the fight fans."

"Where do they come from?" asked Parma, intrigued.

"From all over, but the best are from the pirate fleets. There are a lot of women among the pirates, recruited from Pontus. That's a planet with a female warrior aristocracy. Younger daughters can't inherit their mothers' estates, so they seek their fortunes among the pirates. When they're captured, they bring high prices from the trainers."

For a while, Parma and Victorio relaxed in the shade of the barrack buildings that ringed the practice area, watching the women go through their drill. Parma had to admit that they were as skillful as any men he had ever seen. Once in a while, a woman who was angered or startled by an opponent would make a quick, involuntary grab at her hip. Parma asked Victorio about this curious gesture.

"They're reaching for pistols. On their ships, they wear pistols habitually. Losing them here is a sort of castration for them. Would you care to meet them?"

"Very much," said Parma. The women of his own tribe knew how to fight and did so when the situation was desperate, but they didn't make a specialty of it. These women were different. Victorio led him to the

woman who was obviously the dominant member of
the group. She was a blonde of about thirty, with
aristocratic features marred by a number of small
scars. She had shoulders and haunches like a female
sheepox, and Parma didn't doubt that she was twice
as dangerous.

"Hippolyta, my girl," said Victorio, grinning broadly, "I have someone here who would like to meet you."
The woman eyed him with bored contempt.

"Go away, you miserable little boy-humper." She
turned back to her companions.

"Don't mind that," said Victorio to Parma with a
grin. "She always talks that way to men."

"Not to *real* men," said Hippolyta. She looked Parma carefully up and down. "Excuse me. I may have
misjudged you. I thought you were one of Vic's pretty
boys."

"Speaking of which," said Victorio, "I have one to
meet in a few minutes. I'll leave you two to discuss,
oh, spears, or whatever it is you primitive types talk
about." He left with a chuckle as Hippolyta spat in
the direction of his retreating figure.

"Little sodomite! If he wasn't so good with a net
he'd be useless to anybody. Where are you from? I've
never seen a hairdo quite like yours before."

"Thrax."

"Oh. Our ships never raided there. Nothing on
Thrax worth taking except slaves, and they usually
put up too stiff a fight to make it worthwhile." She
eyed him with puzzlement. "You don't look like the
type who'd give up easy. Parents sell you?"

"I sold myself voluntarily. The tribe was desperate,
and the buyer offered a fortune, at least by my tribe's
standards."

"I didn't think you were a born slave. You stand
straight and look people in the eye."

"How did you come to be here?" asked Parma.

"Captured, of course." Her mouth twisted bitterly. "I was captain of the raider *Amazon Queen*, Cimmerrian Fleet, under Admiral Achillia. We were free-cruising and spotted a merchantman lifting off from Domitian. It looked like easy pickings, so we locked on and boarded. The merchantman was packed with fighting men. It was a trap, the kind they sometimes set to catch pirates. We'd've fought our way out, but they filled the air with nerve gas and shot us with tranquilizer darts. The next thing we knew, we were on the block in Augusta, being stripped and sold. Marius bought us, of course, the bastard." She added a few blistering maledictions in a language Parma didn't understand.

"Won't your admiral buy you out?" asked Parma.

"If we'd been captured in open fight, in a fleet action, she'd have bought us; that's part of the code. But I was on my own, and nobody has any use for a captain who's lost a ship. If I could get free, and steal a ship, they'd take me back. But, more likely, I'll die with a foot of steel in my belly. Mind you, it's not such a bad way to die, I just would prefer to have it come in a boarding action instead of in front of a pack of applauding degenerates. Five of my girls have died already." Her eyes glittered with hatred.

"Were your crew all women, then?"

"Yes, and all Pontines, girls I grew up with in the training camps. Admiral Achillia's a Pontine, and she favors women commanders and crews. The Cimmerrian Fleet's about three-quarters women, mostly Pontines or women born on Illyria, the pirates' home world."

Parma and Hippolyta went to a shaded bench and sat, watching the other women at their training. Occasionally, Hippolyta shouted advice or instructions. Obviously, the women still regarded her as their leader, and she intended to keep them alive as long as possible. The women, Parma noted, all fought as Lights, or with net and trident. Their favored weapons were short, wide-bladed swords and daggers. A few carried short-handled boarding axes or jointed flails, weapons consisting of five or six linked metal bars, tipped with a small spiked ball. All these were favored weapons for shipboard fighting, where the quarters were invariably close.

"I see your women aren't using bucklers," observed Parma.

"No, they're mainly an encumbrance in a deck fight. I've watched you train from the balconies. I've never seen anyone handle the knife and buckler as well as you. Would you drill my girls in handling the buckler?" She added hastily, "Don't worry about giving away your secrets to competition; they never match men against women."

"I'll be glad to," said Parma. He was intrigued at the idea of women fighters. "Now, suppose someone comes at you with an underhand stab, feinting at the belly and then turning his point upward toward throat or collarbone. How do you—"

"You learn to compensate," said Hippolyta. "A woman just has to lean a little farther back to avoid the knife. At least we don't have to worry so much about getting kicked in the crotch." She had a point there, Parma had to concede. "In the fleets, we wore hard plates on breast and belly, but here the fight fans prefer to see us fight without armor. It's an added thrill." She spat furiously. "Wormy little perverts!"

Parma spent the rest of the day training with the women. He was able to improve their shield play considerably. His hardest fight was with Hippolyta. She was tough as a buckler strap and incredibly tricky. Veteran of hundreds of ship fights, she had risen to command of a pirate ship through superior cunning and ferocity. Finally, he ended the fight by stepping in, hooking his right leg behind her shield, simultaneously blocking her knife with his buckler, and bringing his own knife up in a short, vicious arc, stopping so that the point just dimpled the sweaty skin below her breastbone.

"That was a tricky move," she said admiringly, as they toweled off.

"Too tricky for a real fight," he admitted. "I'd be more cautious if my life depended on it."

"That's the best way," she agreed. "I often find myself overcome with conservatism when I'm faced with real action." They paused to watch one of the women practice with the net. She was a small, slender brunette, nearly breastless, with narrow, wiry hips. She looked no more than fifteen, but she handled herself with more than adolescent competence.

"You wouldn't believe she's nearly as old as I am, would you?" said Hippolyta. "That's Medea. She was my second in the *Amazon Queen*. Victorio trained her to use the net. Next to him, she's the best net fighter here." She smiled at the woman proudly. "What that little catamite friend of yours doesn't know about the net isn't to be known." Parma was getting the idea that Hippolyta rather liked Victorio.

From that day, Parma practiced almost daily with the women. Few of the other men would have anything to do with them, fearing ridicule should they be defeated by a female, even in a practice match. Even the trainers resented their Pontine arrogance. It never occurred to Parma to worry about such things. He liked Hippolyta; she reminded him of the women of Thrax, especially of the women of the hill tribes, who often raided alongside their men. The pirate captain responded to him similarly, although she never became flirtatious and neither made any sexual overtures. Any such relationship would be futile in such a place, where nobody's life expectancy extended past tomorrow.

He listened, captivated, to the woman's tales of pirate raids and exploits, and they kindled in him a desire to learn more about the world outside this school and away from this world. He also began to realize what a terrible loss Hippolyta had suffered, snatched from the freedom of the stars to be neck-ringed and penned up here, a mere fighting animal.

Parma's curiosity about the outside world was insatiable, but he found that his ability to learn was severely hampered by his limited vocabulary. Aboard the trader ship, he and the other slaves from Thrax had been taught basic Esperanto by Kreuzer and his assistants, and he had picked up more at the school, sufficient for training purposes. When he spoke to Victorio or Hippolyta about any subject but fighting, though, they had to spend much of their time explaining unfamiliar words to him.

One day, Parma complained to Victorio of his problem, and the netman directed him to a small building in the city where an elderly attendant sat hunched in the midst of a clutter of book thimbles.

"So you want to polish up your Esperanto, eh?" said the old man, astonished to see a games fighter who wanted to learn anything. "What's your native tongue?"

"We call it 'language,'" said Parma.

"That's no help. What's your native world?"

"Thrax."

"The grassworld? My, you are from way out there. Which part of which continent?"

"I don't know."

"Well, no matter, speak a few words of your tongue in this grille." Parma did so.

"Ah, Graeco Balkan, early Third Millennium vintage. Let's see, now." The little old man rummaged through drawers and pulled out a number of thimbles.

"Just sit down on this recliner." The man pulled a padded blindfold over Parma's eyes and placed a sort of helmet on his head. As on the day he had been taken to the hospital, Parma woke, surprised to find that he had been unconscious. When he spoke to the little man he was speaking Esperanto as easily as if he had been speaking his native tongue.

"What kind of place is this?"

"This was once a university," said the old man, "a place where men came to gain knowledge. People are no longer interested in learning things these days, though." The old man sighed. "The only reason anybody comes here is to learn a language. This may be the only operating library in the system."

"Is it possible to learn any subject here? I would like to learn something of this world I've come to. It's all so bewildering."

"Certainly, my boy. Come here every evening when you finish training. It'll be a pleasure to teach somebody again. When you get knifed in one of the games, you'll have the satisfaction of dying an educated man."

V

On entering XV Sector, *Peter's Pence* joined a huge fleet of merchant and clerical vessels, heavily convoyed by warships of the Church Militant. This near the edge of the rediscovered galaxy, any ship that attempted to make a lengthy passage without protection was asking for trouble. It had, in fact, been pirate raids from outside the boundaries of the sector that had betrayed the existence of the Flavian System.

In the vastness of space, scout ships had often passed through the midst of the system without knowing it was there, but a captured pirate had supplied investigators with the name of the system, and a search through the Vatican Library had turned up a few badly deteriorated chart thimbles, one of which had a brief and incomplete history of the system appended, and another that contained, luckily, a complete set of co-ordinates for one of the more obscure planets of the system. Trade had been established

with this minor world, and details concerning the rest
of the system had become available.

It was to this remote planet, Titus, that Miles and
Jeremiah had been taken by a small trade ship ex-
changing machine parts for drugs. From the nearly
desolate spaceport, they had caught a ship bound for
Charun, paying their way with small slugs of tenetrine, a metal that had become disastrously scarce in
the far reaches of the galaxy during the Decadence.

The shuttle dropped them at the commercial spaceport of Augusta, the major city of the planet of
Charun. Miles and Jeremiah had decided on this destination because both the court and the greatest
masses of the poor lived there.

The spaceport was many centuries old, but it was
well kept up. The builders of the Third Millennium
had made almost indestructible edifices, surrounding
fragile materials such as wood and marble with perpetual stasis fields, which protected them from damage and even eliminated the need for cleaning. In the
foyer of the port was a statue of a young man with a
round face that was supposed to be made manly by a
short mustache and pointed beard. Despite the whis-
kers, the face was weak and dissolute. On his head
was a crenelated crown. And he wore long state
robes. An inscription informed all and sundry that
this was Ilya VII, consul of Charun and autocrat of
the Flavian System.

Outside the terminal, Miles and Jeremiah parted
company. "Well, my boy, you should have little difficulty in finding the poor to preach among," said the
priest, surveying the colossal slum surrounding the
spaceport. Stasis fields were expensive, and obviously none had been wasted on the accommodations of
the people hereabouts.

"You may have somewhat more difficulty in working
your way into the court, Father," observed the friar.

"Where there is a will, God will provide a way."
Pax vobiscum, Father."
"And with you, Brother."

Miles walked past rows of dilapidated buildings for many blocks. Everywhere he saw people, shabbily dressed for the most part, standing or sitting or wandering idly about. The overcrowding Miles knew to be deceptive, for the population of the planet had been falling steadily over the past few centuries. The population was heavily concentrated in a few centers such as this in order to be close to the facilities for distribution of food and entertainment. They were idle because there was nothing for them to do. No one starved, but everybody was a little hungry most of the time.

Eventually, Miles reached a large and well-kept park, surrounded by luxury establishments and government buildings. At a bank, he exchanged a few of his slugs of tenetrine for local currency. The man at the money-changing desk raised his eyebrows at the sight of the precious metal, but said nothing. From the bank, Miles wandered into the park and found a kiosk selling reading matter. He bought several periodical publications and sat on a bench to read. The language was one of the forms of Esperanto that had become popular when men began to spread out through the galaxy. The magazines were profusely illustrated, with a scanty, elementary text, from which Miles deduced that the bulk of the population of Charun was semiliterate. There were few news stories, and those avoided politics. The bulk of the reporting concerned the doings of pirates, wars that were being prosecuted with unvarying success by the armed forces of Charun in various parts of the system, and sports. The sports of Charun were obviously the obsession of the populace. From the articles, Miles found them to be brutal, sadistic, and deadly. Also, he found that riots among the spectators caused nearly as many fatalities as the games themselves.

The specialized jargon of the games had Miles puzzled for some time. In one of the games' publications, he found the following:

> "New Year's Games Wrapup:
> Lts; 436k 62dd 371vw 56vu
> Hvs; 355k 92dd 105vw 373vu
> Bst; 210k 891vw 1025vu

Note: Giancarlo, Claudio Victor, Shamyl, and Scorpio won their fights but have died since."

Studying the articles and photographs, Miles came to some sort of interpretation: The fighters were grouped roughly into two categories, Lights (Lts), Heavies (Hvs), plus beast fighters, who did not fight other men. Humanoid constructs also fought, but they were classified as fighting animals. It seemed that they accounted for most of the casualties among the beast fighters. The Lights fought with small shields, or no shields at all, using short swords, daggers, light lances, hatchets, whips, nets, and even lassos. They wore light armor and helmets, if any. The Heavies bore large shields and elaborate helmets, sometimes wore full armor and sometimes none, and their offensive weapons were the long sword, ax, mace, lance, and occasionally the short sword. Apparently the only real difference between the groups was the size of their shields, but the fans supported one side or the other fanatically. In addition, there were many fighters who fell into neither category, but apparently the great games were devoted to Lights and Heavies, the "Classical Forms"; "k" meant killed, "dd" meant defeated but dismissed, "vw" meant victorious but wounded, and "vu" meant victorious and unwounded.

Miles was not shocked. He had seen such situations many times before, and he would have been far more disturbed had he found these people practicing sorcery. Here, the reversion to paganism took the form of petty superstition, not unusual in an urban population that had lost both its sense of purpose and the overwhelming concern with fertility, which is the basis of most pagan religious practice.

Everywhere, Miles saw gambling establishments. In the entrance of each was a small shrine, bearing the image of a fat little deity holding a moneybag in one hand with a pair of scales dangling from the other. From time to time, a gambler would drop a small coin or a bit of food into a bowl at the little god's feet, where it disappeared in a flash of green flame accompanied by a puff of sweet-smelling smoke.

Nearing the edge of the park, Miles heard bells and wandered toward the sound. At its source, he found the last thing he had expected to see in this place: the Gothic spires and arches of a church. Inside, he found a huge, echoing nave, empty except for a dozen or so worshipers, mostly elderly, in the front row. A priest in later middle age, his robes faded and shabby, was beginning Mass. Miles sat in the shadows in the back of the nave to observe. He was pleased with the service. It was of Middle Romano-Coptic Rite, very antiquated but quite acceptable, with no factor condemned by the modern Church. Miles was relieved; often on these rediscovered worlds, cut off for centuries or even millennia by the Decadence, Church services, where they survived, were twisted to the point of heresy, or contained rites long since condemned by Vatican Council as grievous error. When the service was over and the tiny congregation dispersed, the priest set about thriftily extinguishing all the candles except for a small red vigil light. He nearly dropped his candle snuffer when Miles emerged from the obscurity of the nave. For long seconds the older priest stared and said nothing, then whispered:

"God be praised! It is true, then, that Rome has remembered?"

"I was in Rome not six weeks ago, by your time," said Father Miles. "I am Father Miles of Durga, of the Society of Jesus."

"I am Father Stavros, of the Order of St. Cyril. Please come into the refectory, Father Miles." In the refectory, Miles sat at a rickety table while Father Stavros brewed a hot beverage made from some mutated coffee beans. The Charunese priest was visibly collecting his thoughts as he removed and carefully folded his faded but precious ceremonial vestments. "Tell me, Father Miles," he said at last, "is my poor order still in existence outside this system?"

"I know of at least seventeen systems where the Order of St. Cyril is predominant. And now, Father Stavros, I hate to be precipitate, but time is of the essence. I have been sent by Rome to bring this system back into the fold without delay. I must have some information."

"Of course, Father, any way I may help. What do you wish to know?"

"First, tell me who runs all those casinos I passed on the way here."

For a moment the old priest was too shocked to speak.

"Why, they're controlled by criminal gangs, though why you want to know is an unfathomable mystery. These gangs control most activities in the poor parts of the city. There is fierce rivalry among them, and many of the young people hereabouts are attracted to join one or another of the gangs, because of the glamor they associate with violence and because it's the only way most of them can get out of the slums."

"What of the slaves? The report we received said

that slavery was very prevalent in this system."

"Most of them are employed in producing raw materials and foodstuffs on other worlds. The slaves
may be recognized by a thin metal ring around their
necks. Here, probably the only ones you might see will
be the game fighters and the poor victims, male and
female, in the houses of prostitution. Many times we
have petitioned to go among the slaves to bring what
comfort we may, but we were always rebuffed, and
we dared not press the matter. We are barely toler-
ated here, because we are few and weak, and because we keep up our few churches, which would
otherwise fall into ruin and make this city look even
worse." The priest's voice was mournful but tinged
with new hope.

"These things will be set to rights, Father Stavros,
and you will see the Church returned to her place of
honor, and the naves filled with worshipers, and the
seminaries filled with novices, and Rome triumphant
once more!"

"And how will this great work be accomplished?"
said Father Stavros, somewhat dazzled.

"With wisdom, and cunning, and faith, and with
this," said the Jesuit, brandishing his staff. "I must go
now, but you will hear from me soon."

"'Thou shalt bruise them with a rod of iron, and
break them in pieces like a potter's vessel,'" muttered
the little priest.

Without warning, Parma, Victorio, and a group of
twenty others were ordered to the spaceport one
morning after breakfast. They were met by guards, a
trainer, and a doctor, who were to escort them to
their destination, the planet Domitian.

Parma soon found himself standing in the arena of
a public stadium, the benches crowded with more
people than he had ever seen before. He wore ornate,

silver-chased armor and a light helmet with broad
cheekpieces instead of a visor. There were fifty other
men in the arena with Parma, and it was almost like a
practice session in the stadium adjoining the school,
except for the cheering crowd and the fact that he
was holding his Thrax knife instead of a practice
sword. His opponent was another Light, with an oval
shield and a straight dagger. Parma's stomach tight-
ened as he waited for the starting gong. No drugs
were permitted prior to the real fights, and each man
had to face his enemy with whatever courage was
natural to him.

When the gong sounded, the fight was almost an
anticlimax. Almost before the brassy reverberations
had died away, Parma's opponent was on the sand of
the arena, bleeding from a cut to the back of the thigh,
where his armor did not protect him. Parma hardly
remembered the blow. The fight, short as it had been,
had contained at least twenty exchanges of cut,
thrust, block, and parry. The backhand cut to the rear
of the unshielded thigh was one that Parma had practiced hundreds of times in training, and he knew that
he must have made it during one of the exchanges, not
even knowing that the blow had been successful. He
left the man to be attended by the medical staff, who
stood by with stretchers.

The crowd was giving Parma a good hand, which
he mechanically acknowledged by waving his bloodstained knife aloft. Luckily, he was an unknown, and
the fight was early in the day. Otherwise, the crowd
might have insisted that he kill his opponent. The
crowd was distracted by some dramatic moment in
another fight, and Parma walked through the victor's
gate, to be slapped on the back and be congratulated
by Vic, the trainer, and others from the School of
Marius. In the next three weeks he fought four more
times, twice against Lights, and twice against Heavies.

The result was the same: four men with bloody but nonfatal injuries. On his return to Ludus, he was summoned to the office of Marius himself.

He hadn't seen Marius since the confusing first day in Ludus. The school was a very large one, with thousands of men in training, so the owner was a remote and lofty personage. Marius was sitting behind a desk as Parma entered the office and stood attentively just inside the doorway. While he waited for his master to look up, Parma studied his face. Parma was now more than a year older than the bewildered boy fresh from the plains of Thrax, and far wiser; he was able to make a much deeper reading of the man before him than on the first occasion, when he had seen only a dangerous fighting beast.

Now he saw the deep-etched lines of bitterness, and a deep and brutal sensuality held rigidly in check by an iron will. This was a man who would never let his desires and lusts get the upper hand. He could even see, here and there, traces of ironic humor. Parma had inquired about Marius and had found that little was known of the enigmatic games-trainer. He had been born in the great slums of Augusta on Charun. He had risen, through force of personality, shrewdness, physical strength, and ruthlessness to an important position in one of the street gangs that controlled most of the city. After a vicious all-night street battle in which his gang had been defeated, Marius had taken refuge in the only place that provided sanctuary for his kind: a consular recruiting office. To escape death at the hands of the rival victorious gang, Marius had enlisted in the consul's army.

After a year in the brutal training camp of Charun, Marius had been commissioned as an officer of constructs. These beings, fabricated from human protoplasm to be perfect warriors, were excellent, even brilliant fighters on a company scale, with an intuitive grasp of infantry tactics implanted in their genes, but they were hopeless at larger strategy and needed human officers to direct them as well as to take care of logistics, intelligence, supply, and all other matters not involving weapons and hand-to-hand combat. Constructs were also subject to periodic fits of psychotic violence. Only in combat were they stable and safe to handle. The casualty rate was high among young officers, mainly from their failure to take suitable precautions in defending themselves from their charges. For three years Marius had lived among these unholy beings, wearing a uniform of armor cloth, with holstered pistol and dagger at his belt, and always with a heavy, spiked gauntlet on his left hand.

The campaigns in which he took part were little more than glorified plundering expeditions. The planets of the system had been thoroughly looted and were now mostly inhabited by slaves working the plantations, mines, mills, and fisheries owned by the great families. The few semi-autonomous worlds, such as Ludus and Domitian, supplied essential services to the court and the great families, and were left alone most of the time, except for the endless feuding among the great families themselves. From time to time, one of the remaining scout ships would discover some forgotten planet outside the system, and the troopship would be loaded with constructs and return laden with wealth and slaves to keep the tottering economy going awhile longer.

At the end of three years, Marius, not yet twenty-five, his hair already flecked with gray, bought his discharge and signed onto a merchant vessel. Nobody seemed to know where Marius disappeared to in the ensuing five years though some claimed that he was seen captaining a ship that conducted raids from Illyria, the pirate base. And it was almost certain

that, for a while, he was an officer in the hired armies
of the warlord of Cadmus, who manufactured and
trained nearly all of the constructs used in the public
and private wars of the system. What *was* known was
that, some ten years before, Marius had shown up in
Ludus with a large sum of money, bought a long-closed
school, stocked it with slaves, convicts, prisoners of
war, and free volunteers, and settled into the role of
respected businessman. His drive and intolerance of
second-rate quality made his fighters the most demanded in the system. His contacts in the military,
pirate, police, and merchant slaver fields assured
that he always had first chance to buy the most desirable human material.

This was the man who owned Parma and who addressed him with astonishing mildness for one of such
forbidding exterior and reputation.

"Well, my boy, it seems you've done well for yourself in your first fights. I've seen the holos. Five clear
wins and not a scratch on you. Congratulations."

The man's voice and manner held a sort of sinister
joviality that instantly put Parma on his guard.

"I am honored that my poor showing has come to
your notice, sir."

"So, you've learned irony along with fighting. I've
heard that you spend your spare time in the old university." The thick eyebrows went up, the tone was
oddly oblique. The trend of the burly man's speech
escaped Parma so he retained his guarded diffidence
of manner.

"I seek to improve my knowledge of this confusing
system, sir, and I've found that I enjoy the acquisition
of it."

"Yes, quite so. It speaks well for the optimism of
youth that one in your profession has enough confidence in the future to indulge in education. Tell me,
boy, why did you kill none of your opponents on Do-

mitian?'' The sudden change of subject caught Parma off balance.

"Why, it was never necessary to deliver a fatal stroke. I fought until my opponent exposed an unguarded piece of arm or leg, and I struck. There seemed no necessity to kill.''

"Yes, but there was nothing to keep you from killing them after they were down. Didn't the crowds shout for you to do just that?'' The voice was growing impatient.

"They did, but I don't hold it honorable to kill a helpless man, and I was told that the life of the defeated was at the discretion of the victor. I exercised that discretion and spared them.'' Parma's tone remained respectful but firm. The man behind the desk growled with exasperation.

"Damn it, boy, there is no place for honor in the arena, only for survival, and your chances of survival increase with every dead enemy. Men have been killed by those whose lives they have spared. A man always has a far better chance of defeating you in the second fight. As a fighter, you have an obligation to please the audience. They may think it well enough if you spare a man who put up a good fight and gave them a lot of excitement, but if you let a man live who has displeased them they'll turn against you, and if you're defeated, they'll demand your death. Most men will be happy to oblige. Didn't you kill men on your home world?''

"Yes, but that was in open warfare, against hereditary enemies who sought to take our flocks. It's different.''

"There is no difference!'' said Marius, pounding on his desk for emphasis. "Killing is killing, whether done for duty or profit or fun. Why do you think those people like to watch the fights?''

"I really don't understand. Oh, the fighting is entertaining enough, I suppose, I like to watch that myself, but why the people enjoy watching men being killed escapes me." Parma's voice was calm and reasonable, and Marius made a visible effort to keep his own manner cool.

"Well, listen, boy, and I'll further your education." The voice had become a flat, gravelly grating. "It's not philosophy gained from old thimbles, it's knowledge of the human animal gained from years of firsthand experience. The principal, foremost, and oldest pleasure of humanity is to inflict pain and death on a helpless fellow creature. Most people are never able to indulge this desire, because their fellow man might inflict an injury on them in turn. So the answer is a second-best but still enjoyable alternative: to watch someone else taking the risk and doing the killing. A fight is more enjoyable than a simple execution because it adds zest, the element of uncertainty. Also, it gives an opportunity to gamble, and it supplies heroes for the people to idolize, briefly. You will have heard a great deal in your thimbles about the excuses people make for why they fight, kill, and make war. They always lie.

"Mark me, boy, there is only one enemy for a tribe, a nation, or a whole planetary system: He is the man who has what you want, and your move is to kill him and take it from him. If you are a robber, a pirate; your enemy is anyone who has wealth for the taking. If you are a politician, your enemy has power, or a threat to your own power. In the arena, your enemy has the power of taking your life, and you must take that power from him or die yourself. So start killing out there, boy. Mercy is the enemy of survival." He dismissed Parma with a wave, and the young man left the office thinking hard.

On his next visit to the library, Parma sounded out

the old keeper on why the system was as it was.

"Well, things just fell apart," said the old man with a shrug. "Once, all of humanity lived on one world, Earth, though not one person in a hundred these days has even heard the word. They spread out all through the galaxy in the Third and Fourth Millennia, hundreds of thousands of worlds colonized, but Earth remained their spiritual home. Religion, which had been in decline, became very strong again during the Great Expansion. Even after the Earth's own wealth had long been exhausted, it was the home of all the holiest places of mankind. Only Earth had Mecca, Rome, Jerusalem, Salt Lake City, the Ganges, all the sacred cities, rivers, and shrines. There was no central government, but a great network of pilgrimage routes bound together all the worlds settled by humanity."

The old voice was taking on vitality now, beginning to show enthusiasm. "The courts of the great religions became wealthy beyond belief. This paltry Flavian System was once a mighty assembly of worlds, a hundred or more, whose people owed spiritual allegiance to Rome. The wealth that this system alone sent to Rome each year was the full income of ten planets. It seemed that the great star-spanning empire would never end."

"But what happened?" asked Parma, enthralled, caught up in this gigantic vision.

"Things just fell apart," said the old man again. "The courts of religion became corrupt, the expansion stopped, trade stagnated, petty wars broke out. Fewer people each year applied for entrance to universities like this one. The professions that saw to the upkeep of the mechanical systems that provided a good life dwindled away. The machines broke down or ran out of power, and nobody knew how to solve the problem. The arts, literature, all fell off. People just seemed to lose interest."

"Then how does the system survive at all?" asked Parma.

"The men of the old days were mighty builders, and the ships they made in the final years of the expansion are nearly immortal, and they seem to have a perpetual power supply. Also, they are so simple to operate that a moron can use them. One just pushes a chart thimble into the console, and the ship goes to the proper destination. That is why the pirates and the military can go on their plundering forays. The thimbles, themselves, though, are subject to deterioration, and once the last thimble for a particular world has crumbled, that world is lost for good. There are a few scoutships left that can seek out a lost planet, but those are one-shot expeditions, as the machinery for making new thimbles no longer works. Toward the end, many systems who wanted to be free of Earth sent teams of saboteurs to destroy the thimbles and records of their systems kept there. Those raids, and time, have caused the downfall of the Earth Empire."

Parma pressed him further, and described to the old man the interview in Marius's office.

"Your master Marius is a wicked man, and he seeks to justify his wickedness with cynicism. All his life he has lived by victimizing his fellow man, and there is still enough moral sense left in him to make him want to think that all men are his equals in evil.

"The reason why you do not kill is that no sane man kills unless driven to the act by absolute necessity. Unfortunately, there are few sane or moral people these days. The apathy that followed the collapse of the empire of Earth is a spiritual lassitude, an unwillingness to take the trouble to oppose the evil in one's nature with good. All creative urge is inert, even the urge to reproduce has declined. The birth rate has fallen steadily for centuries. Everywhere, destruction has replaced creativity; trade edged out by plunder; statesmanship by tyranny; legitimate entertainment by sadistic spectacle; learning by ignorance; religion by superstition. I suppose that it will end when we are all confined to our little worlds and degenerate into anarchy."

He hesitated in his bitter diatribe. "There may be an answer, though. I think that you are an example of what the old race of man must have been like. You have self-respect, a thirst for knowledge, and a moral sense that will not be brutalized by the arena. Even the horrible Marius seems to have thought about why he is what he is more than most in these last centuries. And I have heard that the consul's sister is a woman of learning and compassion. Can it be that the old spirit is reviving?"

Parma left no less confused, and the depression he had felt after speaking to Marius was still with him. When Parma returned to the school, Vic greeted him with the news he had feared.

"Hey, Parma, we're in luck! We've been picked for the consul's birthday games in Augusta!"

VI

Father Miles looked up at the sign over the entrance of the gambling palace. "RAINBOW'S END," screamed the sign. "CARDS! DICE! RACES! FIGHTS! ALL KNOWN GAMES OF CHANCE! BET A DINAR AND WIN A MILLION!"

Miles walked in past the shrine of the little god. The air was nearly choking with the smoke of a dozen different drugs. Things rattled, spun, whirled, tumbled, and flashed, men and women cheering or groaning at each sound, motion, halting, or change. In a huge holographic pit, fighters were clashing in lifelike three-dimensional projection from Vespasian, another planet of the same solar system as Charun. On a raised platform in a theaterlike room, a huge brute in mailed shorts was challenging all comers to unarmed combat, no holds barred. A sturdy youth accepted, to have his arm broken within seconds. The challenge was reissued.

Miles wandered over to a table that featured one of

mankind's oldest devices. Miles had seen their like in
the Vatican Museum, dug up from the ancient cities of
Sumeria. Four thousand years after the fall of Sumeria, identical cubes had rolled at the foot of the
Cross. Dice never changed. He studied the play, which
was typical. The player rolled the dice: If two, three,
or twelve showed, he lost his bet; if seven or eleven
showed, he won: if four, five, six, eight, nine, or ten
showed, he continued to roll the dice until that number appeared again, in which case the gambler won,
but if seven appeared first, the house collected.

It was a common game, and Miles knew of fifteen
variants in parts of the rediscovered galaxy. This was
almost identical to the version still played on Earth.
Once, Miles had presented the seminar on the history
and psychology of gambling with a paper arguing that
it had been this very game that the Roman soldiers
had played for Christ's garments. Unfortunately, the
dean of the seminar had been Archbishop Scipio,
whose own pet theory was that it had been knuckle-
bones, not dice, that the soldiers had used.

Taking a vacant place at the table, Miles waited
until the dice worked their way around the ring of
gamblers. His trained eyes detected from the uneven-
ness of the roll that the dice were loaded. When his
turn came, Miles felt their balance. The center spot of
the three on one die had been drilled and a tiny rod of
metal inserted. In the other die, the rod had been inserted in the side with the four spot. Neither piece of
metal was heavy enough to affect the roll of the dice
significantly, so there had to be a magnetic plate
beneath the table.

With the dice touching a ring on his right hand,
Miles thumbed one of the tiny knots on his staff, re-
versing the polarity of the magnets in the cubes. Miles
rolled his point: a five. He made several passes, piling
up a respectable number of counters; then he saw a

minute dip of the croupier's shoulder, which indicated that the man had trod on a switch, magnetizing the table. The dice rolled with an almost imperceptible hop and came to a rest, completing Miles' point. The croupier's face betrayed nothing, but, as he swept up the dice to hand them back, he pulled a quick substitution. The result was the same. As the evening wore on, people flocked to the table to see this remarkable run of luck. Finally, a hard-eyed manager closed the table with a false show of joviality.

"The bank is broken on this table, folks. Well, people, there you've seen it! A man can walk in here with a few coins in his pocket and walk out with a fortune, as this lucky gentleman has done! Now, there are plenty of other tables for you to try your luck at, folks, so get at it while luck's still running against the house." Turning to Miles, the manager spoke in a low, threatening voice: "This house belongs to Curio, friend. Nobody crosses Curio's gang. I don't know how you did it, but you won't do it again. Now, get out."

"Tell Curio that I wish to see him." The priest was unperturbed.

"Nobody sees Curio unless Curio wants to see them. I'm in authority here, and I'm telling you to get out!" The manager's face was growing red.

"I don't bandy words with underlings." Miles' voice was concentrated insult, every inflection designed to enrage this vain little bully. "Tell Curio that I have a proposal for him. Tell him quickly or you will regret it." He turned and marched out the entrance in a swirl of black robes.

Within a block, Miles knew he was being followed. There were five of them, so he found a crossing of two streets where there was an overhead light. He stood in the illluminated circle, facing back the way he had come. The men emerged from the dimness in a line.

Miles knew that the little drama was being watched avidly from surrounding windows, so he had placed himself in a position to allow full observation and maximum effect. All the nearby buildings were high tenements.

The man in the center was the beast who had been fighting on the stage in the casino. The others were swaggering toughs of standard breed. Under the armpit of one tunic, Miles saw the outline of a small gun—a rarity in a tyranny where firearms were tightly controlled for fear of insurrection. Another showed the bulge of a knife handle. The hulking brute was first to speak.

"Colouris says you're to be taught a lesson, so hand over the money and we won't do more than break your arms and legs, after which, when you recover, you are to stay away from any establishment belonging to Curio's gang." The ape grinned, seeming proud to have constructed so lengthy a sentence. His companions smirked. Miles answered in his most ringing and clear-pitched voice:

"I am a priest of the Living God, who smites those who interfere with his servants. Today, his business took me to your gambling den. Another day I may be called there again, and, if so, then I shall go there! Do not detain me or you shall suffer!"

The thugs goggled with amazement; then a ferret-faced man guffawed and tapped his temple with a forefinger. Spreading in a circle, two men approached to grasp Miles' arms from behind while another stood before him and slipped on a set of metal knuckles. The staff thrust twice quickly to the rear, and two men went down retching, grasping at groin and belly. It flashed forward once and crushed the larynx of the man with the metal knuckles, who fell writhing to the ground, making horrible strangling noises. The ferret-faced man squawked and drew his gun. He was fast, but the staff was faster, and the gun went spinning, its owner screaming with the agony of a broken wrist. The scream was cut off short by a reverse blow to the jaw. Miles' staff was a mass of complex circuitry, but it was also a perfectly good stick. The big man had made no move to attack, but had stood by with a faint smile.

"So, you're a tough one, eh? You any good without the stick?"

Miles tossed his staff aside. It was not a gesture of foolish bravado.

"God's chosen have been known to wrestle with angels before, and while I am no Israel, you are most certainly no angel. Make your move."

The gangster threw a flying kick, incredibly fast for one so bulky. Miles blocked with an iron forearm and replied with an economical punch to the kidney as the big man spun off balance. Miles felt a metal plate buckle slightly beneath his knuckles: The man was wearing a light body armor. The gangster landed on his feet like a cat, spun, feinted a kick at Miles' knee, but threw a side chop to the neck instead. The priest didn't respond to the feint, but ducked the chop, spinning and sending a reverse kick at the exposed nerve ganglion in the thug's armpit. The man jumped back, his right arm paralyzed. He dove for the fallen pistol, grabbed it left handed, and fired.

Miles had the staff back in his hand, and the thin red beam from the pistol was drawn to its center and expelled harmlessly out both ends as blue light. The man dropped the pistol and leaped in with animal courage for one last try, to be met with a resounding clout on the chin. He collapsed among his fellows.

Miles looked up at the buildings around him from within the circle of his fallen enemies and shouted:

"'He teacheth mine hands to fight, and mine arms shall bend even a bow of steel!'"

He strode out of the light, leaving a ring of groaning, groveling men on the street.

Father Stavros was making coffee when Miles swept into the rectory. The black-robed priest accepted a cup and sat, musing.

"Well, Father Miles, did you have a profitable day?" The priest's voice betrayed equal quantities of curiosity, hope, and apprehension.

"Quite," said the Jesuit, reaching into his scrip and dropping a stack of thin, rectangular golden plaques onto the table. "Send some of this to your Church treasury and use the rest to refurbish this church and help your poor parishioners. You will have more people to preach to soon."

Stavros stared at the golden stack with wonder and stammered:

"But, this is more money than the whole Church of the Flavian System has seen for ten years!"

"This is nothing. Soon the Church of the Flavian System shall be rich, and your position here shall improve immeasurably. Men are much concerned with money here. They respect men and organizations that have managed to accumulate wealth here, where it is so rare. Oh, you'll have people flocking to your gates, soon."

"But, where did all this come from?" said the priest, aghast.

Miles gave him a detailed account of the day's doings. Father Stavros was trembling and wiping the sweat off his brow at the end of the recitation.

"Father Miles, this is most unwise. I go farther: It is foolish. This man Curio is one of the three or four most powerful vicelords in the city. My parishioners go in mortal fear of him. Only God knows how many men he's killed to gain his position. What reason could you have for wanting to see him?"

"It's obvious that in this stagnant society, only the organized criminals are upwardly mobile. If I am to get an introduction at court it must be through one of the gang lords. They will make the contacts among the nobility."

"That, alas, is only too true. Most of the great families have one of the street gangs to do their dirty work for them, and in return the nobles give them the protection they need for their more nefarious activities. But Father, something you have said bothers me sorely."

"What is that?"

"Well, while the Church holds that gambling, in moderation, is not sinful, cheating most certainly is. What you did in that gambling den was cheating."

"There was no fair way to play the game, which was rigged. In any case, my purpose was to forward God's work. I am sure that God will not object to crooked dice when the stake being played for is the salvation of worlds."

"Well, perhaps so," said Stavros, dubiously. It was beginning to dawn on him that this Jesuit seemed of the opinion that God would never dare dispute with him.

"Now, Father Stavros, I must have some information about the court."

"I will tell you what I know, but that is very little. The court is very remote from the lives of the common people, and does not encourage discussion of its activities."

"Who are these great families, in relation to the throne and each other?"

"Well, foremost are the Torreon, the Capelli, and the Broz. These three have marriage ties to the royal family. The royal family itself is very small, because most of the consuls, upon accession, have had their brothers, and sometimes all their male and even female relatives, assassinated. Ilya is the last of his line, and if he and his sister die without issue, it will be civil war between the major families for possession of the consulate. Many of them keep veritable private armies, bought or leased from the warlord of Cadmus. These are mostly constructs, of course, with human officers. These officers, by the way, are mostly from here, the slums of Charun. Aside from the criminal gangs, it's the only way out for most.''

''Is the court entirely corrupt, then? Is there no person of influence to whom I may apply reason?''

''The consul's sister, the Princess Ludmilla, is said to be very learned, at least as such things are defined these days. She has a court circle of scholars and philosophers.''

''Is her brother sympathetic to her, or is he hostile?''

''This I do not know. I can't even say why she's still alive. Ilya has killed everybody else who could inherit the throne.''

''Can a woman inherit, then?''

''Yes, if there is no male living in the direct line of inheritance.''

''Then I suppose it's to this woman that I must apply myself.''

After supper, they listened to Father Stavros' hoard of pre-Decadence Gregorian Chant thimbles.

The next morning, a shifty little man came to the rectory and asked to see Miles. He had come to conduct the priest to Curio. He offered a steel transport, but Miles preferred to walk. He wanted his presence known in the city. This time, as he walked through the park where he had been ignored before, there was much whispering and pointing of fingers. The man in the black robes with the stick was fast becoming a local celebrity.

Curio's house was a luxurious establishment occupying the top three floors of a posh hotel. Miles was conducted past statues and murals of games fighters executed in execrable taste, then led out to the edge of a swimming pool, where a bald man sat in a recliner. The bald man regarded Miles for a few seconds.

"You don't look like so much," he said. "So, Colouris tells me that you jinxed one of his tables and walked out with a stack of plates. He tells me you roughed up five of his boys. Word is you took on the Beast with your bare hands and feet, and you took Jody the Snit's gun away from him. That true?"

"I did so."

"Well, mister, you made me lose a lot of face. That means I gotta either kill you or be friends with you. Personally, I'd just as soon kill you, but Colouris says something about you got a proposition for me. It good enough to make me want to let you live?"

"As for killing me, I doubt that you could. However, there is something I want you to do for me, and in return I will give you something that will enable you to ruin or at least badly hurt your competitors."

"Now you're talking. Sit down and have a drink. What is it?"

"Your houses take bets on the outcome of fights and races conducted on Vespasian."

"Sure. So do Three-fingered Jody's and Giulio's and Fernando's, plus a few small operators. So?"

"Do you know what the lag in transmission is between broadcast from Vespasian and reception on Charun?"

"A few minutes, I guess."

"Between seven and twelve minutes, depending on relative distance. I can give you a transmitter-receiver that will allow you to communicate the results of fights and races instantaneously. You will have a minimum of seven minutes to place your bets in your competitors' establishments.''

Curio's mouth fell open as the possibilities began to dawn on him.

"So," his voice was awed, "you found some old-time gadgets, huh?''

"Something like that.''

"What is it you want from me?''

"I need to establish myself at court. I think that you can furnish me with the proper contacts.''

"Is that all?'' asked the gangster, incredulous. "Sure, I'll take you to see old man Capelli himself. He can get you in. And when I take you to see him, you'll give me the transmitters?''

"That is what I will do.''

"What about the way you jinxed my table? I'll give a lot for that.''

"We'll talk about that later. For now, my business is with Capelli.''

Miles sat at perfect ease amid the elegance of the Capelli palace, on a hilltop outside Augusta. A servant had met him at the gate and conducted him to this small drawing room, paneled in rich, dark, exotic woods and smoothly tanned animal skins. He had been driven out to the palace by one of Curio's men, after a call by Curio had arranged this appointment. He had handed over the small transmitters to Curio's driver as he left the vehicle.

After a wait of no more than two minutes, a white-haired gentleman of dignified bearing entered the room. He bowed gracefully.

"Please pardon me for this delay," said the old man courteously, "but affairs kept me in my office. If I may offer you a drink, or any other refreshment, it will be my honor to extend the hospitality of my house.'' There was a deep charm in the aristocrat's every inflection.

"Thank you," said Miles. "If you have some white wine, it has been a tiring day." Miles played the proper guest, but he was not taken in by the splendidly graceful manners of the old man. Miles was an authority on the reading of intentions and motives through the unspoken attitudes of body and minute variations of facial gesture. Besides this, he had an inborn and highly developed insight that almost bordered on ESP. His every instinct and ounce of training shouted that this man was a merciless old schemer, capable of any treachery that would advance his goals.

"Permit me to introduce myself, my young friend. I am Malatesta Capelli, and my house is at your disposal." He poured a clear wine from a purple crystal decanter and handed the goblet to Miles. "It is the very finest and lightest Chablis-fort, of a vintage raised by my father. I see in you a man of fine sensibility, and I think it will please your palate."

Miles tasted the wine without hesitation. Poison and drugs were not this man's style. If there was treachery here, it would be something more subtle. In any case, the old man had no reason for hostility yet. Miles was just someone to whom his valued hatchet-man owed a favor.

"It is indeed a splendid vintage, sir. I believe that your grapes are a mutated Moselle-Rothschild stock, perhaps the celebrated Teutonic White grape? Am I correct?" Miles affected the air of the slightly jaded, ever so slightly supercilious connoisseur.

"Absolutely correct, sir," declared the old man. "It is encouraging to know that, even at my advanced age, I can still discern a man of taste. And now, my friend, but, I do not think I have your name."

"Please forgive me," said Miles, "I am Father Miles, of the Church of Rome."

"I am most honored to make your acquaintance.

Now, let me see: I am a regular donor to all the temples of Augusta, but I don't remember seeing you among the priests of the Roman Church in the Green Park. You are, I take it, from, ah, elsewhere?" The snowy eyebrows arched in a kindly, grandfatherly manner.

"It is true, sir, I am not from Charun." Miles' voice was perfectly bland.

"I do not wish to pry, of course, but there are rumors that men, members of your religious community, have been seen in various parts of our system, and that these men are from somewhere — outside, as it were, from those reaches of the galaxy that were lost to us so long ago."

"To be sure, I have heard such rumors," said Miles.

"I do hope there is some truth in them," said the old man. "It would be a great thing for us all if the Church of Rome were to be returned to its old position of prominence, and we were to be recommunicated with the great universe beyond." Capelli gave a fine sigh of longing, one that would have been convincing to anyone whose senses were less finely attuned than Miles'.

"It may well be that those days shall come again," said Miles, with heavy significance. "Perhaps, with your aid, that day may be speeded."

The old man's eyes were wide with mock enthusiasm.

"How may I help?" There were a thousand calculations behind the bright blue eyes.

"I need an introduction at court. I understand that the only person there with whom I might gain a foothold is the princess. Could you arrange for me to meet her?"

"Why, of course, my friend. Truly, you would have short shrift from the consul himself, who is only fond of his gross athletes, but the Princess Ludmilla is a young lady of the most delicate taste and the greatest accomplishment. I am sure that such a man as you will be a shining addition to her circle."

They shook hands warmly, made involved farewells, and arranged to meet at the main gate of the palace enclosure on the following day at noon. Miles left the mansion and rode back to the city in one of Capelli's vehicles, feeling like a fly who has picked his way among the meshes of a spider's web.

VII

There had been frantic days of preparation before taking ship for the games. Marius himself had given last-minute coaching, taking an interest in Parma that the younger man did not quite understand. Parma had been issued a new set of fabulously ornate armor, scintillating with jewels, and a gold-plated shield and a cloak of precious cloth trimmed with fur.

On the last day before departure, Parma had slipped out to the library, where he asked the librarian what he might expect. The old man was not encouraging.

"I wish I could say I expected to see you back again, my boy, but I can't." The old man shook his head sorrowfully. "You are going into the pit itself. Out here, where the fighters are trained, people are fond of fighting and value it above simple killing, but in Augusta they love massacres. Instead of single combats, they start a festival off with real battles, and they may not let you spare your opponents.

"The consul, Ilya VII, is the last male of a long and depraved line. He takes no hand in the government, preferring to leave that to his ministers. He spends his time instead at the games, hanging about the training schools in Augusta and surrounding himself with a bodyguard of the most idolized fighters. He needs a bodyguard, too. Plots are constantly being fomented around court. The great families fawn on Ilya but would like to seize the throne for themselves. Avoid the court, boy: It's peopled with predators and parasites. A nice, clean death in the arena is infinitely preferable."

As he lay on his recliner in the ship that was bearing him toward Augusta, the old man's words went through Parma's mind. He was caught between dread and anticipation. He might be noticed in the games, become a favorite of the consul. That was deadly in its way, but it was the path to wealth and freedom. He was not quite sure what he would do with freedom, but when it came he would grasp it. Freedom was what he desired above all else. He had once been satisfied with the abundant food and comforts of the training school, but in the past year, something had happened in his consciousness. He felt the vague, restless stirrings of an ambition he could not name.

He knew that he could not return to Thrax. To the tribe, he would be as foreign as any offworlder, and now that life would be as boring to him as any he could imagine. He realized suddenly that he was doing himself little good in speculating about the future. He had little chance of surviving his first fight. He closed his eyes and slept.

From the port of Augusta, Parma and his companions were taken by transport vehicles to a training school near the palace and adjoining the great stadium.

Looking curiously out through the windows of the
transport, Parma saw a city much like Ludus: dingy,
dilapidated, and full of sullen people. The scene was
livened up by a great many ancient monuments and
fine fountains, some of which still worked, but the
general air was one of decay.

The environs of the palace were another story.
Within the walls of the compound surrounding the
miles-square palace area, all was spotless and glittering. There was hardly a structure not made of some
precious wood or marble, and the roofs shone with an
overlay of silver and gold leaf. In the training school
to which they were conducted, Parma goggled at the
silken hangings, crystal goblets, and golden table-
ware, sniffed incense, and blinked when he was conducted to an incredibly luxurious suite of rooms,
which was to be his for the duration of the games.

"You shall live like a king here, sir," said an attendant, "for a while, anyway." Everywhere there were
slaves in neck rings: valets to take care of their wants;
cooks, waiters; beautiful boys and girls for their
amusement; musicians; porters; and all these to wait
on men who were themselves the lowest of slaves.

No expense was spared to keep the fighters for the
consul's birthday games happy and fit. For several
days they practiced in gymnasia full of sophisticated
equipment to sharpen up skill and timing. Each evening they were entertained at lavish banquets, where
they were served the rarest foods, beverages, and
drugs. Physicians were always in attendance to make
sure that they suffered no overindulgences that might
affect their performance in the fights.

Touring the palace one day, Parma saw his first
constructs, creatures manlike in form but eight feet
tall and having four arms, the fingers of each hand
terminating in two-inch bronze spikes. There were a
pair of them flanking the doorway to the consul's

residence. The next time Parma saw Marius, he asked him a question that had been bothering him.

"If those things are so frightful, why don't the crowds watch them fight instead of men?"

"A number of reasons: First, because it's just not as much fun to watch an artificial construct suffer and die as it is to watch a man. They do fight in the public shows, but then they're classified as fighting animals. You see, human sadism is a complex thing, and it calls for a good deal of subjective identification. The spectator wants to share vicariously the pain and defeat of the victim as well as the triumph of the victor. They can't feel that for a being that just doesn't have human feelings.

"By the way, those guards you saw aren't the true warrior type. They're just for show. Basic human flesh, bone, and tissue are used in making the constructs, and they've never been able to make them much more than seven feet tall without losing all coordination. The nervous system just isn't up to it. Those you saw will be as tame as tabby cats. The real warriors generally have horn carapaces over their vitals, and they can have fangs, claws, horns, or just about any other armaments you can make out of protoplasm, but they're never so overspecialized that they can't use weapons. Excessively long claws get in the way of trigger handling. Being sexless, they miss out on a lot of human motivation, and most of what they do have is ferocity and bloodthirstiness."

One evening, the consul himself came to attend one of the banquets. Parma observed him closely, and did not like what he saw. The young man was of medium height, very well built, from his years of attending and practicing in the training schools, but his face was weak and dissipated. The marks of drink and drugs showed that he indulged in these pleasures far more than any man whose life depended upon keeping his alertness and reflexes.

For all that, the consul liked to fancy himself a fighting man, and in the days after the banquet he often showed up at practice sessions, sometimes throwing off his trailing robe, snatching up a helmet, shield, and sword, and sparring with the fighters. His every move was lavishly praised by the cloud of sycophants who surrounded him like a bad odor over spoiled fish. Parma found him fairly skillful but lacking the split-second timing of the true fighter, and the consul lacked the ability to plan a complex attack and defense pattern several moves ahead, relying on inspiration rather than calculation. He was not very inspired. Parma carefully kept his opinions to himself, making sure not to give the consul too stiff a fight when he was chosen to spar with the dangerously vain monarch.

Instead, after each bout, he complimented the consul politely on his skill and tactfully pointed out how he could improve his fight. The consul seemed to find this a pleasant change from the heavy flattery of the others.

"What's your name, gladiatory?" asked the consul, using the ancient title of the games fighters. "Ah, well, then, Parma of Thrax, we shall take great interest in seeing how you perform in our birthday games, and if you distinguish yourself greatly, we may decide to add you to our private family."

By this, Parma understood that he meant his personal troop of fighters. Once again, Parma felt that strange mixture of elation and dread.

At the gate of the palace enclosure, Miles waited for Capelli's vehicle to arrive. To while away the time, the priest studied the two constructs guarding the gateway. They were, he decided, the most bizarre specimens he had ever seen.

One was covered with striped fur and had bull horns, with a pair of eight-foot tentacles in place of arms. The other looked like a crab standing on its hind legs, with two pairs of nipper-ended arms. Miles recognized them for what they were: scary ornamental bogeymen. The tentacles were obviously nearly useless, and the nippers were comically at odds with the holstered pistol the crablike creature wore, which could not be grasped or fired by such appendages.

In spite of their near harmlessness, Miles could not resist a wave of deep revulsion that washed over him. Centuries of religious conditioning had generated an almost psychopathic hatred of these monsters. To Miles, their very existence was an abomination, and he had to struggle against an urge to attack them. None of this inner turmoil showed in his demeanor.

Aristocratically unpunctual, Capelli at last appeared.

"My dear Father Miles," began Capelli, "I do apologize for my lateness. I trust the wait has not been too tedious? My vehicle will take us to the palace, or, if you prefer, we could walk."

"I prefer to walk," said Miles. "I would like to see the palace area."

The enclosure was laid out somewhat in the form of an Italian Renaissance palazzo. It had been beautifully executed during some classical revival in a previous century. Although it lacked originality, Miles had to concede its excellent taste. He had expected something far more garish and vulgar.

The facade of the palace itself was very similar in design and dimensions to that of St. Peter's Basilica in Rome, and Miles permitted himself the least of smiles when he considered the incongruousness of it. A building like this, designed to impress the populace, was wasted in such a Forbidden City setting. He realized that it must have been built in an era when the people had had free access to the area. With a graceful gesture, Capelli conducted the priest inside.

In the audience chamber, Miles waited with the patience of one who had lived for years at a time within the precincts of the Vatican. One nobody after another was presented to the consul, and when Miles was led forward, the consul acknowledged his presence with bored indifference. From the audience chamber, Capelli led him to a small suite of rooms in a palace annex. There they came upon a small group of men, men of grave demeanor, who sat in a semicircle around a statuesque young woman of great beauty and haughty manner. Capelli walked up to the woman's chair and bowed deeply.

"My lady, may I present the man of whom I spoke this morning? This is Father Miles, a priest of the Roman Church, from, ah, offworld. He is a man of deep learning in theology, philosophy, history, and many other subjects too abstruse for my poor intellect." With a flourish of his arm, the old aristocrat indicated Miles.

"I am most pleased to receive Father Miles, Lord Malatesta. But I should really give a new scholar a private audience, and I see that I have kept you all long past mealtime. If you will all excuse us, and rejoin us this afternoon." The scholars, priests, and philosophers quickly stood, bowed, and left, muttering polite phrases.

"And I, too, shall leave you, with your permission, my lady," said Capelli; "an old man is easily fatigued. With your ladyship's indulgence."

"Of course, old friend," said the princess. "But, in the future, do give us the pleasure of your company more often." She was gracious and regal, almost to the point of self-mockery. The old courtier bowed again and left, turning to go but at the same time seeming to be backing out.

"Capelli is such a sweet old villain," said the princess when he had left, "I am almost going to enjoy having my throat cut by him." Her manner, the patently assumed regality suddenly dropped, was disarmingly frank.

"You are not deceived by his manner, then, I take it?" said Miles.

"Not at all. I know that he plots against the throne and against me, personally."

"Then, by extension, you must distrust me, since Capelli brought me here."

"Precisely." Her tone was quietly conversational, and there was no hostility in her attitude. Miles reflected that those raised in Byzantine courts such as this must grow up a little twisted, at least. It was only remarkable that they did not all turn into bloodthirsty animals.

"May I ask, then, why you are revealing this to me? Surely, if my intentions endangered you, I would be rendered much less effective if I were to maintain the belief that you trusted me."

"You interest me. Whatever your true motives are, they can't have much to do with Capelli. You arrived on Charun only two days ago. The captain of the merchant ship that brought you here says that he picked up you and another man on Titus, a planet suspected of having dealings with worlds outside the system. You paid your way with tenetrine, a metal that had been a state monopoly for centuries. It is forbidden for private citizens to own it. Once here, you parted company with your friend and went to a bank, where you exchanged more tenetrine for currency. You went to the nearly abandoned Church of Cyril on the Green Park and from there proceeded to one of the gambling establishments run by the Curio gang, where you won a very large sum at a rigged table.

After leaving, you were set upon by five of Curio's thugs, whom you overpowered in a most impressive display, and then you returned to the Church of Cyril. Yesterday, you were conducted to see Curio himself, and later the same day you were driven out to the Capelli mansion. Today, here you are in my audience chamber.

"You're not the kind of man I get to meet every day, Father Miles, so I just can't have you thrown in prison yet, can I? Have you eaten? I'm starved."

Miles remained impassive throughout this recitation. He had yet to deal with a court or government that wasn't ridden with spies and informers, both internal and external.

"Lunch would be most welcome, my lady. I assure you my intentions are of the most benevolent nature. I've come to help ease the Flavian System back into the Roman fold, which it left so long ago." Miles saw no reason for not being as frank with the princess as she had proved toward him. She touched a button on a table and servants appeared bearing small, covered platters. Miles and the princess sat and attacked the meal, Miles noting that the princess had the appetite of a wolf but took a care for her health and figure. All the foods were of low caloric content. This suited Miles' abstemious nature. The only beverage was a tart and refreshing fruit juice. When her appetite had abated somewhat, the princess leaned back and regarded Father Miles with a searching gaze.

"Why should the Flavian System want to return to the influence of Rome? The records I've seen indicate that there were good reasons for leaving the old alliance."

Miles knew that she was more eager than she seemed.

"Too many centuries have been spent away from the influence of the Holy Church. Much spiritual suffering has been the result. The advanced state of decadence in this formerly vital culture is a damning indication of that. To return to Rome and reopen the pilgrimage routes will bring about a reawakening of the spiritual force of these people. When they recognize the divinity that is in them, they will once again have self-respect and dignity. More important, their souls will once again have the chance of salvation." The Jesuit's speech was forceful, his eyes gleaming with almost unnatural intensity.

"Have you anything to offer that is of a more substantial nature? Salvation of the soul is a rather intangible commodity, and this is, as you will have observed, a materialistic society." She seemed amused and in a mood to banter. Miles decided to give her a shock.

"How old do you think I am? Charunese years are within a few hours of the length of mine."

She seemed puzzled at the question, but willing to play the game.

"About thirty, I should guess."

"I am eight-six years old."

The princess said nothing for a while, then:

"You may be a liar, but I think not. Has Rome discovered the secret of eternal youth?"

"Not eternal youth, but a treatment that will delay the onset of senescence, perhaps for centuries. There is no drug of immortality. Neither God nor Satan will be cheated of their souls."

"One would hardly expect this from a faith that used to stress the brevity of life and the inevitability of death."

"Death is still inevitable, and the length of life is relative, anyway, always confined between birth and death, the parentheses of our corporeal existence. In any case, we have found that a long life leads to a greater concern with spiritual things, and a turning away from the material."

"You speak persuasively, priest, at least when it comes to extended youth." She was beginning to lose a little of her poise, her voice telling Miles that he now had her captivated. She could not doubt what he said, both because she wanted to believe and because Miles' conviction was such as to compel belief.

"You are attracted by the most trivial of the blessings we offer, my child, but it is to be hoped that, in time, you will come to greater understanding. Will you, then, allow me to attend you, with free access to the court?"

"Of course, Father Miles. I would keep you here, if only to bring me up to date on the universe outside. How is it that Rome has enjoyed this great resurgence? When last heard of, all the faiths of Earth were in the last stages of decay."

"In the year 3520 the fortunes of the Church were restored. From about 2000 to 3000, men spread out among the inhabitable planets of the galaxy. There was a great resurgence of religion in that period, and tithes and the wealth of pilgrims poured into the coffers of the great faiths. Early in the Fourth Millennium the rot set in, and for five centuries the powerful of the Church fought among themselves for this wealth, forgetting their duties of education, spiritual leadership, and unification of mankind. The great unity that was Christendom, bound together by the network of the pilgrimage routes, began to fall apart. First outlying planets, then whole star systems dropped away from the hegemony of Rome. The Muslim and Jewish worlds also became disenchanted with their spiritual leaders, who had become, if possible, even more corrupt than Rome." The priest's tone was somber, as if relating an event that was personally painful.

"Then, in the year 3520, Pope Pius XX, "The Accursed," died, probably by assassination. There was a deadlock for months in the College of Cardinals as to who would succeed. The bribery and pressuring were of unprecedented proportions. Finally, in order to buy a few months of time in which to renew their battle lines, the College chose Esteban Cardinal Montoya, a very saintly old man, one of the few truly religious men in the Church hierarchy. He was elected because he had only a few months to live, being very ill as well as being one of the oldest men in the College.

"At this time, the traditions of the Church were kept alive by a few of the religious orders, such as the Jesuits and Franciscans, and a few secret societies among the Dominicans, Benedictines, and others. A group of Benedictine medical researchers discovered the process of rejuvenation-longevity, which they kept secret, knowing that the bandits who controlled Rome would reserve it for themselves and their favored minions. When Cardinal Montoya succeeded to the Papacy, the Benedictines secretly administered this treatment to him at his palace outside Tivoli.

"Six months later, he reappeared in Rome, backed by the secret societies, some of which were military in nature, such as my own, the Brotherhood Cestus Dei. For a time, there was open warfare in Rome, but so corrupt had the higher clergy become that even their private military establishments had fallen under strength through rampant graft. They were crushed." The Jesuit's fingers curled powerfully into a fist, by way of emphasis.

"Cardinal Montoya, now Pope Leo XXX, went on to reign as Pontiff for seventy-five years, overseeing the cleansing and reformation of the Church. First, the clergy of the Sol system were purged, then those of the outlying systems still bearing allegiance to Rome. After that came the great work, the rediscovery of the worlds that left the fold, the reconstruction of Christendom, which is still far from finished."

"And what of the other faiths?" asked the princess, spellbound.

"When they saw the overthrow of the misrule of Christendom, there were movements to reform Islam and Judaism. Imam Mohammed Shamyl, an obscure goatherd from the Caucasus, marched with his fanatical following on Damascus and overthrew the great pasha. He set up a new capital at Medina, and his dynasty still holds the Caliphate there. A very bloody war was fought in Jerusalem, set off by a secret clique of young rabbis. Unknown to us, an underground movement much like ours had been stirring for generations throughout Judaism. The result was the foundation of a new high priesthood of the Third Temple. Since then, it's been a race to maintain the balance of power among the three great faiths. Diplomatically, at least, we are generally in accord with the Temple, but the Caliphate is subject to periodic fits of military expansionism. Just now, there's a new grand imam, Mohammed Sheffi, who fancies himself a Mahdi. He's been disputing our right to one system after another, and it's almost come to war on some occasions.

"Since this system hardly even classifies as Christian any more, he'd like to snap it up, just to spite us. And, he's especially incensed about the production here of the soulless — your fighting constructs. All faiths denounce it as an abomination and wish to suppress it, but the imam takes particular umbrage at it and is capable of annihilating any planet he catches creating them. His ships may be on their way right now."

"This is a bit too much for me to absorb in one sitting, I'm afraid, Father. You must let me think awhile. You may attend me at breakfast tomorrow, and you will stay among my entourage. I will have rooms prepared for you in the palace. Now, please excuse me." Miles rose, bowed, and left.

Back in the rectory, he found Father Stavros, looking rather bewildered.

"You won't believe this, Father Miles," said the old priest, "but at least fifty people have been here today to ask about the Church. It seems that you are now a celebrity."

"I expected as much. There's nothing like a little showmanship to bring the potential converts flocking in."

"Unfortunately, few of them were interested in the finer points of religion. Most asked if the Christian God would give them good luck in gambling, or make them strong enough to take on Curio's thugs. There were also two arena-fight promoters who wanted to sign you up for the consul's birthday games, which begin in a few days. The sums they offered were quite astronomical."

"Most of these people will trickle away disappointed, but some will stay and their numbers will multiply. These people live in a spiritual vacuum; that part of their spirits that needs true faith is lacking even the counterfeit of political ideology to fulfill them. They will fall like overripe fruit from a tree, to grow into strong new saplings. This system will be one of the easiest we have had to conquer. But it must be accomplished quickly, before the Muslims find an excuse to move in."

The older priest was dubious. This Jesuit took much on himself.

"How went your interview with the princess?"

"Much as I had anticipated. As a frustrated intellectual, she was eager to hear of what is going on outside. As a member of the court, she wanted to know what I was plotting. She was favorably impressed, especially by the longevity treatment. She is an intelligent young woman, capable of cruelty, perhaps, but not a savage beast, like her brother. She has lived every day of her life with the fear of death or hideous torture, not the healthiest milieu for a developing young mind. Throughout childhood, her father, her brother, and other relatives have only been people who have the power and the inclination to kill her. It's no wonder that she isn't like ordinary people."

"Father Miles," said Father Stavros, sorely troubled, "since you arrived, you have tremendously impressed a number of people by winning in a great gambling coup, displaying your artistry at violence, and today you've gone a long way toward winning over the princess by revealing that Rome holds the secret of prolonged youth and life. None of this has anything to do with our faith, with the principles of Christianity. How are you to win the people's souls?"

Father Miles smiled wearily.

"My good friend Stavros, I came here with a Franciscan friar who had the same objections as you. He is out in the city somewhere right now, preaching to the poor. By using that process, the Franciscans might achieve total conversion in about three centuries, but right now time is of the essence. Faith is internal, but it is awakened by external demonstration. This can be something as subtle as the preaching of a holy man or as crude as a battle won by men bearing the Cross as their emblem. 'Give us a sign!' shout the people, doubting Thomases, every one. I am giving them signs, Father Stavros. The power of Rome is greater than the power of thugs, it can overcome even rigged dice, and best of all, it can restore youth and prolong life.

"Soon, they shall see that even the court professes Christianity. There will be a few sincere converts, and many hypocrites, but even the hypocrites will be serving God's ends in convincing the people."

Father Stavros reserved judgment.

"Speaking of my Franciscan friend, have you seen

anything of him? He's stupendously naive, and I worry about him. He's never been away from Earth before, and a city like this is a savage place."

"I've heard nothing of him, but I shall make inquiries," said Father Stavros. "He'll probably be all right, as long as he has nothing worth stealing and doesn't preach against the government. The people are allowed to believe pretty much as they choose, as long as their beliefs don't threaten the court or the privileges of the nobility. He could try to convert among the slaves and get into trouble that way, but there really aren't that many slaves in Augusta."

"Still, please make your inquiries. And now, Father, I must get some sleep. It's been a trying few days, and tomorrow I begin playing the courtier."

VIII

Brother Jeremiah wandered aimlessly about the city of Augusta. He had never imagined that such a slum could exist. Everywhere, vast blocks of shabby tenements stretched, seemingly without end. There were people everywhere, none of them seeming to be doing much. In fact, except for shopkeepers and the like, nobody seemed to be employed at all.

After two days in the city, Jeremiah was still not even sure where to begin. Had he seen signs of starvation, or shortage of medical care, he would have tried to succor the needy, but it seemed that the state provided a bare minimum of food and medical aid — not enough to eliminate misery, but just enough to forestall desperation. In the midst of such poverty, Jeremiah didn't feel quite right about begging. His was a mendicant order, but he feared that begging in this city would be a humiliating experience. He wondered if he was guilty of the sin of pride. Still, he was getting hungry.

The problem was: Just how *did* one go about gaining the attention of these people? They seemed to be total materialists, content to be fed and entertained. In the parks, he had attempted casual conversation with a number of persons, but when the subject turned to religion, most lost interest entirely or, at best, asked if he knew any spells or had any charms to sell that would improve their luck at the games. This sort of petty superstition seemed to represent the high point of Charunese theology.

To crown it all, the iniquity of the city surpassed belief. Aside from the luxury establishments catering to the rich, virtually the only businesses showing any signs of prosperity were the gambling dens, dope shops, bars, and houses of prostitution, and these were innumerable. On three occasions, men armed with knives and clubs had tried to rob him but had gone away discouraged when he had demonstrated that he had nothing to steal.

Now, on the morning of his third day, Jeremiah was beginning to feel the desperation of his position. He sat on a bench in a small park, one of many that dotted the city, and sighed wearily as he saw yet another band of youths approach him belligerently. From behind Jeremiah, a voice spoke up:

"Better leave him alone, boys. He's one of them Roman priests from offworld, see the cross he's wearing?" The boys stopped, turned slightly pale, shuffled a bit, then put away their weapons.

"Sorry, friend," said the oldest, "We thought you was just some out-of-town mark. Come on, brothers." The little group turned away, and Jeremiah turned around, mystified. Behind him was a little, pot-bellied, balding man in a relatively clean blue tunic.

"I thank you for your timely aid, my friend," said Jeremiah, "but I must confess, I fail to understand."

He was, however, beginning to detect Father Miles' fine hand in all this.

"You haven't heard? The whole town's talking about it. A man like you, only with a black robe and a big stick, went to the 'Rainbow's End' night before last and won a big stack of plates. Five of Curio's boys went after him to get them back, and he wiped them out with his stick and his bare hands. One of them was the Beast, and he was a top games fighter in the Unarmed class before Curio hired him for muscle."

Jeremiah smiled ruefully. He might have known that Father Miles would make an immediate impression.

"Let me introduce myself. I am Brother Jeremiah, a friar of the Franciscan order of the Church of Rome. The man of whom you speak is Father Miles, of the Jesuit order. He is my friend and colleague, so to speak."

"I'm Luigi Mangiapane. Say, you look like you could use a square meal."

"I haven't eaten for some time. I have no money, and it seems that one needs a citizenship card here to qualify for the dole."

"Tell you what: I'll buy you lunch, and maybe you can tell me about this Miles character. I have a sort of professional interest in him."

The restaurant to which Mangiapane led Jeremiah was an establishment catering to Augusta's middle class. The decor was mercifully free of games motifs. The menu was varied but priced well beyond the means of the vast majority of the citizens. As a substantial meal settled in his stomach, Jeremiah began to lose his depression.

"You spoke of a profession, friend Luigi. Just what is your profession? So few people here seem to work."

"I'm a handicapper."

"What does a handicapper do?"

"Say, just how far out do you and your friend come

from?"

"Well, we took a ship here from Titus," said Jeremiah, not sure how much he should reveal as yet.

"Oh, that explains it. I guess the games holos don't reach that far out, huh? Well, a handicapper is a games expert who estimates odds and gives tips on what fighter's going to win, or which horse is most likely to come in first, and so on. The big ones are organized and set the payoff rates for winners and like that, but I'm a free-lance. I give my customers tips, and if they win, they give me a percentage of their winnings. It's a pretty good living. Right now is a pretty busy time, with the consul's birthday games coming up."

Jeremiah told himself not to judge. This was not Earth and, after all, this man had befriended him, the first on Charun to do so. Even if he made his living by the blood of others, he knew of no other life.

"Now, about this Father Miles: What makes him such a hot fighter?"

"Father Miles is a priest of the Jesuit order. For centuries, they have been trailblazers for the Church, converting on the most savage worlds. To prepare them for this, they are given the most intensive physical training imaginable. In addition, Father Miles is a member of the Brotherhood Cestus Dei, which accepts only the most capable of the Jesuit graduates. It is a most fearsome fraternity."

The little gambler regarded Brother Jeremiah searchingly.

"I think maybe you come from a lot farther out than Titus. I know a little about the old religions, got a few thimbles from the old days. Sort of a hobby of mine, you know? I'd like to talk more about this, but I gotta go over to the stadium and start taking notes. Care to come along?"

"My religion forbids the taking of life, I couldn't

watch men kill one another."

"No killing today, Brother," laughed Luigi. "It's just practice until the games start next month."

"In that case, I'll come along," said Jeremiah, unwilling to lose the first potential convert he'd found.

In the vast stadium, they sat watching the fighters go through their exercises and sparring sessions, using blunt weapons and battered harness instead of the sharp steel and jeweled armor they would be using in the games. The stands were nearly half full with handicappers from all over Charun making book for the biggest games of the year. Also, there were the inveterate games fans, come to see their idols practicing. Jeremiah noted with shock how many of these were teen-aged girls. It did not seem real to the friar that most of the men down in the arena were doomed, almost certain to die within the next few weeks. Luigi had told him that the consul's birthday games were by far the bloodiest of the year, with little mercy for the fallen. The little man was scribbling furiously in a tablet.

"Now, Brother, you see that young fella down there? The one with the long hair?" He pointed with his stylus.

"Yes, I see him," said Jeremiah.

"Well, he's new, never fought in Augusta before. Name of Parma, from the School of Marius in Ludus. He's only got five fights behind him, on Domitian where the crowd's not too bloodthirsty. Now, most handicappers wouldn't give him a chance in the upcoming fights, but I think different. I know Marius is the best trainer in the system, and he thinks this boy is good enough to send to the consul's games. So, I go to the studio and have them run the holos of this kid's fights. Greatest knifework I've ever seen, and I've been making book on the big games for twenty years. So I'll tell my customers to put their money on him. If he's fighting a man with any kind of rep, they'll get five-, maybe six-to-one odds. They'll win big, and I get 10 per cent of their winnings for the tip. And the beauty of it is, I don't risk any of my own money."

Jeremiah was getting over his revulsion. Luigi was obviously not twisted or sadistic. It was just that the fighters were, to him, no more than dice, instruments of chance and odds upon which to bet. Probably, the friar thought, most of the people here were like that. Nobody had ever told them that there was any other way. As for the fighting, what he could see now was graceful pantomime, not nearly as shocking as the training he had seen on Gravitas. But in a few days, they'd be fighting with real weapons.

"Why do they fight with those obsolete weapons?" asked Jeremiah.

"Who knows? They've been using them for centuries, and I guess they're as good as any. Big shield, small shield, and net-and-trident are called the Classical Forms, so they must date from way back. There's other ways they fight, too, but always with hand weapons. No skill in men shooting each other, I guess. Sometimes they fight animals, or constructs."

"They fight constructs?"

"Sure, you ever seen any?"

"Never."

"Come on, I'll show you where they're kept."

They took an elevator down to the passageways deep under the stadium. The noises and smells told Jeremiah that this was where the animals were kept, before his eyes had adjusted to the dimness. Luigi took him to a set of cages where vaguely humanoid forms stirred in the obscurity. As Jeremiah's eyes adjusted to the light, he gasped. It was an involuntary sound of pure terror.

"Don't worry," said Luigi, "they can't reach you through those bars."

They were creatures of nightmare, things dredged up from man's subconscious fears. In the monastery at Brisbane, there had been an altar triptych, one copied from an original by Hieronymous Bosch. These creatures resembled the artist's hallucinatory images. One was plated all over with scales like a lobster; another had the flexible spine of a serpent. Some had nippers like crabs instead of hands; others were covered in horny spikes. There were claws, fangs, horns, hooves, even tentacles, but always that horrible suggestion of the humanoid.

"They send men out to fight *those?*" asked the friar, aghast.

"Sure, usually two or three men to a construct. These are bred especially for the games. The constructs in the armies are a lot more human looking and more intelligent."

Jeremiah said nothing as they left. He could have told the little man of the terrible wars the Church, Temple, and Caliphate had fought in the systems where constructs had taken over. Some of those constructs had been capable of brilliant generalship, and the wars had been long. Since those wars, creation of the soulless had been anathema to all faiths. As they left the stadium, Luigi asked Jeremiah where he was staying.

"I have no place to stay. The last two nights I slept in the parks."

"That's a good way to get your throat cut. Not everybody's as reasonable as those boys this morning. There's some real weird people in this town."

Jeremiah was willing to allow the truth of that.

"Listen," continued Luigi, "did you know that there's a Roman church in this town?"

"I had no idea there were any practicing Christians at all in this system," said Jeremiah, astonished.

"It's called St. Cyril's, on the Green Park. That's

the big park in the center of town. Run by an old guy called Stavros. Everybody in the neighborhood knows him because he's an easy touch for a handout. You should go by and see him. He'll put you up, I bet." Before parting, Luigi gave Jeremiah his address. "If you need a little money to help you out, look me up after the games. I'll be flush then."

Jeremiah shook his head after the little man had gone. It was difficult to believe that this cheerful, kind-hearted man made his living by predicting which of two men would kill the other. He wended his way to the Green Park and found St. Cyril's. The church was locked, and Jeremiah found the rectory, a small, detached house to the rear of the church. He knocked, and the door was opened by an elderly priest in a threadbare cassock who said:

"Ah, you'll be Brother Jeremiah, then?"

"You were expecting me?"

"I was about to go out looking for you. Come in, come in. Your friend, Father Miles, was inquiring about you."

"He's been here?" said Jeremiah as he entered. The rectory was clean and comfortably furnished.

"Yes, he was here on his first day in Augusta. He spent that night and last night here. This morning he left for the palace, where it seems he's to live at court."

"A fast worker, our Father Miles," observed Jeremiah.

"So I had noticed," said Stavros. "Would you care for some coffee?"

"Decidedly," said Jeremiah. The beverage turned out to be a close approximation of Earth coffee.

"Now, Brother Jeremiah," said Father Stavros, "why is it that you aren't with Father Miles?"

"I'm afraid that his methods are not to my taste."

"I'd thought him a bit precipitate, myself."

"It's not that he goes for a fast conversion, really, it's his disregard for the sincerity of his converts. He thinks in terms of gaining back whole star systems for the Church and not of individual souls. I know his arguments are persuasive, but the Jesuits are famed for that, regardless of the validity of their theses."

"And what are your plans?"

"I was going to preach among the poor, according to the Franciscan tradition, but I've had little success so far," said Jeremiah, with a woebegone look.

"I shouldn't wonder," said Stavros. "The people here are not spiritually inclined, and the popular entertainments are their whole life. I have only a few dozen parishioners, and most of them are elderly. I had feared that when this generation passed on, Christianity would pass with it. Now that you and Father Miles have appeared, though, I've taken new heart. Perhaps, together, you and I may accomplish something."

"I hope that we can," said Jeremiah.

"Will you stay here while you are in Augusta? Father Miles was in and out so quickly that I had no chance to ask him half the questions I wanted answered."

"Thank you for your offer," said Jeremiah, relieved. "I will be most happy to answer any questions you may care to ask."

"Well, first of all, how was the re-reformation of the Church accomplished?"

Jeremiah gave Stavros the same story that Miles had told Ludmilla, with slightly less emphasis on the Jesuits and slightly more credit to the Franciscans.

"So," said Father Stavros, "for nearly five hundred years, the Church has been trying to gain back her lost sheep. And now, at last, you've come to the Flavians. Not before time, I assure you. If ever a system was in need of spiritual uplift, it's this one. And this city, Augusta, is the most iniquitous place in the system, as you will have noted as you wandered about our fair city."

"So I did. How did this place reach such a state?"

"It's a common enough story, here and elsewhere, even on Earth from time to time in her checkered history. A society could not offer its members any value beyond gratification of basic needs. I suppose it comes of the idea that if men are just taken care of — fed, clothed, and housed — they will automatically be happy and docile. It was not true, of course. They couldn't compete with cheap slave labor, and plunder is easier than production. The people's lives were without meaning, and when men are idle, they begin having dangerous, political thoughts. The answer was, of course, to give them something else to occupy their minds. The games resulted. They provided entertainment, emotional relief, and a chance to satisfy the desire for gain by gambling. Between games, they gamble at less entertaining forms of chance or, if they can afford them, use drugs."

"And these are the people we must try to convert," said Jeremiah, discouragement in his voice. "On what grounds can we appeal to them? What factor of our faith will reach them in any way?"

"For one thing, you can demonstrate to them that the Church is still a living entity, not a dying anachronism. It will be a slow process, but I think that progress is at last possible. And there is, after all, your rejuvenation process. That's the kind of thing men sell their souls for, and we're trying to save them instead. Even though we may not care for his methods, Father Miles has certainly brought the Church of Rome to the public attention."

Jeremiah was forced to agree with that. "Where shall we begin?" asked the friar.

"Here, in the church. I've had quite a number of

people come here to question me the past two days, as a result of Father Miles' showmanship. Now is our chance to gain the attention of those whose spiritual need is great. We begin tomorrow."

It was a difficult, discouraging task, but then, Jeremiah reminded himself, it had never been easy to be a missionary. Many of those who came were in search of material gain; some wanted to know if the priests could put a curse on their enemies, and a few Jeremiah was sure were government spies. To all of these, he gave the same message: His creed meant renunciation of the material and its values; the love for one's enemies and all living things. Before he got farther than that, they had usually left in disappointment.

But there were others: the disturbed, the troubled, those who had spent their lives jumping from one petty cult to another in search of some indefinable value. To these Jeremiah spoke, and they listened. He recalled the lessons he had received in the monastery, emphasizing the basic concepts of his faith: love, peace, humility, good will. He knew that at this early stage, it was best to avoid any advanced concepts. Ideas such as Trinity and Transubstantiation were knotty questions for theologians, much less for people taking their first tentative steps into the faith.

Especially difficult to overcome was the problem of the lack of education among those he was trying to convert. Had they been primitives, with a strong concept of deity, his task would have been far simpler. It was at that type of conversion that the Franciscans, with their love of nature and concept of the divinity of all things, excelled. But these were adults with their minds set in habitual patterns, unused to the concept of a supernatural being who did more than affect the roll of dice.

Still, he was gaining. Certain faces kept turning up

again and again as he and Father Stavros continued their earnest preaching. Best of all, they were beginning to bring their children. Jeremiah remembered Miles' words concerning the importance of the second generation of converts.

"Jeremiah," said Father Stavros one evening, as they relaxed after a hard day in the confessional (predictably, the people here had taken to confession with enthusiasm), "we're beginning to make headway." The priest smiled with satisfaction. He appeared ten years younger than when Jeremiah had first met him.

"Still, Father, it's slow. We have only a few score converts, and very tentative ones, at that. I know that a missionary must have patience, but when I see the shape of this city, I despair of ever bringing about a change."

"You misread the situation, Brother. Now, we and Father Miles aren't the only missionaries. Those people we've persuaded are out converting for us, and doing a better job than we ever could. They are the poor of this city, and their neighbors listen to them. Better yet, they see them every day. Those who aren't interested in listening to our preachings will see the example of our converts and be persuaded. Someday, perhaps sooner than you think, people will begin coming to us in droves."

"That's when the persecutions begin," pointed out Jeremiah.

"Hopefully, by that time the good Father Miles will have wrought his flashy miracles among the court and averted such unpleasantness."

"I'm not sure. I think it's more likely to end with his neck on the local equivalent of the headsman's block."

"It's a varied faith we serve, isn't it?" queried the older priest. "Who would've believed that you and Father Miles served the same Church? I suppose it's been that way from the beginning, though. Even the earliest converts could choose whom to follow: the mystical John, the quiet Peter (after Pentecost, of course), the noisy and intolerant Paul. And, later, the founders of the orders: the gentle Francis, the fierce Ignatius Loyola; my own patient, scholarly St. Cyril."

"At least the Church provides something for every taste."

Among those who became habitual attendants of Jeremiah's teaching sessions was Luigi, the little handicapper who had befriended him. The man was an invaluable contact and authority on the low life of Augusta. He always knew when there were government spies in the congregation, and on those occasions Jeremiah and Stavros toned down their insistence on freedom for the slaves and an end to the games, ideas the government would consider seditious. An arrest now would do them no good.

"Luigi," said Jeremiah one day, "you must realize that when Christianity resumes control of this system, it will mean the end of your livelihood."

"I know," the little man shrugged. "I guess there's no help for it. But there'll still be the horses. Besides, if I can live for centuries, like you say, maybe I'll learn some other way to make a living." He thought for a few seconds. "Bet it won't be as good as handicapping, though."

There were others; a woman whose sons had joined the consul's armies to get out of Augusta's slums; a man without friends or luck, an embittered veteran who had lost his legs; a number of free prostitutes. To all, Jeremiah gave consolation, a commodity in short supply on Charun, and a hope for a better life, something they had never known at all. He was beginning to feel the satisfaction of success, even small success, at the life he had chosen.

IX

The Princess Ludmilla was dancing. As recorded music flooded her studio, she leaped, pirouetted, and somersaulted with rare abandon. Miles wasn't sure whether it was a cultural or an athletic exercise. Sweat flew in showers from her dark-skinned body, clad only in a pair of silken briefs. For several days now, Miles had been her constant attendant, to the jealousy of her entourage, who were slighted. Almost every hour of the day, Miles was at her side, answering her endless questions about the Roman hegemony and telling her long stories of his adventures on strange worlds. Whenever he could, he spoke persuasively of his faith, emphasizing those points that his psychologist's analysis had told him were most likely to strike a responsive chord in Ludmilla's mind.

She was as physically obsessed as her brother, but in her the family inclination had taken the form of enthusiasm for personal athletics. Miles had fenced,

ridden, played squash, and even boxed with her, and
now she had asked him to attend her dancing practice, something she normally practiced alone.

Miles admired her skill and grace. She could not
compare with the ballerinas he had seen on other
worlds, her grace being that of a superb athlete, not
that of a born dancer. But her body was lithe and
powerful as a young tiger's, and she made even the
most strenuous gymnastics seem effortless.

Finishing with a slow, writhing back-bend, the princess got to her feet and walked over to Miles, who
handed her a towel. She smiled, panting, as she pat-
ted her dripping body dry. Miles was perfectly aware
that her every gesture was sexually loaded. She was
trying to see what effect her undeniably desirable
body would have on this seemingly inflexible man.
She had worn an aphrodisiac perfume which, mixed
with the scent of her overheated, sweaty, healthy-
young female-animal body, should have sent any non-
eunuch into a state of frenzied rut.

Miles was far from unstirred. He was human, male,
and, physically, at least, he was in his late twenties.
But he was, after all, eighty-six years old, and although priestly celibacy had long been discarded as
essential, or even desirable, he was really more interested in the salvation of her soul. He had often lec-
tured young priests on the attitude sometimes adopted
by young women toward their confessors, as toward
their gynecologists, and he knew of the pitfalls and
complications attendant upon that special relationship. He adopted the attitude of clinical indifference,
while tactfully indicating that, were he not a priest,
his reaction would be far different. This woman had a
touchy ego, and he had to tread a narrow, careful
path.

"Tell me, Father," she said with a lazy grin, "have
you not been attracted to women very much in your

travels? Surely such a masculine man as you must have known many."

Miles was astonished at the clumsiness of her approach. It was an indication of her awe of him, for she could not be inexperienced in such matters.

"I am a man, my lady, and even a priest is attracted to women, but one learns to restrain one's natural impulses when one has a higher mission." He knew that it sounded stiff and stilted, but he had to stay within the frame of reference that she had built around him within her own mind.

"So," she said flatly, "my little performance today has not had any effect on you? A pity—I had fancied myself quite the seductress." She slipped on her dressing robe, an act for which he was duly grateful. He sought a way to spare her ego while leaving no doubt that an affair was out of the question.

"Your charms, my lady, are undeniable, and I assure you that they have had a telling effect. Were I an ordinary man, I would long since have fallen at your feet. But I am not an ordinary man. I am consecrated to a task that precludes indulgence in ordinary desires and even needs. Were I to follow my natural inclinations, I might become so enthralled as to be useless for the great work that demands every molecule of my attention and the absolute concentration of my physical, mental, and moral strength." He was working hard at projecting a fierce repression of carnal desire. She seemed satisfied that she was losing not to an ordinary rival, but to something so powerful that it was no shame to admit defeat.

"Enough of these games, then. From now on, you shall be my teacher and my friend. I will not promise you that I won't be flirtatious now and then, it's my nature to be so, but you are not to take it seriously, just respond gallantly." She walked toward her bath with the air of a woman who has settled a disturbing element in her personal world and put it in its proper slot. Miles felt the relief and satisfaction of a gambler who has taken a great risk for high stakes and found his judgment sound.

The door at the end of the studio burst open, and two of the consul's guards, weapons in hand, entered. They scanned every corner of the room and signaled, bowing. The consul stepped through the door, surrounded by a mob of beefy young men. He ignored Miles and confronted his sister.

"Good day, Ludmilla. I was just on my way to the training school and thought I'd have a few words with my dear sister." His tone was ironic, his smile insolent and malicious.

"Speak then, brother." Ludmilla was cold and formal.

"Tomorrow, you know, is my birthday."

"Happy birthday, brother."

"And it is my desire that you attend my games in the royal dais." The sycophants around Ilya smirked. Ludmilla's dislike of the games was well known.

"Thank you for the invitation, brother, but I fear that I shall be indisposed."

"Come now, Ludmilla, the sight of a little blood will do you good. More than the prattle of your philosophers, I assure you." His tone hardened into threat. "You cannot defy me, Ludmilla; I am consul."

"I shall accede to the consul's wishes." The princess bowed slightly.

Miles was reading the consul as he would have a book. This was the first time he had seen the consul outside his role as monarch, and it was revealing. He could see equal parts of murderous hostility and incestuous longing in the man. He was jealous of her intellectual accomplishments and fearful that she might be plotting against him. In Ludmilla there was only a well-disguised terror mixed with disgust. Her body was literally rigid with loathing. The consul looked sharply at Miles.

"I see you have a new pedagogue. He must be highly favored to attend you here. What is your field, fellow?"

"I am a priest of the Roman Church, Your Grace." Miles felt that the consul knew all about him, was playing some game.

"I hear that you are a dangerous man, a fighter. I like men who can fight. Perhaps you will favor us with a demonstration." The soft voice held an undertone of mockery.

"The rules of my order allow me to fight only in training, or when attacked, Your Grace."

"That can be arranged." The consul was smiling now, and his myrmidons were grinning in anticipation.

"Ilya, you go too far!" The princess was furious. "Don't you get enough bloodshed in your foolish games? This man is my guest."

"I am consul, and I can't go too far. But this fellow would provide little sport for my men." He grinned at his followers, and they responded with fawning smirks. Miles noted one man studying him with intensity. He was a huge blond man of about forty-five, his beard flecked with gray. His bare torso was a massive knot of overdeveloped muscle, seamed with old white scars. The arms crossed over his chest were as thick as Miles' thighs, and they ended in massive, broken-knuckled hands. There was little taper from elbow to wrist. Miles recognized the type: a man raised on a heavy-gravity planet, where generations of natural selection under the killing gravity of a dense world produced a breed like iron. On a standard-gravity world like this he would be unnaturally strong and swift. Reflexes had to be quick to avoid falling objects on a heavy-gravity world. Whatever the consul and the others thought, Miles knew that he was being accurately sized up by this man, who would never make the mistake of overconfidence.

"I'll expect you on the dais tomorrow morning for the first fight, Ludmilla. The people must see that their sovereign family enjoys a warm personal relationship." Whipping around suddenly, the consul strode toward the door; then he hesitated and turned: "Bring your priest."

That evening, Miles and Ludmilla sat in her drawing room, playing chess over goblets of a rare blue wine.

"Who was that blond-haired man among your brother's bodyguard, my lady?"

"That was Hedulio, the captain of the bodyguard. He was our father's guard and friend for many years. He's not like the rest. Originally, he was a gladiator. For ten straight years he was the undefeated champion of the Heavies. Nobody before or since ever even stayed alive in the games for such a span, much less held the title of champion. His owners knew he was worth a fortune, and wouldn't let him buy his freedom, even after he'd accumulated many times his purchase price. Father rescued him from the arena and he swore to defend our family. He's done that faithfully for nearly twenty years. He does try to keep Ilya in line and curb his worst excesses, and Ilya tolerates him because he's absolutely incorruptible. Your move."

"What was your father like?" asked Miles. "And you're in check."

"Damn! Oh, Father was practically the only decent consul of our line. He had little of the family madness, except for occasional bouts of delusion that nobody was plotting against him. He tried to reform the government, curb the power of the great families. He even tried to suppress the arena games, but without much success. Ilya went in eternal fear of him. He always detested Ilya's mindless cruelty."

"What happened to him?"

"He was assassinated, of course. Poison, we think. We were never able to find out who or how, but few consuls die a natural death."

"Why does Ilya let you live?"

"Isn't it obvious? He wants me."

"I saw that when he spoke to you this afternoon. His obsession must be great, to allow you to remain a perpetual threat to his throne. Has he ever tried to force you?"

"No. His vanity is too colossal for that, but he does keep trying. I think he's secretly convinced that I admire him. My life is secure only as long as I hold him off. I fear that he'd quickly find that sex with a sister is much the same as with any other woman, and then do away with me as soon as the novelty had worn off."

"I think he may prove difficult to convert," said Miles.

"Convert?" said the princess, aghast. "You'd have as much luck converting a snow lizard in estrus! That perverted animal isn't worth saving." She snorted in disgust.

"No soul is so base that God will not find it acceptable with severe repentance. And I think that, in time, and properly coaxed, your brother will repent of his sins."

"You disclaimed the ability to perform miracles, Father."

"No miracles. I judge your brother to be extremely unstable, consumed with a guilty lust for you, and dominated by the fear of his dead father. He feels inferior to nearly everybody, which is unsurprising. I must push and bully him into a crux, which will not be too difficult in his state, and, properly guided, his guilt-ridden psyche will push him into the light."

"That's absurd!"

"Hardly. Some of our most illustrious saints began their lives of holiness that way. Checkmate."

The next day, Ludmilla sat frozen and Miles watched impassively as the armies of Light and Heavy clashed, and throughout the long day and the days following they were forced to watch the carnage. Miles could take it calmly. He had seen far worse on other worlds, and suffering of the body was something almost trivial compared to the mental and spiritual torture that men practiced elsewhere. He found the fighters reasonably skillful in their archaic, ritual styles of combat, but he could tell that most of them would not know how to defend themselves properly without their obsolete swords, shields, and armor. There were exceptions, but none of these was in a class with Miles. He had seen only one man here whom he would have hesitated to face barehanded: the massive Hedulio, who combined terrible strength and swiftness with the mind of a true fighting man; one who thought not of weapons, but of himself as a weapon.

When the games were over, Ludmilla said to Miles, sickened:

"What a waste of splendid young men! How can you stand to watch it so calmly? After all, those men are dying with their souls unsaved and unshriven."

"I believe in a merciful God, and I do not think he will judge too harshly men who have worn the perverting ring around their necks. I believe that the soul-enslaving ring is a far greater abomination than all the other vice on this benighted planet. Not content to merely enslave the bodies of men, these slavers even rob men of the hope of escape. Soon the Church

Militant shall proclaim crusade against the slavers,
and then shall they have cause to beg the mercy of
God!" The priest, his voice quiet, spoke with an almost raging intensity, and Ludmilla was very subdued
for the rest of the evening.

Jeremiah felt an incompleteness in his work. The
continued existence of slavery bothered him, and he
felt that he should be doing something about it. He
realized that he and Stavros were almost powerless,
that there was nothing they could do to alleviate the
suffering of the slaves until they had a wider power
base. Even knowing that, Jeremiah felt that he was being cowardly in not speaking out, demanding the release of all who wore the neck rings. As the consul's
games approached, his inner turmoil increased almost unbearably. Within a few days, men would be
butchering one another in the stadium to while away
the boredom of the populace.

He considered going to the training school and trying to convince the fighters not to take up their
weapons, but what good would that do? The men
wore the enslaving neck rings and had no free will to
speak of. Rebellion on their part would be futile.
Should he rush into the arena to separate the combatants, like the monk Telemachus in fifty-century
Rome? That had worked then, when the Roman Empire was tottering and the games dying out anyway,
but here they were the most important influence in
society. Besides, Telemachus had been stoned to
death, and Jeremiah wasn't ready for martyrdom just
yet.

On the morning that the games were to commence,
Jeremiah and Stavros were returning from an all-
night service at the home of one of their new commu-
nicants, a well-to-do hotelkeeper who lived in the
wealthier part of the city, near the palace. He was

the first nonslum dweller they had reached, and Stavros had hopes that the man would help spread the faith into the sparse middle class of Augusta. They were returning to the church by way of Consul's Boulevard, the main street of Augusta, which led from the military barracks at the edge of the city, past Green Park in the center, to the palace area and stadium at the opposite side of the city. As they neared the park, they began to hear music.

It was the consul's procession, headed for the stadium. Cheering crowds lined the streets, waving and shouting. The two priests stopped to watch as the procession passed. First came the consul in his splendid chariot. Jeremiah could see past the august, regal figure to the vainglorious, weak boy inside, strutting and posing ridiculously in his silly, gilt vehicle. Afterward came the heads of the great families. From their aggressive, forthright air, Jeremiah understood who really controlled the government of the system. Then came the fighters in their beautiful cloaks and gleaming armor. It caused Jeremiah grief and actual physical pain to realize that so many of these splendid, vital figures would be reduced to cold meat by afternoon, food for the carnivores that would themselves fight and die with courageous futility.

Next came cages of beasts, all fierce, many beautiful. Then the cages of constructs, creations too demented for service in the armed forces. Last of all, men on horseback, who would fight each other or beasts or constructs, as the whim of the consul dictated.

Stavros saw Jeremiah turn pale and begin to take a step toward the procession. The priest put out a restraining hand.

"Easy, Brother. This has been going on for centuries."

"That was before I got here," said the friar, in

agony.

"Vanity, Brother Jeremiah, remember your humility. You are doing excellent work now. Don't ruin it by attempting the impossible."

But it had all become too much for Jeremiah. The fine, athletic men, the beautiful animals, even the horrible but pathetic constructs filled him with rage and a sick misery. Suddenly, he broke away from Father Stavros, dashed between two guards who were employed in holding the crowd back from the procession, and ran to the mounted men. Seizing one by the stirrup, he shouted:

"Don't go! It's meaningless! This isn't necessary! You're fools to let yourselves be killed this way."

The horseman looked at him in puzzlement, then looked to his head trainer, unsure what to do. The trainer made a quick signal to the troopers flanking the parade route, and Jeremiah was grabbed by several pairs of hands, injected quickly with a tranquilizer, and carried to an ambulance, which delivered him without delay to the transient prison.

Father Stavros shook his head wearily and began to make his way toward the prison. Fifty feet away, the fleeting incident had not even been noticed.

Once again, Parma stood in the arena. This time he stood not on sand but on a kind of ground pyrite that looked like gold dust but wasn't. Parma stood in the front line of a block of five hundred of his fellow Lights. Opposing them were an equal number of Heavies.

The day had begun with a parade, each man in his most glittering, bejeweled armor, led by the consul himself, who was drawn in a chariot and was wearing a dazzling parade-harness. Then the men who were to fight that day had entered the arena either naked or in loincloths, according to personal modesty, and had gone through a series of gymnastic exercises to allow the audience to admire their physiques and the handicappers to calculate odds. Finally, lots had been drawn for the morning battle, and the chosen had entered the arena in full equipment. Each man, as he entered, cut a piece of tissue held by a slave to demonstrate that his steel was sharp. Those with axes or maces smashed stones or old helmets. Besides his personal weapon, each man bore a light javelin and a heavier lance.

An announcer addressed the crowd from Ilya's dais.

"People of Charun, honored visitors: Our beloved consul, Ilya VII, on the occasion of his twenty-eighth birthday, in the tenth year of his glorious reign, wishes to make you a gift of these games. The generosity of our consul is extended even to those of you who see these games elsewhere, by holographic reproduction. The first event will be a grand battle between Lights and Heavies. Long live the consul!" There was a thunderous roar, followed by a tense silence.

Parma found that his palms were sweating as he waited for the gong. He knew that a battle like this was much less even than a single combat. Here, the Lights would be badly outmatched, although they had been permitted to wear breastplates or mail shirts to even the odds somewhat. When the gong came and the lines of Heavies began to advance, Parma thought of retreating but there was nowhere to go; in any case, there were armed men along the walls of the arena to shoot down any who refused to fight or tried to break away from the combat.

The Heavies broke into a short, shuffling trot, stopped suddenly, and hurled their javelins. Parma crouched to get as much of himself as possible behind his small shield. A javelin rang against its surface and glanced overhead. When he straightened, the Heavies were running as fast as their great shields allowed. The Lights hurled their javelins, but few of the Heavies went down. The Lights had taken many losses. Then the lines collided, and Parma had no time to observe the overall battle.

He thrust his lance into a visor, twisting his body to avoid the return thrust. A man on his right fell and was instantly trampled. Wedged in by shields, Parma dropped his lance and drew his heavy knife. A sword blow glanced off his helmet, and Parma made a quick series of thrusts, trying to get at the vulnerable bodies behind the shields. A Heavy thrust from behind his shield at the man on Parma's right. In the instant the Heavy was exposed, Parma stabbed him under his sword arm. Parma was struck with a sudden inspiration: Using his shield to defend himself from the man before him, he used his knife to attack the man engaging the Light on his right. The Heavy's right side was always exposed when he made a thrust, and Parma disposed of five Heavies in this manner, then the lines lost all coherence and degenerated into clumps of men fighting singly or in small groups, with two or three Lights back-to-back against circling Heavies.

Parma was pushed to the edge of the fighting and engaged a fresh Heavy, who had been in the back lines and was unhurt. Parma was tired, and a little slow with his shield. The Heavy's lance point struck him on the breastplate but slipped off. Parma cut the lance in two with his knife, and the Heavy took an ax from inside his shield. The ax swung in a vicious arc at Parma's neck, but Parma ducked and dropped his buckler, leaping in for a clinch. He had no intention of matching weapons with an axman. He held the Heavy's right arm pinned with his own left and tried to stab at the exposed neck below the helmet, but the Heavy hunched his shoulders, and the blade rang off metal. The Heavy threw away his own shield and the two grappled, rolling in the sand, Parma seeking to keep the Heavy's weapon arm pinned. The Heavy managed to grab Parma's knife wrist and gradually began to force the weapon away from himself. Parma was tiring fast. He knew that he must win this fight quickly or he was lost.

Suddenly, hands grasped Parma from behind. Knowing that it must be more Heavies come to the aid of their comrade, Parma sagged into weary despair as he was pulled to his feet. Seeing that he was not killed instantly, Parma realized that men in white tunics were hauling the Heavy erect, too. They were referees separating the combatants. The finish gong had rung, and Parma had not heard it.

As he stumbled to the victor's gate amid the cheering of the crowd, Parma saw that about two hundred Heavies were still on their feet, but fewer than a hundred Lights. Slaves were putting the wounded in small ambulances to be taken to the infirmary, while the dead were stacked on hovering sleds to be hauled to the morgue. Others were picking up fallen weapons and discarded shields, helmets, and armor, and last of all came a squad of beetlelike machines, which sucked up the bloodstained sand with a funnel in front and spewed it out clean through a vent in the rear.

Glancing at the royal dais, Parma saw the consul giving him a friendly wave. Parma managed a sickly grin and a wave of his knife. He wanted very badly to vomit, and feared that he might faint before reaching the victor's gate, but he managed to make it to the infirmary without disgracing himself. There he had his half-dozen shallow wounds patched and was given a tranquilizer. Vic helped him back to his room at the training school, where he fell on the bed and slept for sixteen hours.

In the days that followed, Parma fought several engagements. Luckily, there were no more pitched battles. He fought netmen, Lights, and Heavies, and in one fight, he and his opponent fought with knives alone, no shields or armor permitted. During a day of novelty acts, Parma was sent out, over Marius's protests, to face a man using a two-handed sword. Parma had only his Thrax knife and a four-foot chain with a weighted end to defend himself with. He managed to avoid the whistling strokes of the blade with a combination of speed and timing, and when he saw his opening he whipped the chain around the swordsman's feet and brought him down. Always he spared the defeated, for which Marius continually railed at him, until the trainer realized that the crowds were pleased, taking Parma's mercy to be a show of contempt for his adversary. Gradually, Parma was building up a following on Charun. He even had a fan club in Augusta.

Vic was also doing well for himself. His net play was dazzling, and he never failed to receive a huge ovation from the crowd. The net men never had to fight pitched battles, only set duels with single adversaries. On the day that Parma fought the man with the two-hander, Vic was sent out with his net and trident to fight a construct, a beast seven feet tall with horny plates all over its body. It had the horns of a bull and the beak of a bird of prey, and was armed with a sword and shield in addition to its natural weapons. It was a match so shamefully uneven that even the blood-hardened crowd muttered in protest. The protest changed to cheers when, after a battle lasting nearly half an hour, Vic brought the fearsome thing down with his net, displaying his usual effortless grace and insolent grin. The construct was finished off by a referee with a pistol, since its hide was impenetrable to the trident, and Vic was carried off on the shoulders of a crowd of drunken revelers, the hero of the day.

After the last day of the games came yet another banquet. The number of fighters had been reduced by nearly four fifths, and the relief of the survivors was sufficient excuse to pull out all the stops. In the midst of the revelry, Marius appeared by Parma's side.

"The consul has asked to buy you and Victorio for his personal following. I don't like the idea, you're both worth a fortune, and I'll have to accept his price. Your belongings will be taken to the palace tonight."

Parma's face showed his elation, but Marius cut that off quickly.

"You may think you have it made, boy, but your troubles are only beginning. At court, you'll be at the center of every intrigue. If ever the consul thinks he has reason to suspect your loyalty, he'll have you hamstrung and sent out to fight a construct, at least if he's in a humorous mood. You'll be subject to the jealousy of all the courtiers and parasites who inhabit the palace. And you'd better overcome your aversion to killing people, because the consul uses his fighting train as assassins. Good luck, boy; I don't expect to see you again."

After Marius had left, Parma went over to where Victorio was sprawled on a couch, being fed delicacies by two boys with painted faces and protuberant rumps. The netman waved his two catamites away and gestured for Parma to sit on the couch.

"Did you get the news, Vic?"

"But of course. It only stands to reason that two such stars as you and I should be destined for higher things. From now on, we live like this for good. We fight maybe two or three times a year for special shows, and the rest of the time we protect our lord and master. I can't think of a more agreeable way to live, can you?" Vic popped a candied fruit into his mouth. He had been drinking an aphrodisiac-spiced wine all evening, and it was causing a highly visible reaction.

"It will have to do until something better comes along. Maybe we'll be freed eventually."

"You mean have our rings taken off?" Vic's brows knit with puzzlement. "What would be the advantage of that? You've seen how the people live outside the palace compound. They don't wear neck rings, and they're miserable. We have everything now. Why do you want to lose it?"

In the palace, Parma was conducted by a steward along seemingly endless corridors. In one hall, near the throne room, they saw a tall young woman approaching, trailed by a small knot of men who lacked the cringing, fawning air of the consul's following.

"The consul's sister, the Princess Ludmilla, with her scholars. You must bow very low when she approaches within ten paces, gladiator." The steward's voice was the discreet whisper common to courts and prisons.

Parma studied the woman with fascination. She was golden-haired, tall, and statuesque, and Parma could see in her the carriage of a horsewoman. Also, he did not doubt that she was hard and arrogant. The steward bowed double as she neared, but Parma merely inclined his head respectfully. The graceful princess swept past, staring through the young man with icy contempt. He studied the men who accompanied her. They were elderly men, for the most part, in the gowns of scholars and philosophers. There was one exception: a youngish, dark-haired man with intense blue eyes, who wore a black robe and carried a wooden staff.

X

The riding grounds of the royal family were a walled area of hilly meadows and woodland adjacent to the palace. Ludmilla and Miles rode in silence for a while, enjoying the easy rhythm of the ride. Then she reined in, giving a groan of disappointment: Another group of horsemen, led by Ilya, was coming toward them, with hooded hunting birds and reptiles on their wrists.

"Well met, sister," said Ilya as he reined in beside Ludmilla. "Will you accompany me to the waterfowl marsh?" With an air of resignation, the princess complied, and the two rode at the head of the column, side by side.

Miles found himself near the end, when one of the riders reined in beside him. It was a new man in the guard, a young man with light brown hair in a topknot who rode bareback, a broad, curved knife thrust through his wide belt.

"Your pardon, sir, but I hear that you are a teacher." His courtesy was as foreign to this culture as his coiffure, and he lacked the brutish arrogance and obvious stupidity of most of the other guards.

"That is so, my son. I am a priest of the Church of Rome. Why are you interested in teachers?"

"In the place where I was before this, the School of Marius, in Ludus, I had access to an old university. There were teaching machines there, and I learned a great deal from them, and much that I don't understand. There are no such machines still operating here, and perhaps you could help me to understand some of the things I've learned." He was obviously eager for understanding, a trait Miles had found in few of the inhabitants of the Flavians.

"Certainly," said Miles. "I am usually free in the early evenings, when the princess is practicing music. Come to see me then."

"Thank you, sir," said the youth, bowing. "My turn of guard duty ends at the fifth hour. I'm free then until the seventh hour of the morning." They rode on to the hunting ground.

While the consul and his friends sat their horses on a knoll near a small lake, the young guard would ride out to fetch in the waterfowl brought down by the hunting birds. At a gallop, he would lean from the bare back of his horse and pluck the dead birds from the ground, while balancing a hooded bird on his other fist. The hooded bird always remained level, no matter what the relative attitudes of the man's body and the horse he rode.

As they rode alone back to the palace stables, Miles said, "What business did your brother have with you?"

"The usual. He asked me to attend an erotic free-fall ballet tonight. A private performance. I refused. He was not happy."

"Did you notice that new guard of his? The young man with the topknot who rode bareback?"

"Notice him?" exclaimed the princess. "I've never seen such horsemanship in my life! Ilya said his name is Parma Sicarius, a big winner in the birthday games. I suppose we saw him, but they all look alike in those helmets. Anyway, horseman or no, I suppose he's just another of my brother's tame killers."

Miles remembered him now. In one of the fights he had seen that young man, armed only with a knife and chain, bring down a much bigger man armed with a two-hand sword. He had worn no helmet then, and Miles distinctly remembered the whipping tail of hair hanging from the topknot.

"He spoke to me before the hunt. He wishes to become my student. I've agreed to tutor him in the early evenings."

"A gladiator studying?" she whooped with laughter. "So, my brother has planted a spy on you? Shame on you, Father. I took you for a more cautious man."

"That was my first thought, also, but I found no duplicity in the boy. Somehow, in that hellish school in Ludus, he learned some things from an old teaching machine, and he wants to understand more. No play-acting here; the marks of the born scholar are all over him."

"A potential convert?" Her eyebrows arched sardonically.

"Everyone here is a potential convert, my daughter," remarked the priest complacently.

Back at the palace, Miles ran holographic thimbles of every fight Parma had participated in, from the first offworld to the latest in the birthday games. The Jesuit was surprised and intrigued to see that Parma had never once killed, and only in the milling battle that opened the birthday games had he even struck blows that might have proven fatal. The boy obviously had a regard for life almost unheard of on Charun, and when Parma arrived at his apartment later that evening, Miles was ready with questions that would test what the young man was made of.

He found that the education Parma had received in Ludus had been spotty and erratic, with wide gaps of information and much unexplained material. The man who had aided him had not been a trained educator, just an amateur with an enthusiasm for old knowledge but with no sense of system. He learned of Parma's background on Thrax, his training in Ludus, and his disturbing conversations there with Marius. Miles heard one piece of information that alarmed him.

"Father Miles, the cross you wear has reminded me: On the first day of the birthday games, during the parade, a man in a robe like yours, but gray, rushed out of the crowd and tried to tell the fighters not to go to the arena. He was wearing a wooden cross like yours. One of the trainers told me about it."

"What happened to him?"

"He was taken to the transient prison. I suppose to await trial. Do you know him?"

"I do indeed. He's a friend of mine, Friar Jeremiah of the Franciscan order." That sounds just like Jeremiah, Miles thought, ruefully, heading straight for the symptom and damn the disease. "I must see about this right away. If you will excuse me, come back at the same time, tomorrow evening."

Armed with a pass from Ludmilla, Miles went to the prison, an ordinary building with only a few armed guards in attendance. As he entered, Miles almost ran into Father Stavros, who was leaving.

"Why, Father Miles! Have you come for Brother Jeremiah?"

"Yes, I heard about his predicament not an hour ago. Why didn't you get word to me?"

"I tried, but you are considerably more isolated at court than Jeremiah is in prison. I'd gotten about half-way through the layers of flunkies and hangers-on in my efforts to reach you."

"I see. From now on I'll not be so hard to reach. What charge are they holding the boy on?"

"They aren't really sure. I think they're just holding him until someone can think of something. 'Incitement to mutiny,' I suppose, although the idea's absurd when the mutineers wear neck rings. Can you get him freed?"

"Easily, since he hasn't been charged yet. It may take a few days."

"Praise God. It will be good to have him back. We've been doing so well lately."

"Indeed? He's actually managed to do some converting?" The Jesuit's eyebrows rose until they were nearly hidden in his cowl.

"Oh, yes. Nearly a hundred converts already." The old priest beamed radiantly.

"It seems I underestimated the boy. A hundred! This is splendid. We'll be able to attack the problem from both ends, then. I'll get you a pass to allow you to come to see me at court, and one for Jeremiah, too, when he's free. With me at court and you two in the city, we may be able to solve this in much less time than I had anticipated. Have no fear, Father. I'll have Jeremiah back to you in a few days."

In the prison, Miles showed his pass and was conducted to Jeremiah's cell. There were no bars in evidence. Instead, Jeremiah wore a collar like a slave's but gold in color, which would render him instantly unconscious if he tried to leave. He looked up, astonished, as Miles entered.

"Father Miles! Did Father Stavros finally reach you?"

"No, I heard of your arrest from another source.

You'll be meeting him shortly. What on Earth, or rather on Charun, possessed you to do such a foolish thing?"

"It proved too much for me, Father, seeing all those men and beasts, and even the constructs, about to be slaughtered meaninglessly. I found myself protesting, even though I knew that it was futile."

"Ah, the impetuousness of youth. Well, I'll get you sprung from here, my boy, but it will take a few days, which you can profitably employ in meditation. I suggest you meditate upon the virtue of patience. Do you lack for anything? Aside from freedom, of course?"

"No, they feed at least as well as the titheship, and the facilities aren't primitive. I shall be comfortable as I await release."

"Father Stavros tells me you've been busy in the city. My congratulations. I'd not have believed it possible to make so many conversions in this time."

"Why, thank you," said the friar, astonished.

"Still, it's too little and too slow. All hinges upon getting a sympathetic consul and/or court."

"Well, even faint praise is something."

Ludmilla was having trouble adjusting to Miles' new pupil. He was a courteous young man, very handsome and with a splendid physique, but at the same time he was a neck-ringed slave, a barbarian from some vermin-ridden nomadic tribe on the far side of the system, and one of her brother's loathsome gladiator-bodyguards. She knew the fallacy of such prejudice, but she was still the child of her aristocratic upbringing.

"Father," she asked Miles one evening, "are you really sure this man is suitable? I realize your concern for slaves and such but to have him here, in the royal apartments, being instructed along with me. Is it quite, ah, proper?"

Miles took a deep breath and held it awhile. When he spoke, his voice was as neutral as always when giving instruction.

"Child, do you know how that man came to be a slave?"

"Captured in a raid, I suppose."

"He voluntarily sold himself in order to rescue his people from ruin and starvation. Have you done anything of comparable nobility lately?"

"Of course not," said the princess, flushing. "One hardly has the call to do anything self-sacrificing in this jeweled prison. I wasn't questioning the fellow's virtues, just the fitness of his being educated with me. There are certain concepts I was raised with."

"They are concepts you will have to discard, and quickly. Archaic concepts of birth have no place in the real world. This make-believe feudal-imperial fantasy your system lives in is about to come to an abrupt halt. You say that you've had no chance to prove yourself in this place. You'll have your chance soon. And you'll be standing against that system that raised you, and alongside people like Parma, and Jeremiah, and Stavros, and others of 'low birth.'"

The princess became more subdued.

"It's getting close, then? I've noticed that Ilya's been unnaturally quiet and polite of late. He's plotting something."

"Undoubtedly. Did you have anything better to do with your life until now?"

"No, not really. Well, as well, I suppose, to be executed now for a good cause as later for something else." She brooded a moment. "He'll do away with me quietly, but he'll plan something special for you."

"As long as it's public. Martyrdoms always have a salutary effect on the audience. As some old Earth writer once said: 'For every Christian who dies in the arena, ten leave the stands.'"

"I wish I could be as flippant about it. You were born a Christian; no doubt martyrdom has an appeal for you that I find lacking in it."

"On the contrary, I was twenty-five or so before I ever heard of Christianity."

"I don't believe it!"

"Nevertheless, it's quite true. I was born on a planet called Durga, in the Upanishad System. It was settled by Hindus from northern India in the middle of the Third Millennium. There were few highly educated people among them, and when they lost contact with the rest of the galaxy, religion and culture became debased. Our worship was based on the cult of the goddess Kali, also called Durga, depending upon aspect and time of year. The basic rite of appeasement of the goddess in her aspect as Kali was human sacrifice. Since blood was sacred to the goddess, sacrifice was carried out by strangulation, using a garotte or the bare hands."

"But you didn't participate in these rites yourself, did you?"

"I was one of the holy stranglers. I slew a great many men from the age of fourteen onward. It was a hereditary position. My family were all great stranglers. We were much respected by the community at large."

Ludmilla sat in silence for a moment as this revelation sank in.

"How did you come to be a Christian?"

"Durga was rediscovered about sixty-odd years ago and was returned to Hindu control. The Hindus don't concern themselves much with religious practice on their worlds, believing all faiths to be one, anyway. But the new Hindu authorities put down the worship of Kali in the strangulation cult because they did not tolerate sacrifice of living beings. We practiced in secret for some time. Often we'd ambush parties of the new Hindu administrators and strangle them as grand sacrifices to Kali.

"Eventually the Hindus asked the Jesuits to establish schools on Durga, where the population was fearfully ignorant. The Jesuits have been famous scholars and teachers since the founding of the Society. One night, when I was about twenty-six, I saw one of the Jesuit teachers in our village. I regarded these blackrobed intruders to be the greatest enemies of the goddess, since they claimed that she didn't even exist. I decided to please Kali by sacrificing this priest to her. I tracked him down an unlit street, sneaked up on him from behind, and pulled my garotte from my sash. He broke both my arms and legs and fractured my skull.

"It took me many months to recover, in the hospital the Jesuits and Hindus had set up in the city nearest my village. The priest whom I had attacked came to visit me often, and he began to teach me his faith. Needless to say, I was enormously impressed by him, and I listened to what he had to say with great attentiveness. It was from him that I learned that there's nothing like a sharp object lesson to gain an unbeliever's attention.

"Eventually I saw the light and came into the faith. I felt no guilt for the things I had done in my early life. Those had been done from honest religious conviction and, aside from ritual murder, I was guilty of no crime. Indeed, I was a most civic-minded and lawabiding citizen. I can remember how shocked I was when I heard of a murder and robbery in another village.

"I graduated with honors from the school the Jesuits had set up near my village, and chose to attend the Jesuit seminary on Loyola. There my peculiar talents recommended me to the Brotherhood Cestus Dei, a very exclusive and militant order within the Society. I'm afraid that it enjoys a very bad reputation elsewhere in the Church—just ask Jeremiah—and there are rumors that the Pope would like to suppress us, except, of course, that she often finds us useful."

Ludmilla was more puzzled than ever. She had thought of Miles as a rather reasonable sort of fanatic, a man of intelligence who had been steeped in the mysticism of the Roman Church since birth. A new complexity had been added.

Miles checked his room for bugs, then set all his antispying devices, just in case. He did various things with his staff, pressing and twisting knots and rings. Then he waited. There came a faint buzzing from the staff, then a voice.

"This is Cardinal Van Horn. Are you there, Father Miles?"

"Father Miles here. What took you so long?"

"We've been on a reconnaissance of the world of Cadmus, where the constructs are made. Any progress?"

"Of a sort. I have the sister of the hereditary ruler firmly attached to our cause, and she's in the line of inheritance. The Franciscan who came with me has been doing some good work in the city, but unless you care to wait for a few centuries, it's going to have to be done my way."

"You've always been particular about having your way, Miles. Not all of us are so enamored of your judgment."

"I've been right, so far."

"So far, yes. You'll be unsurprised to learn that the *Glory of Allah* is cruising about the system."

"Maneuvers?"

"What else do they ever call it? We've also had occasional visits from the *Land of Milk and Honey.*"

"I thought the Temple was co-operating with us on this."

"Oh, they are, they are, but you've been a diplomat. Cooperation doesn't mean relaxing one's suspicion or ceasing to look out for one's own interest. Our main problem, though, is the Caliphate. They're treading pretty hard on our toes out here, and word from the UF is that they're agitating for a holy war against Cadmus if the Church Militant doesn't do something soon. It's our system, we couldn't stand for that, so there'll be trouble. You've got to pull one of your famous rabbit-out-of-the-miter tricks or we're facing war over this miserable, wretched handful of benighted flyspecks."

"I'll be ready in a few days, Your Eminence. There's considerable plotting and counterplotting going on just now, and I don't know who stands where."

"Find out quickly and act. Time is running out."

XI

The warlord Bandinegri of Cadmus sat impatiently in the consul's palace in Augusta. He was waiting on Ilya. The warlord was a tall, thin man with a pointed gray-shot beard and a beaklike nose. He looked like a predator, and the look was not deceiving. He habitually wore a jeweled cuirass and helmet, but the pistol and dagger at his belt were functional, well-used weapons.

He didn't like having to deal with Ilya, who was a well-known nincompoop. The consul was nominally his suzerain, but the warlord was, in truth, the most powerful man in the system because he owned most of the armies used in the public and private wars throughout the Flavian worlds. In the laboratories on Cadmus were created the constructs that did the bulk of the fighting. The warlord trained and equipped these creatures, then hired them out to anyone with cash or the prospect of loot. In the rare peaceful intervals, when contracts were few, he sent his forces on raids and plundering expeditions, which he sometimes personally led, just to keep his hand in.

The consul entered in a swirl of brocades.

"Oh, my dear Bandinegri, I am most happy to see you." The consul held out his hand for the customary kiss, which was not forthcoming.

"Um, well, please sit down, warlord, don't stand on ceremony. Will you have something to drink?" The consul clapped once; a slave entered with a tray of refreshments and withdrew at once. The consul must indeed be disturbed, thought the warlord, to enter a room with another man without the protection of his bodyguard.

"What is the problem, Your Grace? I left an important contract to come here at your behest."

"I quite appreciate that, warlord," said the consul, beginning to get nettled. "There is something peculiar going on here in Augusta, and I fear I can no longer trust my nobles and officers."

"You never could trust them," said Bandinegri. "What causes them to be even less trustworthy than usual?"

"Have you heard of the Church of Rome?"

"Of course," said the warlord, puzzled. "It was the ecclesiastical state that controlled the Flavians centuries ago. My ancestor Baglioni Bandinegri, the first warlord of our line, was a renegade bishop of that Church. What has the Church of Rome to do with your problems?"

"Several weeks ago, two men, priests of the Church of Rome, appeared in the city. One established contacts with a prominent gangster, then with Malatesta Capelli, and now he's among my sister's entourage. I suspect him of plotting to assassinate me and put my sister on the throne. The other has been rabble-rousing among the scum of the city, raving about an end to

slavery and the games. Both these men were brought
here from somewhere outside the system, by way of
Titus, which has been having illicit extrasystem dealings for years.''

"So," said Bandinegri, "you suspect that Rome has
made a comeback and is trying to regain her lost ter-
ritories?''

"What else? And what better way than to depose
the reigning autocrat and install a puppet who will do
as they dictate?''

"Why not just plow in here with ships and men and
take over?''

"I think they may be militarily weak, at least this
far from the center of their empire. It's not the Church
I worry about now, but how far they've spread their
insidious doctrines on my home world. I know they've
subverted a member of my own bodyguard. He's no
danger, I have the control to his neck ring, but what of
the rest of my court? What of my army?''

"The answer's simple enough: Get rid of your sister. Kill the bitch and they'll have no hope of putting a
sympathetic ruler on the throne.'' The warlord fumed
at the boy's density.

"I have—personal reasons for keeping my sister
alive, at least for a while.''

"Then kill the rest of them!'' said Bandinegri, exasperated. "Arrest the lot, toss them into the arena, and
have them dismantled by a few constructs. It'll get rid
of your enemies and serve as a wholesome and salutary example to the populace.''

"But there may be others I don't know about. I have
to have time to plant spies among them.''

"And just what do you want me to do in the mean-
time?''

"Since I can't trust my forces any more, I want to
increase my force of constructs. I know I can trust
you, because our interests are the same. There were

two things the Church of Rome was unalterably set against, even in the later, decadent days: private war and the creation of constructs. If they take over here, it's the end for you as well as for me."

That was true enough, the warlord had to admit.

"Yes, I remember the doctrine: 'Usurpation of Divine Function,' I believe it was. No, we certainly don't want the Church back in the system and spoiling all our fun. Who's your intelligence source for the doings of these priests?"

"I have my spy system, and Lord Capelli told me about the interview he had with one of the priests. He's been most helpful."

I'll bet he was, thought the warlord. That explained a lot. He knew that Ilya hadn't the brains to figure all this out by himself. And when the matter of the Church and the unfortunate sister were taken care of, Ilya would be taken care of, and all hail Consul Malatesta Capelli! Definitely, Capelli was the man he would have to deal with. He'd make a better consul than this clown, anyway.

"Good enough, then," said Bandinegri. "I'll send to Cadmus for constructs and officers. They'll be here in a few days, and I'll take personal charge of them when they arrive."

"Excellent! I'll have a suite prepared for you in the palace."

"That won't be necessary, Your Grace. I have a villa outside the city." It would serve, thought the warlord, as a much better place than the palace to hold a few very private meetings.

Father Miles, austere in his black robe, stood in the pulpit of St. Cyril's. A large audience was gathered in the pews to hear him speak. Behind him stood Father Stavros and Brother Jeremiah, plus a handful of priests from other near-deserted churches on Charun.

In the choir loft, heavily veiled, sat the Princess Ludmilla, guarded by Parma, who was off duty.

"Parma," said the princess, "doesn't Father Miles realize that a crowd this size must contain my brother's spies?"

"Assuredly, my lady. I believe that little gambler Luigi has identified at least ten."

"Then why does he go on?"

"This is a public meeting, my lady. Father Miles is not trying to keep his origin or intention secret any longer. It seems he wishes to force the consul's hand."

"I fear he will be most successful."

Father Miles was pleased with the turnout. He knew that he was the prime source of gossip among the lower population. The stories of his miraculous win at the "Rainbow's End" and the skirmish with Curio's men had grown with the telling: At last count, he had defeated twenty thugs single-handedly. And it was common knowledge that he had become a prominent figure at court; he planned to make full use of his publicity. He gauged the tension of the crowd, and when it reached the proper pitch, he began to speak.

"People of Augusta, I have not come among you to teach you to gamble or to fight. I am here, sent by an authority whose power you cannot even imagine, to tell you of what you were, and what you may yet become. You have seen some trivial manifestations of that power, and they are so slight that one day you will laugh that you ever thought them impressive. I am here to take you away from the life of idleness, the meaningless existence you now lead, and to bring you back to the knowledge of the Living God, whom you rejected so long ago."

There was some stirring and fidgeting among the audience. Obviously, a lot of those people out there liked a life of idleness just fine.

"Out there," he pointed skyward, "is the realm of

the reawakened Rome, so vast that your mind could not comprehend it. This Flavian System was once a part of that great unity, but it has fallen by the wayside. Still, God wishes the return of his strayed people, and Rome will open her arms to you if you will only return to her.

"You are the people who went out to conquer the stars a hundred generations ago, and look at you now!" The voice was concentrated scorn. "Men turned away from God and began to worship wealth and power. They reveled in the degradation of their fellow men. They usurped the powers of God, creating imitation men, which they were unable to give souls or the power of morality, the divine spark. Men began to lose their spirit, their drive; they fell into stagnation; even their numbers began to decrease. Look about you! This once-great city is now home to less than one tenth of its former population. Its remaining people, you, live in idle despair. You have exalted the trivial, the foolish, the petty, the worthless, while condemning the true, the essential, to oblivion. Slaves do the work that you should be doing. Men fight and die for your entertainment because you have lost the ability to enjoy anything but horror. As a people, you approach utter worthlessness. You are debased, inert, cruel, and cowardly." Jeremiah, seated now behind the Jesuit, winced visibly. "This will stop!"

"God will not be denied!" Miles pointed an accusing finger at the crowd. "If you fail him again, he will turn away from you, and you will be destroyed utterly. The doom is coming, not in the form of an obscure angel of death, but in ships of war, piloted by enemies of the true faith!" Jeremiah's look became one of dismay. "They will not bring the word of God, but fire and destruction!"

Father Miles' voice slipped smoothly back into its normal tone.

"If, however, you turn back to God, his mercy is infinite. With sincere repentance, he will not refuse any soul, no matter how blackened. You will enjoy the blessings of peace, freedom, knowledge, and prosperity, for the Church is concerned with the quality of this life as well as of the life beyond. In truth, you may enjoy a life many times the length of the one possible to you now!" He gleefully anticipated the effect *that* little bomb would have when it reached the bulk of the population. "You will once again become the race of men fit to conquer the stars. Choose now. Time is running out. Some of you have seen me before; you know that I do not speak idly. God's blessing on you all."

He swept from the podium in his most impressive stalking exit. From the door of the sacristy, he observed the faces of the crowd as they left. Some were stirred, some skeptical, some disappointed. None seemed bored. In all, not a bad result. The city would be buzzing tomorrow. The other priests did not seem so pleased.

"You are rather free with God's opinions," said one.

"Each of us interprets God's meaning within the tenets of Church doctrine," said Miles, unperturbed.

"Father Miles," said Jeremiah, "if the UF ever gets a copy of that speech, the Caliphate will call for your head. Your words will be called irresponsible and inflammatory."

"That is unfortunate, but you will notice that I named no names. If they feel incensed, it's because every word is true."

Later, in the rectory, Miles, Jeremiah, Parma, Ludmilla, and Stavros held council.

"You were a bit scanty in your theology, Father. For instance, I didn't once hear Jesus Christ mentioned. That seems rather a glaring omission for a

Christian priest to make."

"They are not ready yet for too much advanced theology. In any case, I have little hope of really indoctrinating this generation. They aren't primitives with an already established religious sense. A few will convert, but most will remain skeptical and unable to comprehend. What is important is that they realize the danger they are in, and that the power of Rome is all that can save them from that danger. Once we have established schools here, the next generation will grow up in the faith."

"I beg to differ," said Father Stavros. "Jeremiah and I have been having excellent success with the people down here."

"I don't wish to detract from your accomplishments, my friends. You've done splendidly, it's true, but this is still too slow."

"And what," fumed Jeremiah, "was the meaning of that business about 'enjoy a life many times the length of the one possible to you now'? It's against all proper missionary procedure to dangle the longevity treatment as bait to lure in converts. It's a guarantee that you'll never be sure of their sincerity."

"True enough. It's not what I would have done normally, but circumstances force my hand. I've been in contact with the Church Militant. They've a warship in the system now and are ready to intervene upon request from proper authority. The Caliphate also has a warship out here, one of their biggest, a fifty-legion carrier. That means they're ready to dismantle this system given the slightest excuse, to reconstruct it along lines more pleasing to Allah. The new imam is a true fanatic when it comes to the soulless. All the faiths hate the idea of them, and we all suppress their creation, but the imam thinks that killing them and all who have anything to do with them is the most pleasing offering he can make to God."

"I see," said Stavros. "There isn't much time, then."

"Very little."

"What must this 'request from proper authority' consist of?" asked Ludmilla.

"Just a call for aid from the duly constituted government of a system. In the case of autocratic rule, such as you have here among the Flavians, that government is one man, Ilya."

"So much for that possibility, then," said Parma. "I've been living with him for quite some time, and he seems an unlikely candidate for conversion."

"Quite so," said Father Miles. "Given time, I believe I could bring him around, but now I think we'll have to fall back on the second possibility."

"Which is," queried Jeremiah.

"Putting Ludmilla, here, on the throne."

"Meaning that the consul has to die?" said Jeremiah, appalled.

"I wouldn't count on his abdicating in her favor," said Miles, testily.

"Face it, Ludmilla hasn't long to live. She's a threat to her brother's throne and to the ambitions of all the schemers among the great families. In any case, Ilya wouldn't survive an Islamic takeover. They have a short way with rulers who employ construct armies."

"Are you suggesting assassination?" asked Stavros.

"I'm suggesting a popular uprising," said Miles. "The overthrow of a tyrant by his own subjects would be acceptable to the UF as well as being a very fine thing indeed on general principles."

"Father," protested Jeremiah, "you're proposing a violent intercession in this system's affairs. It's not proper and it's not Christian."

"Enough, Friar," barked Miles, at the end of his patience at last. "We're not back on a monastery ship, debating missionary procedure. I was given this assignment by order direct from the Vatican, delivered personally by you. I'm to carry it out as best I see fit, and that is what I'm doing. As for bloodshed and violence, what do you think goes on in that stadium nearly every day? As I recall, you had some strong opinions on that a few weeks back.

"Now, listen," he said, visibly collecting himself. "If we follow the plan I've laid out, we can confine the bloodshed to a very few involved persons, instead of innocent thousands."

"Who are these 'involved persons'?" said Stavros.

"The consul, the head plotters of the great families, a few constructs, and, of course, ourselves."

"What is the plan?" asked Parma.

"The people here are best impressed by physical demonstration, agreed?"

"True enough, I suppose," said Father Stavros. "It's not their fault, but they've been conditioned by generations of exposure to spectacle as the principal form of diversion and the sole manifestation of political reality."

"Father Miles, are you going to give the people a spectacle?" asked Ludmilla with an anticipatory smile.

"That is my proposal. Since I've made myself so conspicuous of late, the consul will have to destroy me publicly to discredit me and emphasize the ascendency of his power above all rivals."

"And what will you do this time that's so impressive?" asked Jeremiah.

"I will fight his bodyguard, Hedulio, in the stadium." There was a shocked silence around the table.

"Don't do it, Father," said Ludmilla. "You're overreaching yourself."

"You wouldn't stand a chance," agreed Parma. "Hedulio's like nothing else on Charun."

"Neither am I," asserted Miles.

"Now it's your turn to discard some vanity, Father

Miles," said Jeremiah. "Jesuit or no, Cestus Dei initiate or no, you can't be that good. Hedulio's a heavy-grav man, his strength and reflexes are inhuman, he can probably take a construct apart like a lobster. Forget it."

"Does anyone have any better ideas?" Miles looked around the table. There were no suggestions. "Very well, then, I fight Hedulio."

"How will you arrange this fight?" asked Stavros, resigned.

"Yes," said Ludmilla, "suppose Ilya just shoots you, or orders you beheaded instead?"

"I'll plant the idea with Malatesta Capelli. He's the one who controls Ilya these days."

"I'll agree to this foolishness on one condition," said Jeremiah. "You must not kill Hedulio. If you're martyred, that's one thing, but if you should by some miracle win, you'd set the cause of Christianity back several centuries by killing the man."

"I had no intention of killing him, just of winning. Besides, it's not just my beating Hedulio that's going to set off the popular reaction; it's when the consul and his cronies try to kill me afterward that the excitement will start."

"Of course," said Ludmilla, "they'd never let you live after such a coup."

"No, they'll try to kill us immediately, before I even leave the arena. That will be the trigger."

"They'll probably succeed," she observed.

"That's inconsequential. The important thing is to get the proper reaction started. Within a few minutes, Ilya should be removed from the scene, either by the mob or through treachery by Capelli. Remember, we still don't know which way Capelli's going to jump. That will leave you, Ludmilla, as hereditary consul, and you must summon the Church Militant forces. I'll give you the signaling device to call them. Their appearance will halt all violence instantly. With luck, some of us may be alive to see it. But the only one of us who is truly indispensable is Ludmilla."

When they arrived back at the palace, Miles gave Parma and Ludmilla some words of advice.

"From now on, children, we'll be watched incessantly. Ludmilla, you've lived at court all your life; you know how to handle yourself in the midst of this kind of duplicity. But you, Parma, must be very careful. I'll be able to neutralize your neck ring soon, but until then you are our weakest link, and you must avoid questioning."

"I'm learning quickly, Father. I'm glad I met you, or I might have decided that corruption and duplicity are the proper standards of men's behavior."

"I rejoice also. Guard the princess well; she's our only hope." So saying, Miles went to his quarters to establish contact with the warship cruising somewhere outside the atmosphere of Charun.

Parma and Ludmilla wended their way to the princess's suite, Ludmilla greeting courtiers with her customary assumed warmth, they responding with the inevitable false courtesy. She sighed with relief as they reached her rooms.

"Parma, I'm so glad you'll never become a courtier." Once she had become used to having the young man around, and after several dressings-down by Father Miles on the subject of snobbery, she found herself speaking to Parma more and more as an equal. "You have no idea how deadly dull the life is, as well as just plain deadly. Pour us some wine, will you? I'm parched as well as terrified."

"Terrified, my lady? What have you to fear now that hasn't been there all your life?" Parma had no awe of the princess, nor of anyone else, except perhaps Father Miles. Parma was a freeborn man of a tribe that acknowledged neither superiors nor inferiors.

"Oh, nothing, I suppose. It's just that it seems so immediate now." She was lonely and frightened, and she felt the need for company. She sat on a divan out on her balcony, under the stars and well away from any listeners, and signaled for Parma to take the chair opposite. To ease her fears, she changed the subject.

"Tell me, Parma, why did you, of all people, choose to follow Father Miles?"

"Well, my lady—" he began.

"Call me Ludmilla. Since we're probably to be butchered together, we might as well be on a first-name basis."

"Well, then, Ludmilla, first, you must understand my background. I came from a nomadic tribe of herdsmen—barbarians, you might call them—but, morally, at least, they were far more sophisticated than this culture."

"I certainly won't contest that. Continue."

"We had certain concepts of divinity: the sky, the sun, the grass, the bones of our ancestors. Animism, I suppose one of your scholars would say. There were certain unalterable rules of behavior among members of the tribe. There were rules regarding war with other tribes, and trade, and behavior at the fairs. All livestock belonged to the tribe, though some herds were nominally the property of certain families. In hard times, all was common property, since the tribe was really one large family. All adult men were warriors, and only in war, or, under very special circumstances, blood feud, could men kill. The only reason for war was when another tribe, usually one of the mountain tribes sought to steal our herds of sheepoxen.

"You must understand that on Thrax, the herds mean everything. Without sheepoxen and horses, a tribe is helpless, without food and shelter, afoot on the wide steppe. It simply means death, and so we fight with a ferocity you wouldn't believe possible to protect our herds."

The princess nodded, captivated by this story of a culture so alien to her own, one with rock-hard values. She was beginning to understand Parma, and, through him, beginning to understand Father Miles far better.

"Suddenly," Parma continued, "there was an end to that life, I was taken to a place where men were trained to fight for the entertainment of other men. I wasn't really sure this was wrong, at first. You see, all my values were tribal. I didn't know whether or not they applied when I was separated from my tribe, but I found that life was decidedly uncomfortable without them. At the School of Marius in Ludus, then later here, I found nothing to replace those values."

"That goes without saying," interjected the princess. "Then you met Father Miles."

"Exactly. Here was a man who had values and standards and no doubt as to their rectitude. Better yet, these values apply to the whole universe, not just to a single people. So I've chosen to follow him."

"You've met Jeremiah and Stavros. You know that they disagree with much of what Father Miles says and with nearly all of his methods."

"That's certainly true," said Parma, laughing. "It's fun to see them arguing. But to tell you the truth, the matters about which they dispute are rather vague to me. I suppose, if I'd been raised in the Church, the differences between Franciscan and Jesuit would seem greater. But from what I've heard from both sides, I incline to the Jesuit. Probably it's the result of being born into a warrior tribe and living an active, violent life."

"And what will you do when this is all over? Assuming, of course, that you're still alive?"

"I've talked it over with Father Miles, and I've decided to attend the Jesuit seminary on Loyola. He says that, upon graduation, he'll sponsor me for initiation into the Brotherhood Cestus Dei."

"So you'll be leaving." Ludmilla was suddenly saddened, though she didn't know why.

"For a while. But against a span of centuries, a few years are not much."

"No, I suppose not," Ludmilla replied. She didn't know what else to say, now that Parma had chosen a path away from hers.

In another room, Miles was once again fiddling with the knobs on his staff, supplementing his efforts with a few unclergymanly curses. He spun around, staff at high guard, as a head, followed by a body, appeared at his window. No man should have been there. The window was at least six stories from ground level. The man slid through the window, and Miles relaxed his guard. The intruder wore the skin-tight black singlet of armor cloth that identified a commando of the Church Militant.

"Father Miles of Durga?" said the apparition.

"If I weren't you'd be dead," answered Miles.

"If you weren't, I wouldn't have been seen, and you'd probably be dead." The man was of medium height, with dark hair and skin, and a long, hooked nose that overhung thin lips. "I'm Commander Father Lame Deer, Dominican order." He reached into his belt pouch and pulled out two small black boxes. "Here are the gadgets you asked for."

"Any trouble getting in here?" asked Miles.

"Are you serious? A bunch of second-year seminary kids could get into this place. Franciscans, even." The Dominican snorted with contempt.

"Excellent. Lame Deer — I've heard the name. From

the Five Systems campaign, I believe. Of course, the action that took the Big Construct and its staff! Father Nkosi told me about it. He was attached as communications specialist on that one."

"Nkosi's a good man," said Lame Deer.

"Do you still have the same team you had then?"

"Most of 'em," said the Dominican. "It isn't a field for men who want to live out their natural span."

"That's for sure," said Miles. "I'm glad to know that Van Horn has your team on tap. Not necessary at all for taking this silly consul, of course, but after this there'll still be the warlord and the Pirate Brotherhood."

"Good to hear it," said Lame Deer. "It's been kind of dull, cruising around this sytem with nothing to do. Care to have me slip a few of my boys down here to help you out? They're getting rusty."

"No, the offer is tempting, but the people here must earn their own self-respect. You know how it is."

"Sure, I've worked a lot of these places myself. That was back in my missionary days. Well, good luck, Father Miles. I've got to get back to the rendezvous point before it starts to get light. *Dominus vobiscum.*"

"*Et cum spiritu tuo,*" said Father Miles.

XII

Lord Malatesta Capelli was being the perfect host. Throughout dinner, he conversed wittily on a number of subjects, none of them involving religion or politics. Now, over snifters of his own excellent brandy, he delicately brought up the true subject of the evening's meeting.

"Ah, Father Miles, you say you are of the Jesuit order. According to my reading of history, this was a most aggressive and militant group. If you are any example, I would say that the order has retained its belligerent predisposition."

"We are still inclined to look favorably upon martial prowess in our training, yes," agreed Miles.

"And this brotherhood of which you have spoken — ah, Cestus Dei, I believe — this confraternity is even more violently inclined than the rest of the order?"

"Not toward the initiation of violence, but toward dealing with it."

"Of course, your pardon. But from the way in which you dealt with those men who set upon you in the street, I must assume that your training far surpasses that of our gladiators and soldiers."

"Yes, from what I've seen of the fighting men here," said Miles, nodding complacently, "their training and methods are far out of date. In fact, I've seen only one man here whom I would be hesitant to face in hand-to-hand combat."

"And who might that person be?" inquired Capelli. Only the slightest change in bodily attitude told Miles that Capelli's interest in this question was far more than casual.

"Hedulio, captain of the consul's bodyguard."

"True, he is a most formidable person. He was a great gladiator once, and I believe that he's rated the most skillful, as well as the strongest unarmed fighter known to this generation on Charun. But surely, Hedulio is getting old?"

"If so, then he must have improved with age. I've watched him at his practice in the bodyguard's training area. No amount of training, however severe, can give an ordinary man the strength and reflexes developed by natural selection on a heavy-gravity world."

"So—" said Capelli, filing that information away for later, "Eh, speaking of age and the improvements attendant there with, what is this gossip I hear of Rome having a drug of eternal youth? Is there any truth to it?"

"Some. It isn't a drug, but a treatment, and it doesn't confer eternal youth, of course, just delayed senescence for a period of three centuries or so. Ordinarily, missionaries are not supposed to reveal this right away, lest people come flocking to the Church purely for the sake of the treatment. However, the people here are most intransigent, and agents such as I are given wide powers of discretion in these matters."

"I will confess, sir, that knowing this already makes your Church seem yet more attractive to me."

Miles could believe that easily enough. Capelli was power-mad, but he was also old. Miles could see the calculations going on behind the blandly smiling eyes. Capelli wanted to be consul, but that would mean having to deal with Rome. But then, Rome had the longevity treatment. Something could be worked out.

"Father Miles," he said at last, "do you really think there is any hope of Rome dealing with Ilya? He is, let us say, not terribly stable, you know, and he's too young to be very tempted by the longevity treatment."

"I'd say there's practically no hope," said Miles. "The Church really couldn't deal with such a person in good conscience, anyway."

"If there were, say, a sympathetic consul in the Flavians, could such a consul find a way to ease that conscience?"

"Under certain circumstances, yes. The freeing of the slaves, the ending of the constructs, suppression of piracy. And, of course, the consul would have to agree to the reopening of the churches and the establishment of Roman schools throughout the system. You were thinking, I take it, of the Princess Ludmilla?"

"Ah, yes, of course, the princess. She is, after all, next in succession."

"Beyond doubt. Well, this has been a most illuminating conversation, my lord. Perhaps we may have more such in the future. Now I must leave you."

"It is my fervent wish to speak with you again, and often."

He showed the priest to a door, where one of his vehicles was waiting to take Miles to the city. In a short time, a messenger was sent out, and later that evening Capelli was back in the same room, repeating to Bandinegri his conversation with Father Miles.

"So," said the warlord, "by co-operating, we get the longevity treatment, but it means the end of our power. Personally, I'll take the short, enjoyable life."

"Not so quick, warlord. Why not take both?"

"How can we have both? Roman ascendency means no slaves and no constructs. Those are the bases of our power."

"First," explained Capelli, patiently, "we must get rid of the priest, publicly."

"Why publicly?"

"Let me explain. We get rid of the priest because he knows us too well. We must get rid of his friends also because he's probably warned them not to trust us. We must get rid of the princess because she stands in our way and will ruin everything.

"I'll suggest that Ilya have the priest killed publicly, by Hedulio, by way of example to his erring people. Ilya will, of course, grossly underestimate the furor of the crowd, among whom this Father Miles has become something of a popular hero. In a mighty show of indignation, I'll have the consul killed and assume power, thus having the throne without staining my hands with blood of the unfortunate priest. In the general chaos the princess will, of course, have lamentably perished."

"And Rome?"

"I will report to Rome my great distress at the deaths of their minions. I will beg that more be sent, sending along a report of the reforms I wish to make. Once we have the treatment in our hands, we can do as we wish. As to the founding of Roman schools and churches, well, delays can be carried on interminably. Our bureaucrats are experts at that. The constructs? They will send observers, no doubt, but observers can be deceived. The slaves? Those, of course, we must keep, only for a short time, you understand, just until we can find employment for them all as well as for those now free, and can get the economy on a more righteous footing. We can spin out these delays as long as necessary, and then, well, we broke from the Roman hegemony once before, and no doubt we can do so again."

"It sounds too complicated, too tricky."

"My dear warlord, the plan is simplicity itself. It was time to get rid of Ilya anyway, and we must do something about the priest and the princess, so why not simplify by combining these necessities in one operation? Rome is a fact, albeit an inconvenient one, and must be dealt with. Let's not commence hostilities with the Church until we have some idea of its military strength."

The warlord brooded for a few minutes.

"All right, I'll go along with it. What do you want of me?"

"Nothing at all—simply that, when the consul calls for your forces to come to his aid, you do nothing. When I assume the throne, you and your men pledge loyalty to me. Only a formality, of course; we'll sign the contracts later."

"Good enough," said the warlord. "If that's all, I'll be going." Capelli saw him to the door, then returned to his drawing room, where he gazed into the fireplace with a beatific smile.

Jeremiah was sorely troubled. On the one hand, he was enjoying his work among the poor. It was the work he had been educated and trained for. He found it fulfilling and spiritually satisfying. On the other hand, there was the near certainty that he would die within the next few days. Worst of all, he was involved in a conspiracy that went against his deepest instincts. True, the consul was hardly a man whose demise was one to regret, and it would save the lives of untold thousands. Still, he was troubled. He could go to the consul and expose the plan, but that would be the cause of many more deaths. Was his conscience so precious that it was worth the lives of thousands to ease it? Oh, well, he thought, I must sin my own sins and do my own penance and live with my own conscience.

He looked out the rectory window and saw Luigi turn from the sidewalk down the path to the front door. The little gambler was now a regular, and today he was wearing a broad smile, indicating that his luck at the races had been good. The end of the consul's birthday games had signaled the start of the racing season in Charun's year-round gambling calendar.

"How much was it?" asked Jeremiah, opening the door.

"Three hundred in my own bets and another five hundred for tips," said Luigi, chortling. "Brother, I wanted to ask you something. I been reading those books you lent me, and I really don't understand this Trinity business."

"The Holy Trinity is one of the Church's most esoteric beliefs. Theologians have been disputing its significance since the beginning of Christianity. You'd need a better one than I am to explain it to you."

"That's a relief," said Luigi. "I thought maybe it was just me."

"The Muslims call us polytheists because, they claim, we're splitting God up into three separate gods. It's one of the most fundamental differences between us."

"Actually, to tell you the truth, that's kind of how it sounded to me. But if you say he's still one, after being split three ways, I'll take your word for it."

"Blessed are they who do not see, yet believe," said Jeremiah.

"Sure thing," said Luigi, puzzled. "But what did you want to see me about?"

"This may sound odd, but, how does the consul's bodyguard, Hedulio, stand up as a fighter?"

"That's an odd question, all right. Well, Hedulio was probably the greatest fighter ever. He's a heavy-grav man, you know, and that gave him an advantage right off. Plus he's smart, got a lot of savvy. He usually fought as a heavy, but he could handle any weapons, and he was tops in all fields of unarmed combat. There was never anything to touch him. You still see him from time to time. Every once in a while some lord'll come up with a boxer or wrestler he says can beat Hedulio, and they'll fight an exhibition in the stadium. The old consul said Hedulio never had to fight any more when he made him his bodyguard, so Ilya don't never make him fight with weapons. Hedulio don't mind the unarmed fights, just to prove he can win. Now, if you don't mind my inquiring, why do you ask?"

"Luigi, this is in strictest confidence."

"Of course."

"What do you think of Father Miles' chances, fighting Hedulio?"

The little gambler sat in stunned silence for a few seconds.

"Oh, man! Would that be a fight to see! The whole city'd turn out to see a thing like that! It'd be the greatest fight of this generation."

"Yes, but could Father Miles win?"

"Not a chance. But he'd give the old boy the greatest fight he ever had. Man, the betting in the stands would be crazy. Before it was over, half the free population would've pledged themselves to slavers to raise a betting stake."

"That's what I feared," said Jeremiah, depressed. "You mean it's actually going to happen?"

"Almost certainly. It's a mad scheme of Father Miles' to gain popular support through popular hysteria, even if it kills him," said Jeremiah, gloomily.

"Hey, that man sure does things in a big way, don't he?" said Luigi, shaking his head in admiration. "But don't give up. He might make it, after all. I'd say he's got, oh," he did some quick calculations, "about a 3 per cent chance of winning. Even if he's beat, Hedulio may not kill him."

"The consul will order him to kill."

"Well, I've never seen a martyrdom before, but I think I'll skip it, because there's likely to be a riot when he's killed. Father Miles is sort of a hero down here in the lower city, these days. On second thought, maybe I will go. It'd be worth the risk to get a shot at that bastard Ilya."

"Shame on you, Luigi. After all my teaching."

"Oh, sure, but you don't mind a little backsliding now and then, do you?"

"It seems I'll have to get used to it." Jeremiah sighed in resignation. "Luigi, I expect to be arrested soon. You and the others had better keep out of sight."

"Come on, now, Brother, no need for that. We'll hide you. I know the lower city better'n anybody, and I've got lots of friends who owe me favors. We can hide you and Father Miles and Father Stavros so the consul's police would never find you."

"No, it's essential to Father Miles' mad plan that we go too. I've agreed to go along, although I don't know why."

"Yeah, that Father Miles is a man with a real fondness for getting his own way."

"Amen, brother," said Jeremiah.

Ludmilla jumped involuntarily when the discreet knocking came at her door. Heart racing, she went to open it, wondering if it was Ilya's police come for her at last.

"Who is it?"

"Parma, my lady."

She gave a long sigh and opened the door with a smile that was not entirely one of relief.

"I never know what I'm going to find when I open the door these days."

"I'm happy to disappoint you," said Parma. "Father Miles gave me this to give to you." He handed her a small black box, perfectly plain except for a tiny red button in its center. The box was no more than two inches square and half an inch thick.

"Is this the signaling device?" she asked.

"Yes, all you need to do to summon the Church ship is to press the button. Of course, you must not do that until you are officially consul."

"Until Ilya's dead, you mean."

"Exactly."

"Just how did he get this? Surely he couldn't have manufactured this himself?"

"It seems that one of his colleagues from the ship paid him a visit last night, with this and another device."

"Past Ilya's security? Well, I suppose it's child's play to these people. What was the other device?"

"A contrivance for neutralizing a slave's ring. Mine has been neutralized." He grinned with new-found freedom.

"Oh, that's wonderful!" She took his hand impulsively. "Now you're free, even if you have to pretend to be a slave for a while longer. How does it feel?"

"Much the same as always, really. I don't think I ever really acknowledged someone else's ownership of me, just their physical power provided by this ring. I never really *felt* like a slave."

"Let's go out onto my balcony. Ilya has his spies to watch us anyway; we might as well go where the whole court can watch but not hear."

Among the watchers was Father Miles, in his own

balcony above and to one side of the princess's. He smiled as he watched. They were young, too young to let so small a thing as imminent death depress them for long. She was beautiful and lonely; he was handsome and brilliant, whatever his background. They were thrown together in a desperate adventure in which there might literally be no tomorrow. Nature would take its course.

In the palace gymnasium, Parma and Ludmilla were practicing in the Princess's personal training room. Parma was teaching Ludmilla how to avoid the knife. Over and over, he would make a stab or slash, and she would make the appropriate block or avoidance. She marveled at this strange relationship. All her life, she had feared assassination and conspiracy. Now here she was, voluntarily letting this man come within fractions of an inch of her body with a knife, and she felt no fear at all.

Suddenly, the door burst open and a number of armed men entered, their weapons trained on the pair. Then the consul entered. Ludmilla looked at Parma, her face drained and white. Parma glared at the consul, his fingers constantly flexing and unflexing on the handle of his knife.

"Don't try it, traitor," said the consul. "Disarm him." One of the guards went to Parma and gingerly took his knife.

"What is the meaning of this, brother?" demanded Ludmilla, knowing the meaning full well.

"Come now, sister," said Ilya, "no foolish banter between us. You know your treason. You shall suffer for it, as shall this slave." He gestured to his guards. "Take them to the princess's suite and place them under close guard."

They said nothing as they were led away. Parma was not particularly alarmed, just ready to do what he could whenever Father Miles gave the word. He looked at Ludmilla and was shocked at the haggardness and pallor of her face. She had lived with this fear all her life, and now that the moment had finally come, she just couldn't believe that she would survive it.

Summoned from his quarters by armed palace guards, Miles was escorted to the great throne room. There he found Ilya, flanked by his bodyguards and the heads of the great families. Before the throne stood Parma and Ludmilla, with Brother Jeremiah and Father Stavros. Miles took his place with his friends.

"Explain yourself, Consul." Miles' voice was cold and contemptuous.

"I am consul!" shouted Ilya. "I do not have to explain myself to anybody!" He was indignant, but his need to gloat soon asserted itself. "You have all been involved in a conspiracy to overthrow my government. I have copies of every speech you've made, priest. Did you think you could keep my spies out of your meetings?"

"There was never any attempt to keep anybody out, Consul. They were public meetings, publicly announced. You could have attended yourself if you had cared to." There was no cringe or conciliation in the Jesuit's voice.

"And you dare to speak treason and foment rebellion among my people?"

"No treason was spoken. No word was ever said against you or your government."

"And yet you came here representing a foreign power! You came as an agent of Rome, of the power whose yoke we discarded centuries ago." The consul was becoming agitated, his grotesque paranoia closing in on him.

"I made no secret of where I came from. I gladly told anyone who cared to ask. It was your own fear and twisted reasoning that prevented you from simply summoning me and asking a few questions. You fear everyone and everything, and so full of deceit are you that you could not conceive that anyone would tell you the truth." Miles' voice stayed cold, and Ludmilla stared at him with horror, Jeremiah with resignation.

"And why did you not come to me?" The consul was almost frothing.

"To what purpose? You are not the government, you degenerate moron! You are a puppet controlled by your ministers, whom you know to be plotting against you. You are a silly, foul, depraved, sadistic, contemptible wretch not fit to clean the streets, much less control a star system." Miles had studied every recording he could find of the voice of Ilya's father, and he was using it now. The words sank into the consul's psyche like so many daggers into his body.

"Kill him!" he shrieked hysterically. "A million dinars to the man who gives me his head!"

The hulking bodyguards stepped forward, grinning. There was much flexing of muscles, spitting on knuckles, and rolling up of sleeves. Only Hedulio remained standing at his consul's side. He had no interest in bounties.

In an instant, Miles was among the guards, giving them no opportunity to devise a concerted attack. The staff cracked into jaws and knees, lanced into larynxes and pits of stomachs, broke noses and cracked pates with rare abandon. Massive forms seemed literally to fly about the throne room, and within a few moments Miles stood alone before the steps, not even breathing hard. The consul stared and cowered in a paralysis of terror.

"Shoot him!" commanded the Lord Broz, a hawk-faced man in his fifties. Miles held his staff aloft. The palace guards already had their guns out, but none had fired yet. There had been no order and, besides, they had enjoyed the humiliation of the despised, arrogant bodyguards. Now pale blue, green, and red beams lanced out, to bend oddly and be drawn to the high-held staff. From the ends of the staff emerged brilliant blue flashes. Standing thus, Miles resembled some ancient lightning-deity.

"'Ye shall be slain, all the sort of ye; yea, as a tottering wall shall ye be, and like a broken hedge!'"

Ilya was too terrified to speak, but the Lord Capelli said calmly: "You don't have quite the upper hand, priest: Look about you." Miles did so, and saw that Ludmilla, Parma, Jeremiah, and Stavros had been hustled away in the confusion. Well, triumph in this room had never been his plan, anyway.

"Your Grace," continued the old courtier, "this man must be destroyed, and publicly, before he becomes a hero to the people. Since we hold his fellow conspirators hostage, he will agree to fight your man Hedulio in the amphitheater, without that stick. If not," he smiled gently and sadly at Miles, "they shall suffer."

"That's it!" said Ilya, his trembling calming and his composure returning. "If you don't agree, priest, your friends, including my sister, will receive such torture as only my tormentors know how to inflict." Miles saw that the consul believed him to have been his sister's lover and was insanely jealous. But then, Ilya would never experience anything sanely.

"'Why boasteth thou, thyself, thou tyrant, that thou canst do mischief?' Weakling! I will meet your mighty man of valor, and tomorrow you and all your people will see that the Living God will deliver him into my hand." He spun on his heel and stalked from the throne room.

Back in his room, Miles began to prepare himself,

mentally and spiritually, for the coming day. He knew that his friends were safe enough, for the time being, and that he had laid perfect groundwork for the contest. There was only one severe variable left, and that was the defeat in hand-to-hand combat of the redoubtable Hedulio. Miles was not sure that he could do it, in spite of his ritualistic speech. His faith was great, but he knew that a man of God could be overcome as handily as any other by superior strength, skill, or treachery.

Miles set his staff to warn him of any approach and lay back on his hard bed. Meditating on the spiritual exercises of St. Ignatius Loyola, he fell into a deep and strengthening sleep.

XIII

The sun was high and bright over the arena of Augusta. The stands were jammed with people, strangely silent. Word had spread about the incredible fight in the palace throne room, transmitted by the consul's heralds as well as by word of mouth. There was no holiday air here, no bloodthirstiness or betting. In other parts of the system, bookmakers were quoting their odds, and people mobbed the holograph pits to watch the unprecedented fight, but most people here had come to see a test, not a show. Those with long-range glasses saw that the princess, in her seat next to the consul, was unnaturally pale, and that she nervously fingered a small, square amulet that hung from a chain around her neck.

In the center of the arena stood Hedulio, looking like some natural feature of rock that the building had been constructed around. Before the dais stood Parma, Jeremiah, and Stavros. Though no official announcement had been made, everyone knew why the priests were there. So far, none knew that the princess was involved.

Parma looked up at the dais. He saw Vic standing there. For once, the netman's face was troubled, and he wouldn't meet Parma's eyes. Parma hoped that he wouldn't have to fight his friend today.

Father Miles emerged from the gate opposite the dais, striding along with his staff like some ancient patriarch toward the little group below the royal seat. When he reached them, he drew off his black robe, which he folded and gave to Stavros. He handed his staff to Parma. Last of all, he handed another little black box with a red button to Jeremiah. It was identical to the one he had given Ludmilla.

"Jeremiah, when the fight is over, push that button. The instrument is set on maximum strength. It will neutralize every slave ring for a radius of two miles. That should prove an agreeable task for you." Jeremiah nodded without speaking, overcome with fear for his friend. Not looking at the consul or the assembled nobles, Miles smiled at his friends and said: "Have no fear, God is my strength." He turned and walked toward Hedulio.

God was not his only strength; he wore the one-piece singlet, midnight black, which was a part of the uniform of the Brotherhood Cestus Dei. Skin-tight, it was of featherweight armor fabric, impenetrable to pointed or edged weapons, more supple than the finest silk. It had rigid plates to protect the groin and the kidneys, and integral gloves and hood. These were usually tucked into the sleeves and cowl of his habit, but Miles had now drawn them over his hands and head. Being supple except for the three plates, the wearer was still vulnerable to clubbing blows of fist or foot, but Miles was mainly concerned with treachery. He had set his staff to absorb any light-beam weapons fired from the stands, but there was still the chance of a bullet. The armor cloth would keep a bullet from penetrating, and spread its force somewhat, but he would risk severe internal injury. Still, it was the best he could do.

He studied his opponent as he neared the center of the arena, and he had never seen a more daunting sight. Hedulio had easily twice his weight, and probably something close to his speed. What Hedulio did not have was the kind of psychological training that Miles had, and the years of practice at the hands of men who were infinitely his betters. It would be a close fight.

There was no announcement and no starting gong. The two men stood at their guard for the fight of nerves, standing statue-still for several minutes. Suddenly there was a flurry of fists and feet, and they sprang apart. There was a red spot over Miles' right eye that would quickly become a swelling. Hedulio was bleeding from one ear. The minor preliminary bout had contained at least a dozen near-fatal blows, but most of the spectators had seen nothing more than that the two men had sprung at each other and then sprung apart. There was another pause of a minute or so, then Hedulio made a seemingly impossible leap and kick to Miles' head, which the priest ducked, rolling on the sand and springing to his feet, rushing in to throw a spinning kick at Hedulio before the big man regained his balance. It was futile: Hedulio had landed with both feet planted as if they grew from roots deep in the bedrock beneath the arena.

For fifteen minutes they sparred in this manner, leaping and spinning, incredibly graceful, striking almost exclusively with their feet, their combat making the fights of the swordsmen look gross and clumsy by comparison. Abruptly, they ceased the dancelike maneuvering. They had each other's measure now, and knew that they were both too swift to be taken in by moves that required so much time to complete. Now they began to fight at close range, with fists, feet, knees, and elbows.

Their styles were different, and they fought for different advantages: Hedulio tried to avoid injury until he could grapple, knowing now that he had little chance of landing a crippling blow on the priest. Hedulio needed the advantage of his greater strength and weight. Miles knew that all men, no matter how strong, possess certain points that are as vulnerable as any other man's: the eyes, the groin, the larynx. Other spots were almost as weak: the kidneys, the nerve ganglia at the corner of jaw and armpit, the ears. These were the spots Miles aimed at, but he had to spend most of his time avoiding the inhumanly powerful and dizzyingly swift blows of the huge, knotted fists. His kidney plates would not be proof against them, and he was wary of getting too close, for he knew that a blow of the man's knee would simply drive his protective groin cup through his pubic bone. Most of all, he had to avoid the grip of the machinelike hands. Once they took hold of him, he would be pulled apart like a roast fowl.

The bouts of close infighting became more savage, more blows beginning to take effect as both men began to tire, each fractionally losing his fine timing. Soon Hedulio began to limp slightly as a result of a side kick to the knee, although Miles was sure that it had hurt his foot more. Miles was nearing the end of his endurance. He knew that this iron man could outlast him, and Hedulio's defense was too tight for him ever to get in a telling blow. The only thing left was a sacrifice play. This meant risking a double kill, but there was no other way. In a few minutes, Hedulio would batter his way past Miles' slowing defense and kill him.

Miles set up his move as carefully as possible: it had to look real, or Hedulio wouldn't fall for it. Above all, the huge man must not try an unexpected attack of his own, destroying Miles' timing. When Hedulio seemed to lose his wariness for a fraction of a second, Miles moved. He slid in for a desperate punch to the midsection, but his foot twisted slightly, and as he fell sideways he threw his arms up to keep his balance. Quick as thought, Hedulio darted in to exploit the opening. As his treetrunk arms closed around Miles' waist for the wrench that would snap the priest's spine, Miles' hands, cupped, slammed down simultaneously on Hedulio's ears. The huge guard dropped instantly to his knees with shock, and Miles' hands, ax-stiff now, chopped the sides of his neck. The great arms loosened and Hedulio went down on all fours, bleeding now from both ears, nose, and mouth, but still miraculously conscious. Miles brought his foot back for a minutely measured kick to the man's jaw that would knock him out without further damage.

The silence in the amphitheater remained unbroken. Throughout the fight no one had shouted or even spoken. Before he could complete the kick, there was a sharp crack, and Miles spun and fell. He began to rise, and another shot sent him sprawling. There was yet another crack, but this shot missed. Through a haze, Miles could see a mob of spectators beating a man at the edge of the arena wall who held something long and thin in his hands. An angry growl spread through the stands, and the crowd began a surge toward the dais where the consul and his nobles sat. Miles felt himself being lifted, saw Parma and Stavros, saw Jeremiah standing calmly in the center of the arena as he pressed the button on the little black box.

With a barely audible *ping*, the neck rings of all the slaves in the amphitheater snapped open and dropped to their former prisoners' feet.

"Kill them!" shouted the consul. "Send in the constructs." To an aide, he ordered: "Call the warlord Bandinegri at his camp outside the city. Tell him to bring his forces to the amphitheater at once."

The gate below the dais opened, and dozens of constructs advanced into the arena. Parma, bracing for the fatal confrontation, glanced back at the dais.

He saw Vic reach into his tunic and draw something out. His arm went forward, and an object arched through the air to land near Parma's feet. It was his Thrax knife in its sheepox-hide sheath. He smiled as he picked it up and felt the familiar bone haft in his palm. Now he had a fighting chance.

Father Miles struggled to his feet and took his staff.

"Are you up to it, Father?" asked Stavros.

"No permanent damage, I daresay. I'm weak, but my staff can compensate." He made adjustments. Here and there, men were vaulting down the arena walls. Many of them were armed. They went to join the group in the center. One of them was Luigi, who carried a short dirk.

"It seems we are not alone, after all," said Miles.

"I guess I owe you one," said Luigi. "I just made a fortune in bets on that fight."

But now there was no more time for talk. The constructs were upon them. A green-scaled gorilla reached them first, but a man behind Parma dropped it with a heavy slug pistol, putting a bullet between its eyes.

Parma stooped and scooped up a handful of sand with his left hand, threw it into the eyes of a catlike creature with striped fur and metal-shod hooves, then disemboweled it with a sweep of his knife. Another construct climbed over its body, a scaly horror with a short sword, its body covered with armor plates and hornlike excrescences. Parma stepped within the sweep of the sword to grapple, struck automatically at the thing's midsection, but his blade skittered over horny plate. A spiked knee slammed into his groin, but his armored codpiece held the pain within bearable limits. Parma wrapped both legs around the creature's waist and bore it to the ground, seeking a vulnerable joint in its home-grown armor. With a surge of animal strength, the construct heaved itself off the ground, getting its sword arm free. Wrenching its other arm loose, it pinned Parma to the ground and raised the sword to nail Parma to the arena floor. Behind the thing's shoulder, Parma saw Miles appear. He merely touched the thing's neck with the tip of his staff. It gave a convulsive jerk and rolled from Parma, unconscious or dead.

All over the arena now, men were fighting the constructs. Only Jeremiah and Stavros did not join in the battle. They were tending the wounded, of which there was no shortage. Jeremiah saw Father Miles, moving a little stiffly now, as he blocked and thrust with his staff. He was absorbing some terrible blows, but he seemed not to notice, fighting on in a kind of ecstasy, a positively beatific smile on his face. Jeremiah realized now what a state of grace was for a Cestus Dei initiate.

Obviously, the men who had joined them were veterans, ex-gladiators or experienced street fighters. They fought with skill and economy, five or six mobbing each construct, dragging it to the ground and finishing it with a stab to a vulnerable spot. Jeremiah went to Hedulio. The man was shaking his head, pushing himself to his feet. Jeremiah mopped blood from his face.

"Hedulio, you had better go protect the princess." That seemed to bring the man out of it. Incredibly, he broke into a run toward the royal dais, seemingly shaking off the effects of the battering he had taken. Two constructs rose up before him. He grabbed their

necks, gave the merest flex of his hands, and they
dropped with broken necks. He paused for a moment
to take a large rectangular shield from one, which he
slung across his back, then picked up a fallen mace,
hanging it from his belt. He took a short run and
leaped at the dais. His fingertips just reached the
edge, and he pulled himself over with a tigerish surge.
He quickly stepped to the princess's side, unslung the
shield, and held it before her, the mace swinging
easily in his right hand.

The consul was turning an apoplectic puce. He
turned to his bodyguards.

"Go in there and kill those traitors for me!" The
bodyguards looked down at the neck rings lying at
their feet, looked at the consul, grinned, and made
various obscene gestures at him, then strolled over to
nearby benches to sit and watch the fun.

"Where is Bandinegri?" screamed Ilya. "I'll have
everyone here killed! All of you! Traitors!" Calmly,
Lord Capelli stepped up behind the consul, took a
small beam pistol from his sleeve, and shot Ilya in the
back of his head. Nobody noticed except Ludmilla.
She closed her eyes, shuddered, and pressed the
button. She was now consul.

In the arena, the battle had turned to utter chaos.
The constructs were being routed. Through a side
gate, the gladiators who had been kept in the cells
within the building for the next games were pouring
in, free of their neck rings and mad with new liberty.
They didn't know whom they should fight, so they just
battled their way toward the exits. Parma caught
sight of Hippolyta, Medea, and the rest of the Pontine
women from Ludus. "Now's your chance, Hippolyta!"
he shouted. "Go find yourself a ship!" She grinned
and waved, then Parma was too busy with another
construct to notice whether the women got out or not.

Suddenly, the crowd stilled. All movement ceased.

A darkness had come over the stadium and the city. Miles and his companions, the crowd, the nobles, the new consul, all looked up in awe. Overhead was a great oval shape, hovering between the city and the sun, crowned with spires and domes, seemingly miles in diameter. It was the Church Militant warship *Gladius Dei*.

Cardinal Mslopogaas Van Horn sat in his command chair aboard *Gladius Dei*, flagship of the Church Militant fleet, XV Sector. Cardinal Van Horn, sector *gonfaloniere*, supreme commander of all Church Militant forces in this sector, was not pleased. He was an incredibly tiny and shriveled man, rumored to be well over three hundred years old. His monster ship contained enough armament to fight an intersystem war, three corps of ground forces, a wing of space-atmosphere craft, ambassadorial facilities, an enclosed park and xenozoological garden, a seminary, a university, an abbey, six parish churches, a full-sized cathedral, and a seventy-five piece orchestra.

Composing himself to hide his displeasure, the cardinal instructed his secretary to admit the two men who waited outside his massive, ironbound oaken doors. When they entered, the cardinal studied them closely. One, walking with some difficulty, wore the black robe of the Jesuit order, clutching in one hand the gadget-loaded staff of a member of the Brotherhood Cestus Dei. The other, half supporting him, wore the white-cowled blue robe of a probationary acolyte. The acolyte had very long, light-brown hair, worn in a barbaric topknot. Somehow, the broad, curved knife didn't look out of place against his ecclesiastical garment. Well, thought Van Horn, it takes all kinds to make a Church.

The cardinal gestured to a chair, and the Jesuit sank into it with a grateful sigh. The acolyte remained standing. Van Horn allowed a moment's pause, then spoke in a voice surprisingly strong for one so ancient.

"Well, Miles, you've done it again."

"I trust, Your Eminence, that God will accept my poor work with favor."

"If so, then his tolerance is even greater than is commonly believed. But pardon my discourtesy; I hope your wounds are not too severe?" The cardinal sounded as if he hoped for a multiple spinal fracture, at least.

"A few broken ribs, Your Eminence, from the projectile weapon, plus numerous hematomas, contusions, and abrasions from the battle."

"You Jesuit fraud," snorted the cardinal. "You dare to walk in here leaning on a stick and an acolyte, with injuries like that? On Spica II you held your command post for six hours with two broken legs and a bullet through your jaw. Don't play on my sympathies, Miles. You've landed me in a fine diplomatic mess, and if Her Holiness sends for your head I'll give it to her on my best platter."

"You wrong me, sir," protested Miles. "All I did was within the law and quite proper."

"Within the law, maybe, just barely. But proper? Never! You took incredible risks, behaved with mad irresponsibility, provoked a serious riot, and had us called in by a ruler whose tenure in office could be measured in seconds. At the behest of this unripe monarch, I'm drawn with a whole sector's forces into what is bound to be a hotly contested system."

"There can be no contest. The legal government of the Flavian system, one Ludmilla I, has opted for Rome. There can be no argument on that score."

"The circumstances of her succession will seem peculiar to all right-thinking clergy, and certainly to our esteemed colleagues in the UF."

"If the current consul replaced one who died by

violence, well, she'd be unique if that hadn't been the case. As for the Caliphate and the Temple, they'll never contest the principle of autocratic rule. A great many of the worlds and systems under their sway are so constituted."

"Oh, enough of this. Now we have the task of rebuilding this system. I have enough Dominican administration specialists to start training a proper bureaucracy here. Just as well; it'll give them something to do, at last. But we'll have to send to Big-Abbey-in-the-Sky for enough Benedictines to get the universities open again."

"Wouldn't Jesuit educators do as well?"

"Never!" said the cardinal. "Half the Church Militant's Jesuit already. Your field work is fine, there's no denying that Jesuits make good soldiers and missionaries, but administration and education are the proper concern of the other orders. Let's see, now. I have a gaggle of Cluniacs left over from the Five Systems campaign. Maybe they could start a fine-arts college. I don't have a wall left for them to fresco or a spare floor to mosaic. Do they make decent wine here?"

"Superb."

"Too bad. I probably won't be able to get rid of my Cistercians, then. Plenty of wasted farmland, though. Maybe the Trappists can put it to use. Can't stand to have them around, anyway. Too quiet. Well, all this can wait. You go get some rest and get patched up. There's still the problem of the warlord. He got away with most of his constructs when we put in our dramatic appearance. And there's the Pirate Brotherhood to be taken care of."

Miles stood and bowed, painfully, and Parma helped him walk from the room.

"Jesuit fraud!" snorted the cardinal.

The council of war was held in a large circular room, with those attending seated around a large, circular table. They were being addressed by a large, circular man, a Benedictine friar from Intelligence.

"The planet of Cadmus, where the Soulless constructs are produced, is a type E planet, orbiting a type G sun, with three satellites, one type Q and two type M." His voice was a mellifluous drone, soothing and easy to listen to. Transmission of information with minimum incomprehension was his specialty. "There are two major continents in each hemisphere, one northern and one southern, plus a number of major islands. The construct-production goes on in the southern continent of the eastern hemisphere.

"The planet is ruled by a warlord-condotierre-capitalist called Bandinegri. He produces and trains his creatures and hires them out to the warring families of some half-dozen planets for their limited wars and raids. For the larger contracts he leads them himself. On occasion, when contracts are few, he conducts raids on his own, taking slaves and loot to sell on the pirate clearing-house world of Melos. His space force is negligible, consisting mainly of transports. He does have a rather strong force of fighting atmosphere-craft, these piloted by humans, drawn from his own planet of Cadmus or hired from other planets or from among the pirates.

"His main strength, though, is in his land force of constructs. These are of a mentally deficient, debased type, grotesque and skilled only in fighting. We will not have to deal with any of the Mastermind class that we faced in the Crusade against the Soulless. His officer corps and much of the NCO class are made up of hired humans. That is as far as our information takes us."

The fat man bowed and sat. Cardinal Van Horn looked around the table. There was a preponderance of black-robed Jesuits wearing the white Crusader's cross on the breast of their habits. Most of the rest were Dominicans in white, with the red cross. The remainder were a sprinkling of other Orders, mostly noncombatant Benedictines and Franciscans.

"Suggestions?" queried the cardinal.

"Frontal attack, Your Eminence," said a white-haired Dominican. "Knock out his atmosphere craft on the ground, drop encircling forces around the camps where he keeps his Soulless abominations and gobble them up piecemeal."

"Thank you, Father Nicholas," sighed the cardinal, "your advice is, as always, directly to the point and simple to follow. Unfortunately, we don't know that the atmosphere craft are kept above ground, and as for his land forces, he seems to have dispersed them when our presence in the system became known. Whatever else has fallen into decay here, the art of camouflage has been preserved on Cadmus. We've circled the place with recon satellites, and all we can see is farmland and meadows. You could mistake it for something out of a pastoral poem. Even the construct labs must be underground."

"If I may make a suggestion?" It was Miles' voice, from the far side of the table.

"I felt sure you would have something to say, Father Miles. Speak on."

"I thank Your Eminence. You have seen my acolyte, Parma Sicarius of Thrax?"

"Yes, what of him?"

"Before he came to Charun, he was kept in a school for fighting-slaves on Ludus. The lanista — or owner — of this school, one Marius, took an interest in Parma, and talked a good deal with him. Parma was able to find out something about him, and I believe he may be of use to us. He is rather a sinister gentleman."

"That's a compliment coming from you, Miles.

You're rather a sinister gentleman yourself. In what manner do you think this fellow may be of use?"

"According to information Parma was able to gather, this Marius was a street gangster on Charun, who escaped into the military to avoid death at the hands of rivals. In the military he gained experience in handling constructs. Later, he seems to have been a pirate, and it is almost certain that he was on Cadmus for two years or so as one of the hired officers. With the abolition of the games, he'll be at loose ends and probably ready to cooperate."

"Cooperate!" spat the cardinal. "A man like that should be hanged, not offered a chance to cooperate. He's a gangster, pirate, mercenary and slaver. Oh, the degrading compromises we're forced to in God's service. Very well, send for him."

"I've already taken that liberty, Your Eminence. I can have him here after morning Mass."

"Never a wasted minute when you're around, Father Miles. Very well, we will now adjourn for Mass, and will reconvene here immediately afterward, to confer with this unsavory character." He rose, and the whole assembly filed from the room in strict order of precedence.

Marius eyed the circle of clergymen warily. He wasn't quite sure just what they were, but he knew that some of the ones with red or white crosses on their robes were among the hardest-looking men he had ever seen, and he had tangled with the roughest men in this system. The loss of his training school had ruined him, and he had been on the point of rejoining his old colleagues among the pirates when Ludmilla's police had showed up on Ludus and hustled him to a ship which had taken him to Augusta. There were two faces here that he recognized; Parma, who had been his property, and the black-robed man who had fought the astonishing battle in the amphitheater of Augusta just before the monster ship had showed up.

"You are one Marius. Any other names?" The speaker was a tiny, raisin-like man in a red gown, white coif and wide red hat.

"It's the only name I have. It must suffice." His voice was defiant but wary. He could see that false humility would cut no ice with these men.

"Do not be too spirited, young man. Your life dangles by a thread. An evil life, it is, and a thin thread. Now, we have been informed that you have contacts among the pirate fleets, and that you have experience of the planet of Cadmus. Is this so?"

"I was once a pirate, and I was an officer of constructs on Cadmus." It was obvious that there would be falsehood-detecting devices trained on him, so he didn't bother trying to lie.

"Truly, you have led a most deplorable life. However, we are here to eliminate the evil you represent, not to punish its practitioners. So, as long as you refrain from these reprehensible practices, you will be safe enough."

"If that's the case, why should I aid you?" His tone was not defiant, merely reasoning.

"Safety from us is not necessarily safety from everyone. If you refuse to cooperate with us, we shall do nothing to you, simply let you go. At the spaceport of Augusta, to be precise. A most unsavory district, that. Controlled, I believe, by one Giulio, a former colleague of yours. Without the protection of your erstwhile wealth, how do you think you would fare?"

"And if I cooperate?"

"Then you will have the protection of the Church, which is not inconsiderable. You will have a chance to restore your fortunes, *legally*," the voice snapped out the word, "which a man with your energy and abilities should be able to do easily. Personally, of course, I am but a man with a man's frailties, and would prefer to see one such as you roasting over a slow fire. But, since that is probably to be your fate eventually, I am too old not to have learned patience."

"What do you want to know?"

"You will betray your former friends?"

"A man like me has no friends," snorted Marius.

"The logic of that does not escape me. First, the dispositions of the defenses on Cadmus, approximate numbers of constructs and human troops, locations of aircraft wells, anti-air-and-spacecraft artillery and troop concentrations."

Marius took a deep breath and began to recite. He asked for a holo of the planet of Cadmus, and with a pointer gave detailed information, dating back to the time, several years before, that he had left the planet. There was no reason to believe that any significant changes had been made. It quickly became apparent that Marius must have held a position of some importance to have so detailed a knowledge of the planet's defenses. Also, he had a marvelously retentive memory and a true, if untrained, talent for transmitting information.

When Marius had finished, Cardinal Van Horn appointed a team of tacticians to work out the details of the attack. He then appointed a commando team to attempt a capture of the warlord himself.

"Once he is in our hands," said the cardinal, "all effective resistance will cease. Thus, we may accomplish our holy work and avoid needless bloodshed. You will be well enough to lead this force, Father Miles?"

"Your Eminence honors me with his confidence. Yes, I am almost mended." There was no irony in the Jesuit's tone now. This was the kind of work he found most spiritually fulfilling.

"Well, then, you may have Commander Father

Lame Deer and his team. Will that be satisfactory?"

"Absolutely."

"You may also have such other men as you choose, Father Miles."

"Thank you, Your Eminence. I'll take Parma ..."

"Do you think that wise?" He paused. "Well, you know best, and I suppose it's just as well that the young get used to doing the Lord's work early. Still, he's hardly trained ..."

"And I'll take Marius."

"What!" The cardinal was stunned. "Whatever for? You can't possibly trust him! Besides, we may need him for the campaign against the pirates. Got to have the spacelanes safe for commerce or we'll never get this system pacified."

"Naturally, Your Eminence, I don't trust him, but, if you follow me, I think I know to what extent I dare not trust him. The interior of the warlord's palace is a maze, and Marius is familiar with it. Besides, he seems a very competent man, and I think he would be handy in the mixup."

"I'll grant you his competence, but how do you know he won't betray you?"

"To whom will he betray us? There's only the warlord himself, and he's already betrayed that gentleman to us."

"This Marius strikes me as a man quite capable of carrying out just such a complicated treachery, and successfully too. Oh, well, whatever you like, but only you would do such a thing," the Cardinal concluded, shaking his head.

All parties were then dismissed to ready themselves for the coming fight.

The warlord Bandinegri of Cadmus sat in his palace, contemplating his maps of his planet. Around his small conference table sat his most trusted officers.

He had called them here to discuss the greatest crisis that had arisen since he had inherited the mercenary-estate from his father. Word had come from the Church Militant of Rome, transmitted by the legal government of the Flavian System.

The message had been simple. Surrender all military forces under his command. Dismantle all laboratories for the production of constructs. Remove the neckrings from all slaves within his dominions. Cease all contact with pirates or raiders. Accomplish all these demands, and no action would be taken against him; he would go as free as any other man, and no crime he had committed in his past life would be held against him. If he did not comply within two days' time, he would be attacked by the forces of the Church Militant.

The warlord was a tall, thin man, who habitually wore a dress cuirass and plumed helmet, both chased, jeweled, and of immense value. The pistol he wore was not ornamental.

"Have all the constructs been withdrawn from Domitian?" The warlord's voice was clipped, military.

"The last have returned from all foreign contracts, Marshal," replied one of the officers. He was a moderately young man, like most of them. "The moneys for broken contracts have been refunded, and there is no cause for complaint. There is, naturally, some displeasure. We are, after all, taking away the wherewithal to fight some long-cherished feuds." There was mild laughter around the table.

"And the raiding teams?"

"All in," said another officer. "The force has already returned from the raid on the newly-discovered Aurelian world, and the expedition to Sempronius was cancelled."

An older man in scarred harness spoke up. "Our forces are at maximum strength, Lord. We're faced with a pack of chanting priests. There is nothing to fear, this'll be good practice for the new constructs just out of the tank."

"Oh, think you so?" said the warlord, thoughtfully. "Did you see the broadcast from Charun, how that priest beat Hedulio?"

"Mere chance, my Lord. The combat could have gone either way," spluttered the old soldier.

"The point is that there was any contest at all. Hedulio should have been able to defeat any living being with ease, and that priest beat him. Not with brute strength, nor merely cunning, but with both, plus the ability to risk all on a do-or-die gamble. It is such men that we must fight. But we shall win, simply because we have no choice." The meeting broke up and the officers returned to their posts.

The warlord himself walked restlessly through his palace. Every room was decorated with the loot of hundreds of campaigns fought by the warlords of Cadmus in centuries past, when there had been thousands of worlds to plunder. In those days, Cadmus had possessed construct labs that could turn out pilots capable of planning and fighting space battles, strategists that could plan campaigns spanning systems of stars and scores of years. Now, he was left with his few divisions of defective constructs who were scarcely better than animals, his remaining atmosphere craft, and his hired human troops, whom he knew would probably desert or surrender at the first hint of superior force. They were used to small campaigns in limited feud-wars, and raids on helpless victims. What was coming was all-out war on a planetary scale, something that had not been seen in this system in three centuries. The constructs would fight until all were dead, but they would not be effective without firm leadership. Once their officers were gone, they were likely to start killing one another.

Bandinegri entered his drawing room, where he kept his finest treasures. Here were paintings, sculpture, jewels, weapons, and furnishings. He gazed at his face, slightly distorted, in the silver shield once carried by an emperor. From a cut-emerald decanter he poured ancient wine into a diamond goblet, taking it to his favorite couch, a genuine Louis XIV from Earth, looted from the palace of some long-forgotten potentate. He regarded the painting on the wall opposite the couch. It had been commissioned in the days before all art had become stagnant, and it represented Bandinegri's remote ancestor, Baglioni Bandinegri, surrounded by his officers and construct guards. The scene was the end of the campaign that had won the planet of Cadmus and founded the fortune of the Bandinegri. The warlord mused; those were the great days, the glory days. If it was all to end now, well, it was better this way, and it had certainly been worth it. He raised his glass to Baglioni and drained it.

XIV

Parma had been assigned to a barracks-room among other enlisted service monks of the acolyte class. He found the austerity of life irksome at first; he had been living in relative luxury since leaving Thrax. The simple habits of the nomad quickly reasserted themselves, however, and Parma soon began to enjoy the clean simplicity of this rigorous life.

Less easy to adjust to was the discipline and regimentation of military life. All personnel of the enlisted ranks were lay brothers and sisters, acolytes, novices, and monks or friars of less than five years' service. The non-commissioned ranks were made up of senior monks, friars, nuns, and deacons. Officers were ordained priests, male and female. Being a new man, Parma was assigned a senior monk to instruct him in military-religious customs and usages.

Hand-to-hand combat came easy to Parma, but projectile and light-beam weapons were more difficult.

His experience with missile weapons was limited to javelins. On Thrax, his tribe had not even had bows. It was most difficult to adjust to the difference between the trajectory of a solid-missile weapon and the line-of-sight aiming of a light-beam gun.

Each morning the men were awakened by the bell for morning Mass, after which they ate a frugal breakfast in the refectory. The morning was spent in drill and combat training. After the midday meal, there were lectures on military theory and the history of the religious campaigns, followed by hand-to-hand training and weapon maintenance. Then came the evening meal, which consisted of concentrate-enriched bread and unenriched water, followed by theological lectures and debates. After evening Mass, they were permitted to retire to their wooden-slat bunks for five hours' sleep. Exhaustion made the beds seem comfortable. The men did all their own cooking and cleaning, taking turns in the kitchen and laundry. Very little was mechanized. The company commander conducted Mass and acted as confessor to his men.

For weeks, they were given special training in fighting constructs, for most of these men were far too young to have fought in any of the campaigns against the soulless. Some of the classes were conducted in gigantic auditoriums or holographic theaters, with Marius himself lecturing. Parma found it decidedly odd to see his old master suddenly on the side of the angels.

There was to be a preliminary wave-attack by skirmishers, to test the strength of the defenses, in which Parma was to take part. If resistance did not immediately crumble, the attack was to be withdrawn, with a show of being beaten off, and Parma would then be detached from his company to join in the planned commando raid on the warlord's palace. The deadline for surrender had been extended repeatedly, but the warlord had taken this as a sign of weakness and used the time to further consolidate his defenses. The order for attack came.

There was much orderly bustle as the troops assembled after communion and confession, and filed by companies onto the vast boarding deck where they would be assigned their landing craft. It was almost like a training exercise but for one small but ominous note: a small black box strapped to the back of the commander's orderly. It contained the CO's extreme unction kit, which some of them would almost certainly need before the end of the day.

There was a lengthy wait before Parma's company boarded, and he was surprised to see Father Miles walking down his rank.

"There you are, Parma! I just came to wish you good luck in your first battle for the Lord." The Jesuit's eyes glowed with enthusiasm.

"You aren't coming, sir?" asked Parma.

"No, more's the pity. I'm not commissioned in the conventional forces and they won't let an ordained priest serve in the enlisted ranks. Try to preserve yourself unhurt and we'll have a crack at the warlord himself later. That mission comes under Unconventional Warfare, so anybody can take part." He was almost boyish in his eagerness.

"There's the bell for my company. Goodbye, Father Miles."

"God bless and keep you, son, and all your companions." He made a cross over Parma's forehead, then the troops were filing into their craft, almost indistinguishable in their blue, hooded coveralls with the white cross on the breast. Soon Miles stood alone on the echoing, plainlike deck.

The landing craft had dropped in a great circle

around the enemy's largest camp, near the capitol city. Their missiles had been ineffective against the shielding of the craft, and the landing was accomplished without casualty. Singing the ancient battle hymns, the troops disembarked onto the grassy meadows of Cadmus, taking up their prearranged positions. There was high-trajectory shelling, which began to inflict damage. When all were in place, the armored support vehicles rolled down the ramps and into their allotted places among the ranks. A screaming flight of atmosphere craft, flying low, began to spray rockets and deadly beams among the Church soldiery. The heavy-duty masks absorbed most of the beam weapons, and the rockets caused relatively few casualties among the men, who wore armor cloth coveralls. A wave of space-atmosphere craft from the ship drove into the enemy formation and the combat in the air broke up into individual dogfights. Then the order to advance came.

Parma, as a new man, was in the rear ranks of his company's advance, holding a solid-projectile rifle, with a beam-pistol and his knife at his side. He wore a close-fitting bubble-helmet which protected against projectiles and poisonous vapor, gas and spray. He had a beam-absorber in his belt, but it could overload if struck by a heavy-duty projector. Parma hadn't been so frightened since the mass battle of the birthday games.

For the first few minutes of the advance, the men met little direct fire. But as they moved in closer to the trench and bunker line surrounding the camp, nightmarish balls of multicolored lightning came bouncing along the ground. The Cadmians were using a fireball generator, a weapon long obsolete in the rediscovered galaxy, but still lethal. The balls had to be ducked or dodged until they had discharged their power, and the consequence of failure to judge rate and direction of bounce was incineration.

When they were within six hundred meters of the trenches, small-arms fire became intense. Bullets and shell fragments whined through the air, while light-beams in rainbow hues crisscrossed and occasionally touched a piece of unprotected equipment, which would disappear in a spray of white-hot molten droplets. Here and there, as they crawled closer, a number of beams would lock onto a single soldier, overloading his beam absorber and sending him off in a brilliant blue flash. At one hundred meters the fire of small arms, beams, fireballs, and light artillery became so intense that further advance was impossible. Pinned down, they dug in, planting a circle of trenchers around the camp at three hundred yards. The trenchers blasted their circular gouge, set up collapsible roofs, and installed firing-stands. The advanced troops then fell back into the trenches and a high, grounded fence was set up to protect against fireballs. The attack had been going on for six hours.

Parma sat on his firing-step, worn out. A monk passed by with packets of food, handing one to each man. Another brought covered jars of some hot, sustaining drink. Parma ate and drank gratefully. To his surprise, the combat rations were better than their daily fare. He rested after eating, waiting for the order to attack again. Plainly, they were meeting with far tougher resistance than had been anticipated.

Suddenly, the enemy fire stopped. Jumping to his feet and grabbing his rifle, Parma faced out over the scarred no-man's-land that had been green meadow just a few hours before. The man next to him was turning up the power of his beam gun. Everyone else seemed to know what was about to happen.

"On with your helmets, prepare for counterattack." It was the voice of the Standard-Sergeant.

When the counterattack came, it was with unnerving suddenness. First, there was an open field; in an instant, tubes buried in the ground belched forth a dense black smoke. The Church forces opened fire into the fog, stitching random patterns, laying down a dense field of fire. With incredible speed, the constructs were pouring out of the cloud. They appeared to have covered the whole distance at a dead run. Creatures out of a nightmare, they were designed to appear frightening as well as to be functional, fighting animals.

A picture came into Parma's mind: the altarpiece of the ship's cathedral, a copy of one centuries old by Hieronymus Bosch. These constructs resembled those hallucinatory demons from the artist's subconscious. Here was one plated like a lobster, its head a skull of solid bone with eyes peering out from inside; there was another covered in striped fur, clutching a beamer in clawed talons, with a foot-long ripping beak in place of a mouth. Others had pincers, tentacles, bone-club tails, metal-shod hooves, spikes growing from knees and elbows, horns like bulls or rams, fangs, and claws, all in infinite variety and combination. None were much less than seven feet tall and many were more.

The monsters fought skillfully and with complete disregard for death. They destroyed the fence with grenades and poured onto the trench embankments, their numbers savagely decimated but seemingly unstoppable. Parma fired until his rifle ran out of self-propelled pellets, then dropped it and drew his pistol with his right hand and his Thrax knife with his left. All along the trench line, men were dropping shoulder arms and taking up handguns for the close fight, with a dagger, short sword, light axe, mace or jointed flail in the free hand. Even in the Fifth Millennium, war quickly reverted to the Bronze Age when distances closed.

A crab-like creature appeared before Parma and he burned a hole between its eyes with his pistol. He managed to mow down three more before a kick from a bone-tipped foot knocked the pistol from his hand. He disemboweled the kicker with a left-handed sweep of his knife and kicked it aside as he tossed the knife to his right hand. Suddenly, a grey scaly monster was upon him, attempting with its powerful tentacles to wrest Parma's knife from his grasp. They struggled for several minutes; then the construct, with a mighty heave, knocked Parma to the ground, pinning him there with a huge webbed foot and raising its sword for a neck-crushing stroke. Twisting his head to the side, Parma saw the upraised arm of the Standard-Sergeant, wielding a flail: a short wooden handle to which were attached six jointed steel bars, each six inches in length and the last tipped with a spiked ball. The sergeant had to bring the jointed staff down on the creature's head five times before it let go of Parma and collapsed. Hauling Parma to his feet, the sergeant shoved a rifle into his hands and pushed him back on to his firing-step. The acolyte had to stand on a sandbag to see over the pile of construct bodies in front of him. The field was clear, the last of the smoke screen blowing away in wisps. There were no more constructs — all had been killed. Most of their officers had escaped, fighting heavily-armored and retreating as soon as it became obvious that the construct-wave attack was not going to sweep the trench.

Parma looked about him, shaking his head. Medics were loading the human wounded onto stretchers for evacuation, and there were far too many stretchers. Casualties, mostly from the clubbing effects of the constructs' hand weapons, were more than forty per cent. The constructs could not be taken alive, for they fought until completely incapacitated by their wounds, then died.

"Sergeant," asked Parma, "why isn't the camp shelled or rayed from the ship, or bombed by the atmosphere craft?"

The Standard-Sergeant stared at Parma with scorn and horror.

"Where were you during the Holy War lectures? It's against canon law to direct indiscriminate fire on a site which may hold civilians. For all we know, that camp's full of slaves."

"Sorry, Sergeant, I must have missed that lecture." Parma was chagrined.

"Slept through it, you mean," barked the sergeant. "I'd assign you a penance, but you acquitted yourself well today, so I'll just give you extra kitchen duty when we return to quarters. We'll all be pulling extra duty, anyway. We've had twenty five killed in this company, and seventy more in the infirmary. Now, stand to your post and keep eyes to front!"

There were, however, no further attacks that day, and during the night orders were given to pull out. Silently, the men filed back to the landing site to re-board their craft. The roofs were dismantled, the trenches collapsed and, by sunrise, the Cadmian officers stared bewildered over a scarred but bare field.

Back aboard ship, funeral services were held for the dead and prayers said for the wounded. When Parma returned to his bunk, he was appalled at the number of empty beds. His company had suffered some of the highest casualties of the day's fighting. Exhausted, he fell asleep.

In the war room, there was no sleeping. Cardinal Van Horn was most displeased.

"This skirmish today was far too costly. What happened, Monsignor Ortega? You were in command and on the spot."

Ortega, a Dominican, was still in battle dress, dirty and slightly wounded.

"Firstly, Your Eminence, there were the antiquated weapons; nobody has seen fireballs for centuries, and it took time to have the grounded fences put up. Secondly, there were the constructs themselves. They were far better provided with natural weapons than any we have ever come across. Their appearance gave them a decided psychological as well as physical advantage in the hand-to-hand fighting. Then there was the smokescreen, a tactic unused for millennia. The constructs came pouring out of it like ants. Still, we held the line. There was no panic and the men fought superbly. That is all, Your Eminence." Ortega fell back into his chair, exhausted.

"Thank you, Monsignor Ortega," replied the cardinal. "I do not believe that any blame attaches to you, and certainly not to your men. It was, after all, a strength-testing skirmish, and we did plan to pull out if the enemy were too strong. Our retreat turned out to be more convincing than we had planned. Now, to our second plan."

"I have a question, Your Eminence." Bishop Mangiapane spoke up.

"Pray ask."

"Why did Marius not mention these weapons, the smokescreen or the bizarre constructs?"

"An excellent question, Bishop. Marius, will you explain yourself?"

"Gladly," said Marius, unabashed. "When I was an officer here several years ago, these forces were used entirely for offensive purposes on other planets, never to defend the home world. I had never heard of the fireballs or smokescreen because the warlord himself probably didn't know about them, until he received your ultimatum and dug out his old defense plans. Those weapons were probably installed centuries ago and forgotten. The only instruction we were given was the locations of the camps and forts and how many beings they'd hold. We all pulled duty in them, but we never had to unlimber the defenses, except for the anti-space-and-aircraft rockets and beamers, when pirate ships got too close. You noticed that my information on those defenses was perfectly accurate."

"Perfectly," said the cardinal. "Continue."

"As for those horror-show constructs, I never saw any like them except for ornamental ones — palace guards and the like. Those monstrosities were probably brewed up in the labs especially for this fight. It only takes a few days for hand-to-hand combat skills to be imprinted on the genes. The ones I commanded here and on Charun were much more human in appearance. You couldn't fit most of those we saw today into standard space suits."

"Very well," sighed the cardinal, "we'll accept that for the present, but you're on your good behavior until we have the warlord. Now, Father Miles, you have your mission planned?"

"Completely, Your Eminence." The Jesuit's voice was clipped, official. "The warlord's palace is in the center of a large park in the city of Dragonsteeth. It consists of a large number of rooms, filled with treasures, following no particular plan. It may have had a coherent architect's plan at one time, but wings have been torn down and rebuilt, rooms added according to whim: in short, a labyrinthine nightmare to find your way around in. Somewhere underground is the warlord's command room, linked to all posts and aircraft on the planet. Marius here assures us that he can guide us past the defenses at their weakest points and take us to the command room. I think he can be trusted." He favored Marius with a look that boded ill for any betrayal of that trust.

"With Father Lame Deer's team of twenty men, plus Parma, an unexcelled knifeman, Marius and myself, the mission is quite feasible. A small craft, heavily shielded and masked, will take us to the rear of a blind knoll half a mile within the park, in a densely-wooded area. Entrance to the palace compound will be effected using boosters to get over the wall, first removing the sentries. With luck, we should be within the palace itself before the alarm is raised. Marius claims that the palace doors aren't fortified, so it will be mostly a matter of fighting our way past the guards to the command room. The door to that room will be fortified and beam-shielded, but Father Lame Deer's men are equipped to deal with that. Once inside, the warlord, the palace, and the planet will be ours." Miles seemed supremely confident.

"Well," said the cardinal, "there's nothing excessively technical about that. Any questions?" His gaze swept the table. "If not, then I adjourn this conference. Go get some sleep, all of you. A light diversionary attack will be mounted tomorrow, using men who were not in today's battle. Father Miles' mission leaves tomorrow night."

The warlord sat at his conference table, stroking his short, pointed beard. It was a gesture which signified that he was feeling very confident. He looked around at his principle officers. They were flushed and smiling.

"Two attacks successfully beaten off, gentlemen, and our forces scarcely diminished. What is your opinion?"

"I think these priests have greatly exaggerated the size of their forces, my Lord," said a bulky young man in scarred armor. "They hoped to terrorize us into submission, but we've matched them easily, so far."

"But we've lost most of our aircraft and pilots,"

countered Bandinegri.

"True," said another, "but their craft are of more advanced design than ours. They haven't used aerial bombardment, and there's been very little strafing. I think they used up most of their ammunition in the dogfights on the first day, or they'd have attacked the city from the air."

"But," put in an older man, dubiously, "what about that great ship of theirs? It could hold scores of divisions."

"That's been the basis of their terror policy," said the first man. "I think it's a leftover from the old days, like the warships the pirates have. They may have no more men than we've already seen. Why else would they delay an all-out offensive? If I had a ship like that, and it was as powerful as it looks, I'd have annihilated this city and all the camps surrounding it."

"Why else, indeed?" said the warlord. "I think we're all agreed, then, that there's no cause for alarm at this stage. Return to your commands now, and sleep at your posts. They've tested our strength, and found us too tough for their liking. In all probability, their next move will be a night attack. Be ready for anything." The officers stood, saluted, and filed from the command room, the massive door sliding shut behind them.

Bandinegri chuckled with satisfaction. He poured himself a glass of wine spiked with an alertness drug, for he didn't plan to sleep until the fighting was over. Plenty of time to sleep later. His relief was great, and he felt almost amused at his early forebodings.

"Paper tiger," he muttered, chortling.

Aboard the commando craft, the landing party gave their equipment a last-minute check. Nearest the landing-door sat Commander Father Lame Deer. He was an Amerind, one of the few remaining racial

ethnic groups left. His ancestors had been among the
first to emigrate en masse at the beginning of the
Third Millennium, to preserve their customs and
racial identity. He had been raised on the planet of
Aztlan. His face was round, flat, and dark and his
hair coarse and black, in an antiquated tonsure.

In a double row along the sides of the narrow craft,
facing inwards, sat Lame Deer's men. They were
twenty hard-faced senior monks, whose skills and
talents made them invaluable, but whose tempera-
ments were unsuited to conventional operations. At
the end of these two rows sat Parma, Father Miles,
and Marius. Parma was equipped as he had been for
the battle of the first day, except that he now had an
officer's bubble-helmet, loaded with gadgets, and a
short beam-rifle.

Miles was in the black armored garment he had
worn for the fight with Hedulio, but he now wore a
harness which held a pistol and dagger, truncheon,
small grenades, and a variety of small weapons and
tools he had judged might come in handy for the
night's work.

In Marius, the change was startling. He was no
longer the well-dressed, urbane, slightly sinister gentleman he had seemed a few days before. Clad in
plain gray armor cloth and light steel helmet, he had
no bubble or visor. His belt had a powerful heavy-slug
pistol and a long, broad, single-edged knife. Hooked
around his waist, above the belt, was a jointed flail,
and on his left hand was a heavy steel gauntlet, with a
flaring cuff almost to the elbow and a thick reinforc-
ing band over the knuckles, studded with half-inch
pyramidal spikes. He was a picture of raw, brutal
armed force, and any group of men but this would
have kept a wary distance from him.

The small craft flew silently down through the
atmosphere of Cadmus, heavily shielded against

detection. A dense cloud cover had been arranged over the city of Dragonsteeth as further cover, and the craft settled down in the park without being noticed. One of Lame Deer's men jumped from the craft to reconnoiter the area, while the ship stayed poised for instant escape. The man returned and signalled all clear.

In single file, the commandos, the acolyte, the Jesuit, and the lanista left the vessel and merged with the forest. As they progressed through the woods the commandos conversed in the clicks, grunts, finger-snaps, twitters, and low whistles that passed for a language among their brotherhood. Even at close range, the sounds could be mistaken for those of animals, insects and birds. There was a series of clicks, and all halted. The point man returned to report that the edge of the wood had been reached and the palace was in sight.

From the edge of the wood, they surveyed the palace wall. It was highly ornamented, twenty feet high and topped with a wire fence, probably charged. On their bellies, the attack force inched their way toward the wall, taking advantage of every bit of cover, the men in front using scanners to detect buried weapons.

Apparently, it had been so long since the warlords of Cadmus had needed to think of their palace as a line of defense that they had allowed their mine-fields to lapse. The few mines the commandos came across were many centuries old and inert. Nevertheless, the men took no chances, and it took them three hours to cover the hundred and fifty meters to the wall.

To mount the wall, they needed "boosts," jointed frameworks which fitted from waist to feet and could multiply the power of a man's legs manyfold. One of the monks leaped to the top of the wall, clearing the charged fence. There was a muffled shout, a brief scuffle, and silence. Then the monk gave a low whistle, and the rest followed him to the top of the wall, Parma and Marius almost falling on the other side, unaccustomed as they were to the apparatus.

On the wallwalk lay an inert form, a human guard, unconscious and securely trussed. A monk was left to guard the retreat path while the rest crossed the courtyard to the palace proper. The doors were substantial, but Lame Deer's team were skilled at making doors open. Once inside, a monk was posted to guard the entrance, and all the beam rifles were left in his charge. It had been decided that lightbeam weapons were too chancy to use within the building, and each man had a heavy-caliber slug pistol, almost silent, but throwing a pellet which would fell any man and most constructs with a single hit.

Marius led the way through seemingly endless corridors, past rooms unused for generations and over ramps and stairways thick with dust. This wing had been chosen as the point of entry because Marius knew it to be long vacant. As they neared the center of the palace, the men came upon rooms carelessly heaped with treasures, undisturbed for years and unguarded. One room was filled to the ceiling with precious metals, another knee-deep in jewels. Many were full of fine works of art, most of them having miniature stasis-field bands attached.

Suddenly, they came upon a room in which four constructs and a human officer sat. All five jumped immediately to their feet, reaching for weapons, but slugs felled them before the man could even shout. Miles stepped over the toppled forms of the constructs and knelt by the officer, who was bleeding from a shoulder wound and nearing a state of shock.

"'Tell us where the warlord is, and we can still save your life. The longer it takes us to find him, the longer it will take to get back here and evacuate you to our hospital."

"I think—maybe—war room—or maybe—big painting room—" The man fell unconscious.

"Marius, where's the big painting room?"

"It's the warlord's private drawing room. There's a short corridor connecting it to the war room. I can get us there, and if he's not in his drawing room, he's sure to be in the war room."

Led by Marius, they continued through the labyrinth, stopping now and again to avoid parties of humans or constructs. The humans were mostly slaves, men and women, wearing identical blue loincloths, and nothing else except for their neck rings. It was not difficult to avoid detection, for the palace was so vast, and so thinly-populated that, had there not been a need for haste, Lame Deer's men would have moved about for weeks without being seen or heard.

Finally, Marius raised his hand for them to wait. There was a faint mutter of voices from a room across a corridor which intersected the one down which they had been surreptitiously making their way.

"That's the warlord's office. Beyond that is the drawing room, then a short corridor, then the war room. I don't know who's talking in the office, but he probably has some guards or orderlies with him in a time like this."

"We'll have to take them," said Lame Deer. "Pistols and blades, but we're to take the warlord alive if possible. Take no risks, though. If he gets too dangerous, kill him. I'll explain to the cardinal."

There was a muted rasp of steel being drawn as the team drew their secondary arms. Marius, his heavy pistol in his right hand, drew his long knife with his gauntleted left. Hunching his shoulders, he charged, barely hesitating to smash the door in with a powerful kick, then he was in the room, with Lame Deer and Miles close on his heels. Inside, they surprised a dozen humans and an equal number of constructs. Unwittingly, they had arrived just as guard was being mounted. Marius was firing as he entered, and the guards recovered with astonishing speed and reached for their weapons. Then, all the monks were in the room. A few more shots were fired before the action turned to a silent, deadly struggle at close quarters. Miles was wielding a short truncheon with economic skill, backed by Parma with his Thrax knife. Beyond the melee, in the next room, he glimpsed a tall, bearded man in a cuirass firing into the combatants with great coolness until his pistol was empty. Then he turned and ran through a door on the far side of the room.

Miles fought his way out of the guard room and into the drawing room, but Marius was quicker, charging into the corridor beyond, several yards ahead. As he saw a massive door sliding shut at the end of the corridor, Miles knew that he would never make it through but Marius, quick as a lizard, was in. Lame Deer, Parma and a half-dozen monks who were still on their feet appeared beside Miles.

"Charges on that door!" barked Lame Deer. Two monks drew small packets from their belts and began to scan the door for proper placement.

Meanwhile, those outside had a full view of what was going on inside through a diamond-crystal plate which made up the center of the door. They could even hear, since there was an address system inside which was reporting everything said within the war room into the corridor and guardroom, and probably all over the planet.

The warlord was shouting into a grille on a small dais, "Enemy in the palace! Send troops to the palace at once!" Then Marius was in the room with him.

Dropping his now-empty pistol, Marius ripped the flail from around his waist. Twirling it, he approached the dais in a wary crouch.

"Well, if it isn't my old comrade-in-arms, Marius," said the warlord sardonically as he drew a pair of short, curved swords. "Last I heard of you, you were running a fight school on Ludus." He swung a cut at Marius' head and another at his knee. The lanista blocked the head-cut with his gauntlet and jumped over the other, sending back a whistling sweep of the flail.

"I've come up in the System. Military advisor to cardinals, no less. Sorry to be doing this, but it's your world or me, so your world goes."

Bandinegri dodged the flail. "Well, we all work out the best deal for ourselves that we can. I never liked you much anyway, Marius." Those were the last words spoken. The fight was brief, sweaty and grueling. A smashing blow of the flail caught the cuirass, knocking the warlord off balance, another brought him to his knees, and a hammer blow of the spiked gauntlet crushed in the side of his jeweled helmet.

Marius struck the switch that opened the great door, and the monks rushed in. Miles stepped to the warlord's side. The man was barely conscious, and obviously dying. Miles shook his head.

"Do you have a last confession to make, Warlord Bandinegri? It is not too late."

The warlord seemed to return to full consciousness for a few seconds; his eyes focused briefly. His mouth began to work, and he attempted to speak. Miles leaned forward to catch his words.

"It's been worth it," whispered the warlord, and died.

XV

The banqueting was over, and the host and his principal guests sat in the consul's receiving-room in the consular palace in Augusta, drinking vintage wine and conversing in the cool of the evening. The curtains had been drawn back, to allow a view of the three small moons to enter the room, along with the pleasant night air of Charun. On one side of the low table sat Cardinal Van Horn, flanked by Father Lame Deer and Monsignor Ortega. On the other sat Father Miles and Parma Sicarius. At the head of the table was Princess Ludmilla, now the consul.

"Well, my friends," said the consul, "now that the curse of the soulless is eliminated from our domain, what is next on the agenda?" Ludmilla was eager to be about God's work. Van Horn was gratified at the conversion of the government of Charun, but still a bit suspicious nevertheless.

"There remains, Your Grace," said the cardinal,

"the problem of the pirates, who will prove a far tougher nut to crack than the late Warlord of Cadmus."

"How so?" queried the consul. "Their ships are antiquated and number only a few hundred, while yours are modern and await in the thousands. Their bases are few, having only two planets, Melos and Illyria, neither of them as well defended as was Cadmus."

"The problem, if Your Grace will excuse me," replied Ortega, "is one of Church law regarding Holy War. According to our rules, all military force must be aimed solely at any armed power consciously directed against the Church or those peoples who enjoy the protection of the Church Militant."

"Then surely these pirates come under that category," countered consul Ludmilla. "What is to keep you from annihilating them?"

"The problem, saving Your Grace's favor," said Lame Deer, with unaccustomed diplomacy, "is that these pirates number only a few thousands at most, while they hold slaves, prisoners, civilians, and noncombatants of various sorts in numbers probably exceeding a million. We may not proceed against them if our actions would endanger those innocents."

Ludmilla frowned. "Yes, of course, we must not kill the innocent. What do you suggest, Father Miles?" The consul greatly esteemed Father Miles, and would never forget that she owed her current position to his valuable teachings and bravery and strength.

"Certainly, Your Grace, we'll have to infiltrate this nefarious organization from within. That means that we must get a few good men to be accepted in the rather loose brotherhood of pirates for a little judicious sabotage. Our friend Marius assures us that he can accomplish this."

"Excellent!" cried Ludmilla. "What is your plan for this glorious mission?"

"Marius has a ship, the *Samnite,* bearing a crew of twenty-five. He has had connections with the pirates in the past and it will not seem odd to them that he should seek to rejoin them, now that he has lost his school of fighters on Ludus. The crew, of course, shall be made up of our own agents: myself, Father Lame Deer and such of his men as have come through the Cadmus campaign without serious injury, Parma, and a few others.

"We must devise a ruse whereby we may bring the pirate fleets to battle in such a manner that we can inflict a decisive defeat on them without endangering the large number of innocents they hold. Above all, we must not let them know the advantage that having these hostages gives them. We have to destroy them before they can gather too much intelligence about us."

"Father Miles," said Ludmilla firmly, "I would like to go along on this mission, as head of the royal family."

"Surely, Consul," interrupted the cardinal, "that is not wise. This will be a dangerous, cutthroat mission, no place for a young woman." The ancient prelate was scandalized.

"Actually, Your Eminence," said Miles, "That might not be such a bad idea. I can vouch for the consul's ability to take care of herself. Her face is hardly known yet outside the palace, and she would serve as first-rate protective coloration."

"Excellent idea!" cried Father Lame Deer.

The cardinal shook his head, knowing himself to be in the midst of a pack of madmen.

Marius took a chart-thimble from a small box attached to the console of his vessel, the *Samnite,* a small cruising yacht once used as a scout-ship in the days when the Flavian System had a space navy worth boasting of. Placing the thimble in a small hole below a screen, he pressed it in with his thumb until there was a faint click and the screen lit up with a column of coordinates. Marius was one of the few captains left who could actually read the figures and know what they signified.

When the ship was spaceborne, Marius summoned his "crew" to the messroom for their briefing. The soldier-monks no longer looked like the disciplined, dedicated men that they were. Their garments were extremely varied, from simple belted tunics to voluminous trousers to near nudity. Skins had been stained or bleached, hair dyed, false hair implanted or scalps shaved, and paints or tattoos applied. Bracelets, anklets, arm bands, necklaces, earrings and nose rings glittered and flashed with jewels and precious metals.

Ludmilla had dyed her golden hair black and straightened its wave. Her skin was dyed a deep olive and her blue eyes covered with membrane-lenses to appear deep brown. Beside her was Hedulio, brought along at Miles' insistence to keep guard over the consul. The famous warrior's face had been surgically altered, so that he now could pass for an ordinary heavy-grav man. Parma was back in his belt, boots, and loincloth from Thrax, but his face, too, had been altered, having become rather well known through the birthday games. Miles was in the simple tunic and soft boots of a common spaceman.

"Our destination," began Marius, "is the planet of Melos. This world is the great clearing-house for the pirates. There they sell their loot at huge year-round markets, and much of the inhabited area of the planet is taken up with slave compounds. These will be packed right now, since the consul's proclamation outlawing slavery has caused a slump in the market. On Melos, we'll make contact with the pirates."

"Why not go straight to their home base?" asked

Lame Deer.

"The only chart-thimbles for Illyria are owned by the pirates themselves. When I left the brotherhood, I had to turn my thimble back over to the head of my fleet."

"Explain the organization and customs of the pirates, Marius," said Father Miles.

"There are five main pirate fleets; the Cimmerian, the Yellow Skull, the Hellhounds, the Dragonships, and the Corsairs. There are about twenty minor bands, comprising five to twenty vessels, but the five great fleets have among them at least a thousand ships. There's no overall command, but there is a council of the leaders of the fleets. This council allocates new worlds to be raided and flotas of merchant craft to be plundered, in order to eliminate needless competition within the brotherhood itself. Despite that, there is often internecine bloodletting, pirates being of a rather volatile nature.

"About half of the pirates were born to the profession, and the command of the best ships and fleets are usually hereditary. The rest are made up of recruits from all over, part-time pirates, who double as merchants when they aren't in a position of strength, and occasional hired specialists for difficult circumstances. Once, when I was among the pirates, we had to hire a whole team of heavy-gravity men for a raid on Buchinsky's Planet."

"Which fleet are we aiming to link up with?" asked Lame Deer.

"We'll try for the Cimmerian. It's one of the two strongest, the other being the Yellow Skull. The Cimmerians are commanded by Achillia, a woman formerly of the female-warrior aristocracy which controls most of the North-East continent of Pontus. She's one tough old bitch, and you'd best watch your step if she ever comes your way. I worked with her before, and I think she'll be glad to have me back, since it's coming to a showdown with Rome.

"On Melos, you're to spread out among the dives and stews there, making yourselves known and ingratiating yourselves with as many ship's crews as you can. Relay all information you pick up to me, Father Miles or Father Lame Deer. You've each been provided with a 'background,' though it probably wouldn't stand up to close scrutiny. Fortunately, it isn't customary among the pirates to inquire too closely into a man's past. If anyone pries too much, you have an excuse to challenge him. Dueling is common among the pirates. As far as they're concerned, you are former fighters or trainers of mine, street gangsters or down-and-out merchant crewmen. There are lots of those who join the pirates. When a merchant vessel finally wears out there's no repairing or replacing them these days, so unless a man's lucky, the only space berth to be had is among the pirates."

"What will Ludmilla's status be?" asked Miles.

"She's to pose as my mistress. There are plenty of women among the pirates, but the consul looks too decorative to seem functional, and as the mistress of a ship's captain, she'll be spared the unwelcome attentions of other men. Unless, of course, some other captain chooses to challenge me for her." His grin left little doubt as to the outcome of such a duel.

"On Melos you may go armed openly. Most men do, and with good reason. There is no law on Melos. Within the market areas, order is maintained, so that the merchants and bargain-hunters can feel safe, but outside those areas anarchy reigns. The streets are alive with establishments designed to separate pirates from their earnings. Travel nowhere in groups smaller than three. Old scores get settled in the streets and back alleys, and there are always desperate men looking for an easy mark to restore their fortunes. Wear armor vests beneath your clothing whenever possible. Don't let your holy vows give you away. Gamble a lot; all pirates do. And do a little whoring, or it'll look suspicious. Since you're on God's work, the Old Man shouldn't hold it against you come Judgment Day."

"A little less levity on these subjects, if you please, Marius," protested Lame Deer, a notorious prig. He was upset at the anticipatory grins he saw on the faces of some of his men.

Ludmilla examined herself as she dressed, prior to debarking on Melos. The change was rather stunning to her. Although the only changes were in her coloration, those were enough to turn her into a complete stranger to herself. Even her body hair had been dyed black. She pulled on a one-piece garment that would cover her from neck to crotch, leaving her arms and legs bare. The body suit was of armor cloth, skin-tight and supple, with rigid plates protecting her breasts and lower belly. Even women had to dress for the vicissitudes of life on Melos. She took up a plate of thin, gold-colored metal and placed it over her face. It was a half-mask, covering her brow and temples, with side pieces which curved down and forward to cover her cheeks. It was exquisitely molded to conform to the contours of her face, with eyebrows inlaid in green stones, and a large, oval green gem set in the center of her forehead. The mask, besides being a piece of jewelry, served to protect her face from scarring if she should be caught in a brawl. A wide band around her head held the mask in place, and her now-black hair hung over the band in a shaggy mane to her shoulders. She was adorned with gold bands around her upper arms, gold filigree bracelets that extended from wrist to elbow, green stone eardrops, and, last of all, a jeweled belt from which hung a similarly jeweled dagger and small beam-pistol.

Ludmilla was almost embarrassed at the picture she presented in the mirror. She no longer resembled a cloistered princess, but looked instead just like a pirate's woman in this barbaric getup, right out of a holodrama.

She was both nervous and excited. Life, which had been a dull round of boredom relieved by moments of terror, had suddenly become exciting and full of purpose. All her life she had only known two types of men; the brutes surrounding her brother, and the scholars, mostly elderly, who were her mentors, and who, until recently, had gone in fear of her brother. Now Ludmilla was consul, on a mission to protect her people, and she had met men of an entirely different stamp, truly fascinating men. There was Father Miles, with his strange, fearsome, almost inhuman dedication, so sublimely confident and without physical fear. Then Parma, with his simple integrity and quick intelligence, formerly a neck-ringed slave of the class she despised the most, but who was so much better than all the nobles she had ever known. And such a horseman! And now, Marius; a dangerously fascinating creature, nearly as self-confident as Miles, a man of powerful ego and ruthless self-interest, a formidable fighting animal. And yet, he had a redeeming humor, unsuspected moments of self-deprecation, a cynical appreciation of fate, and more sheer animal magnetism than she had ever encountered in a man. In spite of her almost arrogant poise, Ludmilla was strongly attracted to these men. She shivered a second, then slid her door open and stepped out into the corridor.

Miles, Lame Deer, and Marius walked abreast along one of the sidewalks of Melos, which was the name of the principle market city, as well as that of the planet itself. Miles had expected a noisy, raucous spacer-town, but Melos was nearly silent, and rather picturesque in the cool evening. The buildings were stone on the lower stories, carved wood on the upper floors. The streets were illuminated by gaslights burning in globes made up of many small, colored planes set in a soft-metal matrix. The windows of the buildings were similarly made, giving the place more the look of a rustic village than that of a pirate hangout. Melos was a world of great forests, and there were many fine wood carvings about. Even the sidewalks and streets were of planed wood.

From time to time, groups of men would approach the three, eyeing them appraisingly. Always, they would look a second time, then give them wide berth. Occasionally they could hear scuffles in the alleys, muffled screams or groans, but Marius always signalled for them not to investigate; "First rule here: mind your own business." Their slug pistols were loose in their holsters, and Marius retained his gauntlet at all times.

Marius was looking for a tavern he knew of where he hoped to contact the Cimmerian pirates. He stopped at a sign bearing the likeness of a winged animal. Over the door was an angular lantern with a top of elaborately-carved wood. They descended a short flight of steps into a spacious room divided into two sections. In one, men sat at tables of rich, dark wood, eating, drinking, and imbibing drugs. In the other, quiet but intense gambling was going on at well-filled tables. They took a table which gave them a good view of the room and the entrance. A young woman in a neck ring came to the table.

"Your orders, gentlemen? The lorp soup is very good today."

"We'll begin with that," said Marius with the assurance of experience. "Then Purchie steak for three, with corblies and frups."

"Very good, sir," replied the waitress.

Miles was a bit apprehensive of just what Marius had ordered, and he filled in the time before the food arrived by, among other things, reading a sign which stated, in ornate letters, the rules of the house.

"NOTICE TO ALL CUSTOMERS. THE FOLLOWING RULES MUST BE OBEYED OR THE MANAGEMENT WILL BE FORCED TO TAKE STEPS:

1. No beam weapons allowed inside.
2. All arguments arising within the premises to be settled in the alley to the rear of the building.
3. Winners of such arguments to remove any body or bodies from the alley at their own expense.
4. Gambling debts to be paid before leaving premises.
5. All deaths arising from defaulting on gambling debts to be regarded by the management as justifiable homicide.
6. No sexual molestation of employees or chattels, male or female.
7. Management asumes no responsibility for loss of property, life or sanity within premises.
8. Women and men are not to occupy lavatory booths simultaneously.
9. Killing, injuring or mutilating any employee or chattel is forbidden.
10. No spitting.

Marius noticed Miles reading the sign.

"Those are the 'Ten Commandments'" he remarked. "You'll see a sign like that in every joint on Melos."

"I thought you said there was no law here," said Lame Deer. "What do they mean by 'justifiable homicide'?"

"If the management thinks what you did wasn't justifiable homicide, they kill you."

The discussion was interrupted by the arrival of

dinner. Miles found everything delicious, and questioned Marius about the excellence of the cuisine in an outlaws' dive like this.

"All services are good on Melos," said Marius. "The pirates raid for slaves everywhere, both within and without the system, and all the slaves end up here for sale. In times of a glutted market, the proprietors here can pick up highly-skilled slaves at incredibly cheap prices. A place like this probably has a kitchen staff that would be the pride of a luxury hotel on a resort world."

"Cooking's just like home," agreed Lame Deer. "This was cooked over charcoal."

"Two things in abundance on Melos," said Marius, "are wood and natural gas. Very little else." The door banged open and a small group of men strode in, led by a big, bearded man in disreputable reptile-hide clothes.

"Mucius!" shouted Marius. "Hey, Mucius, over here!"

The bearded man peered through the gloom, caught sight of Marius, and burst out with a joyous shout. He rushed over to Marius, threw his arms around him, and bestowed a sloppy kiss on each of the lanista's cheeks.

"Marius!" he shouted, when he had breath. "We've been waiting to hear from you since we heard about the games being closed down. Good to have you back."

"Mucius," said Marius, "I want you to meet Miklos," he indicated Miles, "and Skraeling." These were the names they had agreed on earlier. "Both good men. I have a crew of prize roughnecks, eager to try their hands at free-cruising."

"Pleased to make your acquaintance, boys," said Mucius. "Still the *Samnite?*"

"Same ship, Mucius. Boys, Mucius is the captain of

the *Badlands,* meanest ship of the Cimmerian fleet, except for Achillia's flagship, the *Hippolyta.* By the way, where is the old lady?"

"She'll be here within the next few days," said Mucius. "One of the scouts turned up a planet out in the Fifth Sector that's been lost for five hundred years, so she took her own ship to raid. She'll be here soon with a cargo of diamond-crystal slabs. You ready for the showdown with these people from Outside?"

"Not quite yet," answered Marius. "The *Samnite* had all her armament stripped years ago, when I went respectable." Mucius threw his head back and laughed uproariously.

"You, respectable! Well, we'll take her back to the shipyards on Illyria and get her arms reshipped. It's a good thing you're getting back in with the Cimmerians, Marius. The other fleets are caught short, just now. You see, boys," said Mucius, turning to Miles and Lame Deer, "everybody's been raiding for slaves the last few quarters, and now our biggest market's fallen through, what with Ilya being killed and that saintly sister of his being consul now. But the old lady's had us all out raiding for essential equipment and minerals, stuff that's needed on the outlying planets, so we've got plenty of customers."

"Clearly," said Miles, "this Achillia is a woman of uncommon business acumen. I look forward to serving under so astute a commander."

"Smart boys you got here, Marius," said Mucius. "Now, what do you say to a little game of craps?" And the men drew their purses and settled down to a long evening of serious gambling.

In the *Samnite,* a group of monks sat at the mess table, comparing notes. Brother Simeon, a very handsome young monk with a superb physique, was carping. He wore only the moccasins, belt and scanty loincloth common to the herdsmen of Drivas.

"I think I've been propositioned by half the pederasts in the pirate fleets. They're a talkative lot, though. Just roll your eyes and they spill everything." His comrades burst into immoderate laughter. "Laugh if you like," he said, blushing, "but I've learned that all the pirate fleets are being recalled to Illyria for an extraordinary conference."

Ludmilla, escorted by Parma and Hedulio, was out shopping in the main bazaar of Melos. She wandered through shops and stalls that were selling jewelry, fine fabrics, works of art; everything that the most jaded buyer of luxuries could desire. She was not really interested in buying; rather, she was relishing the very atmosphere of being a pirate in a pirate's lair. She moved among the outlaws, accepted as one of them. It was quite a heady sensation for one raised within the confines of a palace. Here was open friendship and hostility, instead of the Byzantine corruption and duplicity of the court.

Often, she was approached by some swaggering bravo, intent on the conquest of such a prize, but any such was quickly stopped in his tracks by the glares of Parma and the formidable Hedulio. Ludmilla could enjoy the air of danger while knowing herself to be protected.

"Urso," she inquired, using Hedulio's adopted alias, "what do you think of this crystal vase? Do you think it would go well in my room in the ship?"

"Whatever pleases you, my lady," grumbled the giant. Ludmilla wondered vaguely why she had asked. Indeed, Hedulio never seemed to have an opinion of his own. It was just something to say. Still, the vase was exquisite, and she decided to buy it. It weighed at least fifty pounds, but Hedulio picked it up in his great paw as if it were made of paper. They found a well-appointed restaurant, one frequented by merchants, and the consul crisply demanded a good table. When they were seated, she ordered for them with authority. She felt more sure of herself in these surroundings, with the luxurious tapestries on the walls and the priceless carpets covering the floors. Water tinkled in a fountain of jade-like stone, carved centuries before on some forgotten world.

"Pollux" — this was Parma's new name — "what do you think of this place?"

The young man sat awhile in thought.

"Men live well here, my Lady. Better than slaves, anyway. There is some dignity in being an outlaw, but what they do here is ignoble. They take from people who have worked for what they have. They take the people themselves and sell them as slaves. It is no virtue to escape slavery only to become a slaver yourself. That is what first attracted me to—" He looked around quickly, realizing that he might be overheard.

"Tell me later," said Ludmilla.

Fleet Captain Achillia pored over her account books and tables of organization. She knew there was a war coming up, and she had to determine the exact strength of her fleet. She was a handsome woman of about fifty, but immoderately hard looking. She had been raised among the aristocracy of Pontus, a society of soldier-women who kept huge estates worked by slaves. Picked slave men were used for breeding stock, all impregnation being by artificial insemination and all male fetuses aborted immediately upon analysis. Girls were raised in brutally harsh camps and the weak were allowed to die.

Nobody knew how the customs of Pontus had originated, but it suited the Pontines well enough. The slaves, who made up the great bulk of the population, were never asked what they thought. Achillia had

had an older sister, and so couldn't inherit. So, like many of her companions, she left Pontus to seek her fortune among the pirate fleets. She found that she had the qualities needed to keep a violent, hairtrigger band of men and women in line and profitably employed, and she was not long in rising to officer rank. Soon she was in command of her own ship, and then a small fleet, which her organizational talents built up over the years into one of the most powerful of the pirate fleets.

She rang a bell to summon her secretary. An armed young woman in armor cloth entered and bowed. "Yes, Admiral?"

"Send invitations to all the captains of the Cimmerian Fleet to a banquet, to be held at my Melos villa this evening. They may bring as many of their officers and ladies as they care to. Are there any new arrivals?"

"Captain Marius, formerly of the Cimmerian Fleet, is here, admiral. Word is that he wishes to rejoin."

"Splendid. Marius is a good man, as men go. Invite him, too."

"At once, Excellency." The girl bowed again and left.

A slave at the door announced each new arrival, and Achillia greeted them as they entered her banquet-room. She was wearing a sheer gown of light, filmy material. It was not an attempt to appear seductive; in fact, for the first twenty years of her life she had never worn clothes. The warrior-girls of Pontus had trained naked in all weathers, and not even shoes had been permitted. Now, after the passage of years, she was still not used to the feel of clothes, and when forced to wear them, she wore the lightest garments possible.

"Captain Marius of the *Samnite*, with his lady and

officers." The slave's voice was not loud, but it carried to every corner of the room.

"Marius, my old friend, it's wonderful to see you again." She took his hand in both of hers.

"My joy at seeing you again overwhelms me," answered Marius. "Achillia, I would like to present to you my companion, Milla, and my officers, Miklos and Skraeling."

Achillia bowed briefly to the officers, taking a somewhat longer look at Marius' "companion," who was wearing a shimmering black gown and a silver-filigree half-mask, set with black stones. She guided them about the spacious room, introducing them to her captains and officers. When dinner was announced, she took them to her own table, seating Marius on her right. Miles and Lame Deer she paired with two of her female officers.

"Come, Marius," said Achillia. "Tell me what's happened to you."

"Very simple, my dear. The new consul, Ludmilla I, has outlawed the games. I had everything tied up in my school on Ludus. When that was closed down, I had nothing left but my ship."

"Why did you take so long to come here?"

"I had numerous affairs to settle. Also, I had to round up a crew, and I found quite a good one. I'll match it against any in your fleet."

"I wouldn't take a bet like that. You were always a good judge of men."

"My ship needs arming, though. I had to get rid of her guns when I began using it as a private yacht."

"The *Spitfire* went out of commission last year, plus a couple of others. When we get back to Illyria we'll put the *Samnite* in the yards and salvage some of the armament from the hulks."

"When will we be going to Illyria?"

"You'll get word, but it will be soon. This will be a

working voyage, and we've word of a merchant flota leaving Demetrius shortly. We'll hit it as it leaves system, before going hyper. Let's see, now, since your ship has no armament, will your men be available for boarding party duty?"

"Of course, my dear. It'll give them a little practical experience and give me a chance to get back in condition after all these rusty years."

"You've never been rusty to my knowledge," remarked Achillia. "You just want an excuse to mix in with the looting yourself."

Ludmilla was conversing with a young officer who sat on her left. He was handsome, knew it, and kept surreptitiously reaching for her thigh under the table. He didn't worry her much, but she had no doubt as to the significance of the look that Achillia had given her when she arrived. Ludmilla began to wonder whether all the people here, male and female, lived in a state of perpetual rut. Personal vanity was the rule here, men of the officer class favoring parti-colored hose in brilliant contrasting colors, with codpieces bearing intricate designs in metallic embroidery. Women wore anything at all and tried to show as great an expanse of skin as possible. All wore lavishly-jeweled weapons, but the decorations never interfered with the weapon's function.

Miles fared somewhat better with the young woman officer who had been matched with him. He found that all the officers and crew of Achillia's personal ship were women. This one made it clear that she, for one, did not share her commander's aversion to men.

"And what did you do before coming here?" she asked. "If you don't mind my asking, that is," she added hastily.

"Not at all," replied Miles. "I was captain of Marius' yacht and part-time instructor at his school for fighters on Ludus. When the games ban went into effect, I was out of employment, and Marius offered me the chance to come with him and join the pirates. I've always wanted to do that since I was a boy, so here I am." Miles was faking a slight tipsiness. He noted that most of the men here were getting a bit tight, so he decided to follow suit.

"And how does such a lovely young lady as yourself come to this admirable trade? Mind, you don't have to tell the truth."

"I was born on Illyria. My parents raised enough to buy a Guild membership for me and I was apprenticed to a ship at thirteen. I took part in my first raid at fourteen and fought my first space action at sixteen."

"How do you come to be with Admiral Achillia?"

"She favors women for her officers as well as for— other purposes. I was rising slowly in rank on ships with mixed crews, so, when a place opened up on the *Hippolyta*, I applied for it. I had to fight two duels with other applicants before I got the position." She smiled sweetly under her gold half-mask. "But, that's enough about me. We're so glad to have you and your ship here. Captain Marius has been away for years, but everyone knows him by reputation."

"Indeed, he is a man of parts," agreed Miles. "But, surely the approaching fight with these outsiders is not as critical as all that. My captain says that Admiral Achillia has over two hundred vessels and that, with all the rest of the pirate fleets, there will be over a thousand, possibly fifteen hundred ships."

"But, you see, the bulk of those are transports, along with scouts." She was getting a little tipsy and talkative, herself. "Achillia has only about twenty-five actual fighting ships of the first class. That's why we need all the new men who've been coming in."

"Have there been many?"

"Oh, yes. All the part-timers, a lot of the great families who own raiding ships, out of work merchant

spacers, even some of the consul's Army and Navy
men have made off with some of her ships. Nobody
wants to see these outsiders come in and take over.
They'll ruin everything."

"They certainly seem to want to spoil all the fun,"
agreed Miles. "What do people here think of them?"

"Well, some think they may prove unbeatable.
They have a ship as big as a city, and maybe more of
them. Others hold that they're all show."

"But they took Cadmus."

"True, but then, they captured the warlord's palace by a ruse and his constructs destroyed themselves. They couldn't do that in a space battle. Besides, we don't rely on constructs. In any case, win or
lose, most of us would rather die fighting than live
with a pack of priests regulating everything."

"A dismal prospect, indeed."

After dinner, Achillia regaled her guests with dis-
plays by recently caught entertaining-slaves, dancers,
musicians, and mimes. The evening was livened up by
a few duels among some junior officers, which many
of the guests adjourned to the garden to watch. The
party broke up when a majority of the guests had become too drunk or drugged to be amusing any longer.

When Marius, Miles, Ludmilla, and Lame Deer had
returned to the Samnite, Marius announced: "We
leave for Illyria the day after tomorrow. And we'll be
doing a little pirating on the way."

XVI

Off the planet of Demetrius, the dozen ships of the Cimmerian Fleet waited for the flota which was to be their victim. The detection instruments on the planet were few and antiquated, but the fleet lurked on the blind side of one of the planet's satellites just to be safe.

Marius had given them their instructions immediately after leaving Melos. "You're now part of the pirate fleet, so you have to start behaving like pirates. We're going to take some merchant ships, so you'd better overcome any inhibitions you may have regarding theft."

"Will there be bloodshed?" asked Lame Deer, a little anxiously.

"Probably very little. If they can't run, merchant ships usually don't fight. The captains and crews don't own the cargoes, and it's the cargoes we're interested in. We don't want to damage the ships unnecessarily; there are few enough left as it is. We may want to rob these again some time."

"How will the action be carried out?" asked Miles.

"When the ships take their fleet formation after leaving the planet, prior to inserting their chart-thimbles, we jump them. This can be done by eyeball piloting. If they try to run, we cripple them with rockets or beams. Before they have a chance to start thinking, we close on them, match airlocks, and we're in. Boarding parties can carry hand weapons and low-velocity slug guns, but no high-velocity stuff or beams. Some of these old ships are pretty fragile. Even a bullet fired inside might cause irreparable damage, maybe even get us all killed. If there's resistance, though, it'll have to be met with force. You can't fake it, or we'll give ourselves away."

"But," said one of the monks, "if we injure or kill innocent people, our own souls will be lost." There was a mutter of agreement among the others.

"Take your choice," said Marius, grinning with cynical malice. "What's more valuable, your twenty-odd souls, or the lives of a million or so prisoners held by the pirates?"

"We are not accustomed to think of our morals in quantitative terms, Marius," Miles remarked grimly.

"If there were one innocent, and a thousand of us, the problem would be the same," added Lame Deer.

"Well, do your soul-searching and theological hair-splitting some other time — there's the signal." Marius pushed himself from his chair with his arms, reaching for his helmet on its rack. The others followed suit, and Marius went forward to the control room while the crew filed into the airlock. Sitting in his control-chair, he gave the readiness signal, to be answered by an order to advance. He locked on to the lead ship, which was the *Hippolyta*, with Achillia in command. After twenty minutes of carefully masked maneuvering, they came within nonmagnified-sight of the merchant flota. Marius was instructed in code to take the smallest of the ships with his yacht.

Suddenly, the space before the flota was brilliantly lit by flares, burning with the intensity of miniature suns, warning the ships not to move. Achillia's voice broke interspacecom silence for the first time since leaving the protection of the small moon. "Remain where you are and prepare to be boarded! You are now the prisoners of the Cimmerian Fleet. Flight will result in the crippling or destruction of your ship. Armed resistance will result in death."

Marius broke lock with the leadship and piloted his craft into the flota to match airlocks with his assigned victim. It was a very tricky and skillful piece of piloting, and one which most captains, used to leaving all the work to the thimbles, would have found beyond them. When the locks were firmly mated, Marius left the control room and rushed to his own airlock, picking up a heavy-duty cutter in case the other ship decided not to let them in. The precaution proved unnecessary. The hatches separating the ships opened, and the "pirates" rushed in, to find the crew of the other vessel assembled, unarmed and resigned. Obviously, they had been through all this before.

"No trouble and nobody gets hurt," barked Marius. He stepped up to the man whose white coverall proclaimed him to be captain. "What're you carrying?"

"Furs, timber, fabrics, and ceramics for Barsam Brothers." The captain was sullen but cooperative.

"Tell Barsam Brothers that they should keep their payments up to date. Then they wouldn't be losing a valuable cargo. So, you lose your commission for this trip, but you keep your ship and your life."

Achillia's voice came over his helmet-speaker. "Any trouble with you, Marius?"

"Ship secured, Admiral, no resistance," answered

Marius.

A large, unarmed carrier locked on to the cargo lock of the merchant vessel, and machinery went to work transferring the cargo from one hold to the other. Achillia's voice came over Marius' helmet-speaker again. "Ask the crew there if there are any who want to join us," she commanded.

"Any of you want to quit being kicked around and be pirates, instead?"

To the vast surprise of Miles and the rest, five young crewmen stepped forward, grinning.

"Get aboard the cargo ship, then," said Marius. The merchant captain shouted, red-faced, "You men will regret this! You'll never ship on any vessel of this line again. I'll post your names throughout the fleet!" The men made various obscene gestures at him and strolled away to pick up their belongings.

"Anyone else?" asked Marius. There were no more takers.

Back aboard the *Samnite*, they sat sipping some tea-like herb.

"Was that a typical operation?" inquired Miles.

"About ninety percent of pirate jobs are like that," replied Marius. "Why should ordinary spacers risk their lives and ships for somebody else's cargo? Of course, if the captain or crew own the cargo, as is sometimes the case, there may be fighting. Some of the merchant ships are licensed to carry arms, and they've actually tried a few times to ambush boarding parties. An enterprising captain can get rich by the capture of a pirate ship. First, there's the value of the ship itself, which he can sell. Then, there's a bounty on pirates, and those that aren't executed he can sell as slaves. Besides all that, if he's lucky, the pirate ship may be carrying a valuable cargo, which can't be reclaimed. So, there's a powerful temptation to the more adventurous spacers to try their luck at pirate-catching."

"And those men who joined the pirates, does that happen often?"

"We don't often give them the opportunity but, when we do, there's never any lack of volunteers. Ordinary spacers live dull lives, because the ships practically run themselves. They aren't paid much, the food is skimpy; in short, they really don't live much better than slaves. They get even less when their ship is pirated, so they're often eager to try the other side for a change. There are always more spacers than berths for them, as the number of ships declines. The pirate's life is interesting, rewarding, and carries a prestige that ordinary spacing lacks."

"When do we arrive on Illyria?" asked Lame Deer.

"Within ten Standard days. I still don't have a chart-thimble for Illyria; we'll pick one up when we get there. Right now, we're travelling locked on to the rest of the fleet."

"It would help matters greatly if we could get one of these thimbles to the Church fleet off Charun," said Miles.

"No chance." Marius shook his head. "From the time we arrive on Illyria, we'll be in the company of other pirates. This is to be a war conference, and once all the pirate fleets are gathered, there'll be no personal raiding expeditions. If we try to lift off-planet without leave, we'll be burned before we clear atmosphere. Illyria is one planet that hasn't let its defenses lapse."

"Once we've seen the place and gotten a good idea of its defenses and fleets, some of us, at least, will have to get back to our own fleet," said Lame Deer. "How do you propose we do that?"

"That's your problem," replied Marius, grinning. "I undertook to get you there, but it's up to you to get back."

"You know, Miles," remarked Lame Deer drily, "there was a time when his scalp could have decorated my lodge."

"The idea has its attractions, I agree," nodded Miles.

"What happens when we get to Illyria?" Ludmilla interposed. She did not want to see a falling-out among these peculiar allies, who had worked well together so far.

"We'll put down at the main shipyards," Marius continued, "to have the new armament shipped. While this is being done, I and my principal officers will attend a round of conferences on the problem facing the pirate brotherhood. Between conferences, we'll attend more banquets such as the one at Achillia's villa on Melos."

Lame Deer looked appalled, Miles stoical, and Ludmilla delighted.

"Are they all as dissipated as the orgy on Melos?" asked Lame Deer with some trepidation.

"Oh, no," Marius assured him. "Most of the pirate chiefs are far less inhibited then Achillia, who is something of a prude."

Lame Deer blanched. While he could look forward to a bloody battle involving almost certain death with joyous anticipation, he feared moral temptation more than most men fear being boiled in acid.

The shipyards of Illyria looked much like shipyards anyplace: a confused jumble of derricks, pits, heavy machinery, and gutted ship carcasses. Perhaps there were more pits and derricks standing idle than in most ports of the rediscovered galaxy, perhaps more dead and cannibalized ships. Still, it was by far the most active and prosperous place that Miles had seen so far in the Flavian System.

Miles and Ludmilla took a land-shuttle into the

main city of Illyria, while Marius remained aboard to
direct the placement of his new armament. The city
was called Port Royal, and Miles smiled inwardly. He
was probably the only man in the system who knew
the origin of the name. Since the distance between the
shipyards and the city was great, all the officers of
the Cimmerian Fleet were to take up quarters in
Achillia's palatial villa in Port Royal. Miles and Ludmilla were to try to get there early to get favorable
accommodations.

To Miles' relief, the villa was made up of a number
of small buildings surrounding a huge courtyard-
garden, in the center of which stood a large house,
where Achillia herself lived when she was on Illyria.
Miles chose a convenient bungalow near the surrounding wall with several exits, and ordered three
of Lame Deer's men to guard it against all comers. He
didn't think that any of the other ships' captains
would challenge his right to the place, considering in
whose name he was claiming it. Marius did seem to
have something of a reputation hereabouts.

With nothing to do till evening, Miles and Ludmilla
decided to see something of the city. They found, to
their surprise, a well-kept and well-regulated munici-
pality with wide, clean streets and every evidence of
prosperity. It appeared that the pirates restrained
their lawlessness here, probably reserving it for
other parts of the system. Miles reflected that nearly
everywhere predators make sure never to foul their
own lairs. Here the pirates had their homes and families. There were a number of uniformed police in evidence, who it turned out, were mainly there to curtail
the exuberance of the part-time pirates and recent
recruits.

They stopped to have lunch in a rooftop restaurant,
overlooking a park where children played about a
fountain. Ludmilla had, reluctantly, left behind the

swashbuckling lady-pirate outfit she had worn on Melos and was now dressed in a demure belted gown, with all weapons tucked out of sight. Miles had adopted the colorful hose-and-doublet outfit favored by pirate officers. They ordered from a menu printed in several languages. Ludmilla had been wanting to ask Miles about something she found disturbing, but she didn't quite know how to phrase the question. Finally, she decided to just go ahead and ask.

"Miles, do you really think that Parma should become a priest?"

"I see no reason why not. Of course, he may choose to be a monk or friar." He knew perfectly well what she was leading up to, but he decided to let her talk it out first.

"But isn't he a little ... well ... ignorant and naive to be a priest? Of course, I realize he's brilliant, but his background is so limited."

"He will be educated at seminary, and it's not uncommon for students to be illiterate when they first arrive."

"Isn't it a bit late for him to be learning Christian morality? You said yourself that it was far better to start with children."

"That is so in the case of Charun, where a debased and exploitative society had destroyed all traditional values. Parma's case is different. He was raised in a tribal society which had a very strict moral sense. Their morality was primitive, applying only to the tribe itself, but as Parma gained a wider view of the universe, he began to apply his morality to the rest of mankind. Unlike our friend Marius, for instance, Parma is a virtuous creature, and education in Christianity will give him a philosophic and spiritual base for that morality."

"Damn it, I don't want him to go!" blurted out Ludmilla at last. She could have bitten her tongue. There it was, right out in the open.

"So," Miles raised his eyebrows in mock surprise, "the princess has fallen for the peasant boy, just like in the stories."

"Don't you make fun of me, you sanctimonious hypocrite. You just want more converts to stack up extra credit for you in heaven."

"My dear, I have no desire to come between you and your long-haired paramour. In any case, the day is long past when priests were supposed to be celibate. There's no reason why he can't have you and his cassock both."

"But he'll be away for years!"

"True love should endure through a trifling few years. Speaking of which, does he know about this passion of yours?"

"Well, not yet. In fact, I've only been really sure myself for the last few days. Since Melos."

"Perhaps you are being a bit hasty then. People usually are, the first time around. How did you happen to settle on Parma, if I may ask?"

"At first, I was attracted to you. All my life, I was surrounded by old scholars, slaves, and the animals who followed my brother. The only men of my own age group who were at all attractive or interesting were the young nobles, and they were such a scheming, depraved lot that I hated all of them. Then, suddenly, you showed up. I began meeting men who were strong without being cruel, intelligent and proud. I was even fascinated by Marius. He's ruthless and brutal, but he has a mind and a charm all his own."

"A dangerously attractive fellow, Marius," agreed Miles. "It strikes me that you are infatuated with the very idea of desirable men. It might be well to approach this situation with extreme caution. But why Parma, in particular?"

"Back on Charun, I was repelled by him at first. He

was one of my brother's fighters, and I was disgusted with all such. Also, he was a slave. I was a product of my raising, and I found it difficult to overcome my aversion to the lower classes, even though, intellectually, I knew these distinctions to be absurd. What first impressed me about him was his horsemanship."

"Men have been found attractive for far less worthy reasons."

"Then, when he came to be your student, I discovered he had a fine mind. We spoke often, usually about what we were learning from you. His comprehension astonished me, and I began to realize that what you had said about the irrelevance of social origin was true. On Melos, he told me why he had chosen to follow you into the church service. He said that, since he had left his tribe on Thrax, he had been searching for the kind of peace and contentment that he had felt when he was a part of an integrated society, with rational rules of behavior and a humane regard for fellow beings. He knew that he'd found something close to what he'd known before, only incomparably more sophisticated and far-reaching; something that supplies rules which apply to the whole universe.

"I couldn't believe that this was the sheepox herder from Thrax speaking. His grasp of the concepts you'd given us was far greater than I'd imagined. And besides all that, he had such a beautiful body!"

Miles smiled at that. "I somehow felt that it wasn't just his intellectual accomplishments which attracted you. Yes, it's true that Parma is a remarkable young man. And background is as inapplicable to teachers and philosophers as it is to slaves and princesses. Socrates was a stonecutter, Mohammed a camel driver, and Christ Himself a carpenter. Buddha was a prince and Confucius a noble. All human beings have the same potential. Faith is most easily inculcated in the very young, but it can come to a man at any stage of life."

"I've valued your teaching, Father Miles, but I can't say that you have taught me faith in your God."

"It shall be as God wishes."

The meeting hall of the pirates was a huge, ornate single room with a high ceiling and great exposed rafters. It was nearly as booty-crammed as the warlord's palace on Cadmus. Miles craned his neck to study the specimens which commemorated famous expeditions of bygone generations. There were precious silk hangings and paintings covering every inch of wall space, and battle flags hung in profusion from the rafters along with crystal and gem chandeliers. On stands and in niches, statuary competed for attention with fabulously-jeweled weapons and armor. The name-plates of captured vessels covered a huge central pillar.

Marius and Miles had arrived early for the meeting, which was for fleet commanders, captains and first officers only. Standing near the door, Marius could identify each important officer as he came in and relay the information to Miles. Marius knew most of the important men in the fleets, but there were a number of new faces, as age, duels, and the hazards of the profession had taken their toll. They were a barbaric group: tough, scarred, yet dressed and bejeweled lavishly. Some of them wore their hair to the shoulders, others wore braids, and still others were shaven-headed; a few wore a roached strip of hair fore-and-aft from brow to nape. Women were nearly as numerous as men, a preponderance of them being Achillia's sisters of Pontus.

When all were assembled, the commanders of the five great fleets took their seats at a high table running the length of one of the end walls. Flanking them sat the commanders of the minor fleets, some eighteen in number. The ship's captains and first officers sat along a table which ran from the dais to the central pillar. Marius and Miles, being new men, sat near the very end of the table. Food, wine, and ale were set out, but this was not to be a banquet; rather, it was a serious business meeting. The refreshments were to keep stomachs from grumbling, and piratical attention from wandering too far.

The spokesman for the pirates, one Admiral Cato of the Yellow Skull Fleet, pounded for order on the table, using the butt of an ancient, ceremonial pistol. "Order, order," he shouted. "The Summoning of the Fleets is hereby declared to be in session. All business, recreation, gambling and fighting will now cease until this Summoning is adjourned." Having spoken the time-honored words, he took up a paper and addressed the meeting: "This Summoning has been called in order to meet the problem of the Outsiders, calling themselves the Church of Rome, who have arrived to challenge our supremacy in the spaceways of the Flavian System. The floor is now open to proposals, starting with the Fleet commanders here assembled at the High Table. I will begin first." He cleared his throat.

"Fellow pirates, we have all heard of the Church of Rome long before this. Some of our more reckless brethren," he turned to glare ferociously at Admirals Horatio, Paolo and Stepan, who commanded the Dragonship, Hydra and Buccaneer Fleets, respectively, "have been raiding into a sector which they've had under their control for several years now. They did this against my advice. I said long ago that we do well enough for ourselves in our own systems. Why stir up trouble with people who forgot we existed centuries ago? Well, they've done it, and it's too late now for the wisdom of my advice to do any good. My proposal is, hit 'em hard right now, drive them out of the system, and maybe they won't come back." He sat down to hearty applause from about a third of the audience. Then the commander of the Hellhounds stood. He was Admiral Sestos, a blocky, shaven-headed man with a face like a keg of nails.

"I think we're worrying too much about these priests. Our activities are frowned upon by every established planetary or multi-planetary authority in this system; why should we let this bother us? If we let these people come in unmolested, there'll be more trade than this system has seen in centuries: more flotas to loot, richer settlements than we now have available for raiding. Best of all, it'll be a chance to capture ships. When my grandfather was Admiral of the Hellhounds, there were twice as many pirate ships as there are now. It used to seem that they'd last forever, but every year now more of them fail. In a couple more generations, maybe less, there'll be no ships spacing in this system. So, here's my proposal: Let's negotiate with these people, be cooperative, even promise to be good, if necessary. Then, when they've brought trade back to the system, go back to our customary way of making a living." He sat down and received about the same applause as Admiral Cato had. The next speaker was Achillia.

"What my esteemed colleague, Admiral Sestos, has overlooked, is that one of our most important trade items has always been slaves. If these people are allowed to reinfest the system with their trade, the first thing they'll bring in will be machines; machines that will make slave labor redundant. As the old machines broke down human labor, and cheap human labor, became a necessity throughout the system. We've grown fat supplying that demand.

"I must agree with Admiral Cato. We have to drive these people out immediately, if we can. The question is, are they in a position of strength, or are they bluffing? Nobody has ever been aboard that monster ship of theirs to tell us..." She sat and her place was taken by Admiral Horatio of the Dragonship Fleet. He was a thin, elderly man with dagger-blade eyes.

"As our good friend Cato has pointed out, some of us have been taking ships within the Roman Church sphere of influence for some time. We have been able to find out very little about this organization, because they have only recently come into that sector." He rummaged around in his doublet and finally pulled out a long piece of paper, drawing on a pair of spectacles. He cleared his throat.

"These are the facts about these mysterious priests that my intelligence officers were able to come up with:

A. Their center of organization is the city of Rome, on the planet Earth. This is the same Church which held sway over the Flavian System centuries ago, and seems to be enjoying some sort of resurgence.

B. Their true military power is unknown, because they continually move their forces from one place to another.

C. They have some sort of ritual taboo against killing, except under very circumscribed conditions.

D. Their space navy is largely employed in convoying vessels directly engaged in the church's service, especially for what are called tithe-ships."

With these last words Horatio's voice held a particular emphasis. He took off his spectacles and put away his paper. "These tithe-ships are the vessels which collect the yearly revenues of the Church of Rome. I spoke to the captain of an extra-system pirate vessel, who told me that he had taken part in an expedition to capture one of these tithe-ships. An emergency in another sector had drawn off its convoy, and a band of twenty pirate vessels had attacked it. They lost six ships, and many of the pirates were killed in the hand-to-hand fighting aboard the ship. It seems that these priests don't believe in sensible surrender. The treasure they found aboard was staggering: more than a billion ounces of precious metals, a thousand hold-chests of jewels, works of art, spices, drugs, and perfumes in volume so great that they were forced to leave much of it. They captured easily twice the entire income of the whole Flavian System. I agree with Admiral Sestos. Let them come in! With wealth like this, we can do without the slave trade." He sat down amid shocked silence. The mention of such overwhelming wealth sent the pirates into ecstasies of greed. The very thought of so much loot was almost a religious experience to them. Finally, another speaker stood. He was Admiral Josip Harelip, of the Corsairs.

"My friends," he declared, "we argue to no purpose. The wishes of our various leaders here assembled are not incompatible." He spread his hands in an appeal to calm reason. "One party desires that we drive these outsiders from our system, for the excellent reason that, if we do not, they may destroy us instead. The other party wishes to allow them in, so that we may get at their wealth and, more importantly, that we get a chance to capture new ships. Now both of these arguments have merit, so I propose a compromise: Let us drive these priests from the system now, to insure our own safety. Then we may raid to our heart's content in *their* trade lanes. Some of our fleets have already established contacts in the Roman sphere, so let's take advantage of these contacts. In clearing out the Roman ships, we may capture many of their chart-thimbles, thus providing ourselves with settlements of theirs which we may raid. However strong they are at home, they must be weak and thinly-spread so far from the hub of their empire. This, I believe, is amply demonstrated by

Admiral Horatio's account of the captured tithe-ship.
There is no reason why we cannot retain our hold on
this system, and plunder theirs." A tumultuous applause erupted as he finished his speech. Obviously,
the bulk of the pirates favored his proposal, but the
debate continued until every last ship's captain had
his say.

When the evening had worn very late, and the arguments became more and more vociferous, Admiral
Cato lurched to his feet and pounded the table with
the ancient pistol once more. "Order, order! I hereby
declare this Summoning adjourned, on the grounds
that you slobs are by this time too drunk to carry on
an inteller—intellent—intelligent debate. Clear out
and be back here in two days' time." He fell back into
his chair, cross-eyed.

The pirates crowded out of the hall, still shouting
and waving fists. Some retired immediately to the
dueling-ground, to continue the debate in a more forthright manner. Miles and Marius returned to Achillia's
villa, to discuss their next move. When they arrived,
Lame Deer gave his report on the condition of their
house.

"I've been over it thoroughly, and there are no listening or observation devices. I've rigged all the en-
trances and windows so that nobody can get in but we
can escape easily. We found a tunnel beneath the
building, leading under the wall to a river bank. I've
installed charges on the nearest wallgate, in case we
have to get out that way in a hurry, secured climbing-
holds at three points on the wall that are invisible
from the main buildings, and established covered
routes to get to all of them unobserved."

Marius gave a low whistle. "My apologies if I've
been a little rough on you, Lame Deer. You do seem to
be a man who knows his job."

Lame Deer favored Marius with his customary

level stare. "I try to do my duty as best I can. Regardless of whom I am called to work with."

"At least," interrupted Miles, "the pirates will be occupied for some days with their debate. That gives us time to formulate some sort of plan of action. Marius, what do you think their next move will be?"

"Well, their greatest weakness is that they know far too little about the Church and its forces. They're going to realize that pretty soon, and start casting about for a way to gain some intelligence."

"We could take advantage of that. Marius, it's now your job to convince as many of the leading pirates as you can that you're the best man available to send to Charun to collect intelligence concerning the Church forces."

"That was my thought also. You will, of course, have some plan for me to relay to the cardinal?"

"I'll give you the details of that when the time comes." Marius knew that Miles was hedging, did not trust him. That suited him. He didn't trust any of them, either. He was trying to formulate some explanation for their actions and motives that would fit them into his own bitter philosophy and view of the universe. He had concluded that they were much the same as the people he had always moved among, substituting masochism for sadism, asceticism for license, and self-righteousness for cynicism. Two sides of the same coin. He could not see that they were preferable to the gangsters, pirates and tyrants he was used to, but they did seem stronger, so he was willing to play along.

Marius sat on a couch across from Achillia. A small table bearing flasks and glasses of great value stood on the floor between them. Marius was admiring the woman opposite him. She still had the body of a woman half her age, and she cared for that body as she cared for her ships. Her face was clear, handsome and unlined, and her hair, clipped short, showed no gray. She was the kind of woman Marius would have been attracted to, had her desires not so obviously worked in other directions. Marius, for all his lack of principles, had never been promiscuous, preferring certain qualities in women to mere quantity of attractive flesh. He had once known a woman something like Achillia, but she was long dead.

"You are uncharacteristically silent, Marius. Where is your old charm? Why are you not flattering me? Surely there is some advantage you wish to gain, some little moral ascendency to throw me off my guard?" She smiled with feline self-contentment.

"Forgive me, old friend. I was woolgathering. For a moment you reminded me of somebody else I used to know, a long time ago." His voice held an odd, wistful note.

"Ah, now you do want to throw me off my guard. Marius overcome by sentimentality, indeed. Next you'll tell me I remind you of your long-lost love."

"To be sure, it was a clumsy attempt. You are far too perceptive for me, Achillia. I should know better than to keep trying." The admission told Achillia that she had drawn blood. How strange that even Marius had memories. She had a few, herself, but she would never have let such weakness become known. She wondered what had caused Marius to lower his guard and allow such personal revelation.

"Well, let's stop fencing and start planning." She was all business now. "I've decided to throw my support behind Horatio. He has more brains than all the others put together. I want your support when it's put to the vote, and your backing, with your men, if it comes to open fighting with Cato and some of the others."

"And my reward?"

"I have a number of the minor fleets in my pocket. The Black Knife, the Jokers, the Wolves and the Nasties are yours, if you stick with me. I know you are the most capable of my commanders. Support me, both now and during the fight with the Outsiders, and when we've won you'll have those fleets. Think well on it. Fourteen good ships and crews, plus their transports, to begin your own fleet with. In a few years, you could have a fleet bigger than mine, or the Yellow Skull."

"Why are you so anxious for me to set up in business? I'll be ten times the rival that Cato ever was."

"There's no reason for us to compete. When we've beaten these Outsiders, there will be plenty for everybody. What I mainly need is to know that you won't be plotting against me right now, at this crucial time. Are we agreed?"

"Agreed," said Marius, without hesitation.

Miles arrived at the shipyard in the hours just before dawn. He had left the villa by one of the climbing-spots Lame Deer had provided. He made a circuit of the berth where the *Samnite* now lay, bristling like a pugnacious boar with her new armament. When he was sure he would not be observed, Miles made a dash for the entry hatch. He worked the combination-lock quickly, without even having to use his tools. Once inside, he took the companionway up to the control room. With a small tool, he removed a plate from the base of the console and reaching inside, he pulled out a small, metal box which was unmarked, but which bore the unmistakable look of manufacture by the Benedictine School of Space Engineering. Miles pressed a combination of spots on the sides of the box, and a small opening appeared in one side. He gave it a shake, and an object fell out into his hand; it was a new chart-thimble, which would now guide any ship unerringly to Illyria.

XVII

The Grand Ball was being held in a mammoth room in the center of Port Royal. The low ceiling was supported by slender columns of crystal, and there were no walls, all sides being open to view the extensive parklands and inevitable fountains. The pirates were dressed in their gaudiest finery for this event, to which all were invited. The room was packed to overflowing, the crowd spilling out onto the lawn and among the trees. There were even a few swimming in the fountain.

Ludmilla sat on the edge of one of the fountains, periodically dipping her goblet into the basin. This particular fountain was filled with a fine golden wine. She was dressed in another of the lady-pirate costumes, this one in silver and black, with low boots sporting inch-long silver spikes on their toes. She was accompanied, as usual, by Parma and Hedulio, and she could see Miles and Marius talking earnestly with some shaven-headed captain.

The music was wild, and people were dancing, talking and politicking, or just watching the festivities. The air was heavy and fragrant with a dozen different types of drug-smoke, while food and drinks were being carried around to the guests on trays. Those with arguments to conduct had a fine, spacious dueling-pit to settle them in, with plenty of space for spectators to watch and place their bets.

Ludmilla realized that she had never been happier. She was living life at its most dramatic and romantic, amid spies, outlaws, and men and women who lived dangerously and with a total lack of inhibitions. She knew that she was witnessing the passing of this wild, free, fearsome way of life. There would be no room for such in a galaxy regulated by Rome. A colorful phase of her world's history would soon be gone forever. She was somewhat saddened at the thought, but she remembered what Parma had said about the pirates and was a little cheered. At least they would finish well, she knew. They'd die with a fight and a curse and a few drinks, not much caring. Their lives were all sensation, with little thought and no future. She drank a silent toast to them.

A man approached. He was the young, handsome officer she had seen on Melos, the one who had been so objectionably familiar with her thigh. He grinned like a cobra. "Well, we meet again," he leered, breathing wine in her face. "Why not accompany me to my ship, where I will shower you with the loot of my latest expedition." Without further ado, he began pawing her. Parma had drawn his knife, and Hedulio had unfolded his arms in preparation for a little agreeable homicide, when Marius appeared. "No, lads, remember whose woman she is." He glared at them warningly. "This is my challenge. Well, captain, . . . ah, Polycarpio, is it?" His voice was dangerously friendly.

"Will you explain yourself? This lady is my companion, you know."

The handsome young captain turned on him with unmistakable sobriety. "If the noble Captain Marius has no objections, the pit is over there." His eyes glittered with bloodlust. Marius saw some ferocity-inducing drug at work there, along with fear-suppressants and reflex-speeders. They were the standbys of the professional duelist. The man would be deadly dangerous. There was a ring of silence spreading around the two men. Marius began to pull on his gauntlet as Miles looked on with grave concern.

Suddenly, Ludmilla's booted foot shot out, to land squarely in the young captain's crotch. The metal spike on her boot-toe glanced off armor, but the kick still had sufficient force to double the man over. Her next kick, with the side of her foot, caught him under the chin, sending him in a backward arc to splash into the fountain. There was a momentary silence, then the sound of Achillia's deep, mannish laughter. The crowd broke into howling mirth as well. Admiral Cato ran up, shouting, "Get him out of there, quick, he'll spoil the wine!"

Captain Polycarpio was hauled from his fragrant bath, head lolling, to be borne away by friends. Achillia walked up, still laughing. "I could use a woman like that on my crew, Marius. Would she consider joining?"

"She's free, ask her." Marius shrugged.

"I'm flattered by your offer, Excellency, but I'm quite content with Captain Marius." Ludmilla shivered at the caress in the Admiral's eyes.

"As you should be, no doubt. But do keep my offer in mind. Come, Marius, let's find some of that Ophelian wine." She took his arm and led him away. When they were out of earshot of the rest of the crowd, she whispered to him, "That little coxcomb came primed to kill. Who put him up to it?"

"I was wondering that myself. I've narrowed the list down to no more than five hundred."

"True, you're not without enemies. People here have long memories."

"Not to mention that word of our little talk and your offer may have leaked."

"Only if you did the leaking," retorted Achillia.

Ludmilla wandered over to Miles. He was sipping a very rare blue wine, wondering idly how many lives it had cost. He favored her with a smile. "Congratulations. That was splendid. You've gained a lot of admirers, and from now on they'll be polite and careful."

"Including our hot-eyed Admiral, I'm afraid."

"I've been hearing about how Achillia was raised. Much similar to the old Spartan system, but applied to girl children instead of boys. Sexual inversion is inevitable when one sex lives entirely separate from the other. Pity."

"I find it hard to pity any of these people, although I can admire and hate some of them."

"Really? I think it's a great pity. These are splendidly vital people, entirely without the apathy and defeat we've seen elsewhere in this system. Consider Achillia, and Marius, too. Look at the potentialities they had twisted and crippled by their background. Achillia has the force of character to run a pirate fleet, surely one of the most formidable of tasks. She could have risen to any position open to a person with drive and intelligence, but her desires were perverted by a ruthless militaristic upbringing.

"And Marius, with the mind of a philosopher and the morals of a street gangster. He was born into the horrid slums of Charun, where the only way out was through the criminal gangs. In any sensible society he'd have been a teacher, a statesman, a captain of industry. Instead he's just an uncommonly gifted criminal, denied the crucial ability to discern between right and wrong. I'd have valued such people as friends, but for them, it's too late. Their minds are too far gone into psychopathy. I may even have to kill them.''

"But, Marius is our ally! He fought alongside you on Cadmus.''

"We can't trust Marius, because there's no faith in him. He's betrayed his former friends to us and he'll betray us just as easily. We can only trust him to act in his own interest, but what he thinks that interest to be is something which lies entirely in his own mind, and it's a mind I can't fathom.'' He sipped his wine morosely, depressed for the first time since Ludmilla had met him. The glitter of the scene began to fade for her, and she sensed doom closing over the gathering like the wings of some great bird of prey.

Admiral Cato called yet another meeting to order. This time, only the admirals and the most important of the ships' captains were present.

"We have unanimously decided, after expending a lot of hot air, that we should clean these strangers out of our system, but not too far out. Now, the first order of business is to acquire some intelligence concerning the real power of these priests. Admiral Achillia has suggested that we send her captain, Marius, on this mission and I back her choice. We all know that he can talk his way into a dragon's belly and out again. Of course, he can't take his ship, but we can send him as far as Melos, where he can take a merchant ship to Charun. He assures me that he can get aboard the big ship and back again within thirty Standard days. That's about thirty-six days, Illyria time. All pirating activities to be suspended until then. Any objections?''

He raised the ancient pistol over his head. "Done,'' he cried, as the pistol-butt slammed down onto the table with finality.

Miles rolled up the paper and thrust it into a metal tube, closing up the end with a blob of sealing-wax. He stared at it for a few moments, then handed it to Marius.

"This is written in code. If you're discovered, somehow, we won't be giving anything away. And take this." He handed Marius a short dagger with a smoky yellow stone in its pommel. "This is a weapon issued only to priests of my order. If it were taken away from me against my will, it would auto-destruct. I have set its mechanism so that it will remain whole for twenty Standard days. It must be in Cardinal Van Horn's hands by that time or your mission will have failed, as will ours. Go now, and Godspeed."

When Marius was gone, Lame Deer turned to Miles.

"You don't trust him, do you?"

"Not a bit. But we haven't much choice, have we? We must hope that Marius will decide that his most profitable course is to throw in his lot with the Church."

In his cabin aboard ship, Marius took out the tube and dagger and examined them. He carefully steamed off the thick lump of sealing-wax and removed the rolled-up paper. The code was none that he was familiar with. After several hours of attempt at decoding, he gave up. Obviously, the message was only decipherable to one who had the key. Carefully rolling the paper back into the tube, he replaced the wax, resealing the edges over a candle with minute care. He turned his attention to the dagger.

The story about auto-destruction was obvious nonsense, and it could have no use as identification that would not be equally well served by the coded message. He took the dagger to the ship's infirmary and employed the see-through on the dagger's handle. Inside, beneath the yellow-stone pommel, was a tube of lead. The handle itself was intricately booby-trapped against examination. This was what he had been looking for. He ran a further series of tests on the dagger and found, under ultra-violet light, a microscopic group of figures incised into the ricasso, the flat part of the blade immediately in front of the guard.

Marius sat back with a satisfied sigh. This was sort of like the intriguing he had done in his days on the wrong side of the law. It was something he had missed. He copied out the figures and took them back to his cabin for decoding. It was a long, weary task, and it occupied the whole trip back to Melos. In the room which he had rented in the city of Melos, he continued the task. He was firmly convinced that the figures somehow gave the formula for opening the dagger-handle. The code was a dense one, but it was similar to some of the ones he had employed in the past, and it was only a matter of time.

The day came, on the ship bound for Charun, when the dagger lay before him, the traps neutralized and the yellow stone removed. He tipped the little lead cylinder out of the handle and unscrewed the cap, finding exactly what he had expected to find—a tiny cone of feather-light metal. It was a chart-thimble. Somehow the wily Father Miles, or maybe Lame Deer, had contrived to steal one of the pirates' treasured thimbles, or else, through some technology unknown to him, they had made a new one. He smiled and lay back on his bunk. What to do now?

"Miles, we've got to get away from here soon." Father Lame Deer was fuming with righteous wrath. "My men are enjoying this duty entirely too much. Give them another two weeks of this, and they'll forget the Church and join the pirates!"

"Calm yourself, Lame Deer. Marius is surely back on Charun by now, and the Church forces are probably on their way." They were in the yard behind their house at Achillia's villa. Twenty feet before them was a standing post. Lame Deer was throwing a pair of short-handled tomahawks at an inch-square spot painted on the post. He would glare at the spot, then his arm would be a blur as one of the little axes would appear, bisecting the spot. He seemed to be taking out all his hatred for the sinfulness of the universe on that little spot. He felt his side nudged by Father Miles, and turned to see their hostess approaching.

Both men turned to face her, bowing. She was wearing her arms-belt over the usual filmy gown, which probably weighed less than one ounce. A pair of knives with short, broad blades and flat handles on her left hip balanced a small beam-pistol holstered on her right. All were devoid of jewels, as was she herself, except for a pair of wide metal bracelets which were more protective than decorative, as was a broad, metal-link collar which encircled her neck and covered her shoulders.

"It's good to see my officers at training," Achillia remarked. "Most of them are besotted or drugged to the eyeballs. You're very handy with those tools, Officer, ah, Skraeling, is it?"

"Skraeling it is," answered Lame Deer. "You are very gracious, Excellency, to so compliment my small skill." He threw his other ax, and it landed solidly into the target, a quarter-inch from the first. Then he went to retrieve his weapons.

"First Officer Miklos," she continued, "why don't we see Skraeling at our parties more often? He seems an engaging enough man."

"Well, Excellency, he's not as handy with his other tools, if you take my meaning. Only cares for fighting, really." He had feared that Lame Deer's puritanical temper might land them in trouble.

"Oh, a pity." She shook her head in sympathy as Lame Deer rejoined them. "Let me have a try at that." She drew her knives, throwing them so quickly that the second was on its way before the first had even reached the target. She threw them by the handles, using only her arm, her shoulders staying perfectly level. Both knives landed solidly in the target area. Miles' eyebrows went up a fraction of an inch. He moved to the target, withdrew the blades, and returned them to their owner.

"May I speak to you in private, First Officer Miklos? It's a business matter."

"Of course, Excellency, I am yours to command." He gave Lame Deer the signal to keep close guard. He didn't want his conversation with the Admiral to be overheard.

Once inside the house, she came straight to the point: "Miklos, do you recall the man who tried to push a duel with Captain Marius at the ball a couple of weeks ago?"

"Clearly, Excellency. A Captain Polycarpio, I believe?"

"Exactly. He is captain of the light cruiser *Fire Dragon* of the Dragonship Fleet. The commander of that fleet, my supposed ally, Admiral Horatio, was probably the one who put him up to it. I am now going to take you into my confidence." She explained the details of her offer to Marius. "I thought, at first, that he was hired by one of the officers of the smaller fleets that will be consolidated under Marius' command: one who had hoped himself to command one of those fleets. My inquiries in that direction were fruitless. It seems that Admiral Horatio has contrived to plant a listening device in my quarters, so I suspect that it was he who called on his captain to challenge Marius. Polycarpio is a notorious duelist, even among this crowd. Twenty-two dead men to his credit this year. I want you to investigate this matter and deal with Polycarpio. I can't have allies plotting against me at a time like this. You must ingratiate yourself with Polycarpio and, if possible, get to Horatio himself. I must know the extent of his plans."

"I am most flattered by your confidence, Excellency, but, why me? Surely you have many officers whom you know better." Miles was cautious and suspicious.

"First, Marius vouches for you, and I know him for a fine judge of men. You wouldn't be his first officer unless you were competent. Second, as his first officer and most trusted lieutenant, you are the one most likely to sell him out, so you will seem less suspicious to Polycarpio." Miles nodded at the wisdom of that. "Third, all of my most trusted officers know entirely too much about me. If I gave them a chance to betray me to my enemies, I would be taking entirely too much risk. Last of all, there is a good chance Polycarpio or Horatio will kill you. To be honest, you wouldn't be much loss to me."

"That is most clear and logical, Excellency, and removes any doubts I may have harbored. However, it leaves one important question to be answered." Miles made his eyes swim with greed.

"Of course. What is to be your reward? Marius tells me that you were captain of his yacht. Can you actually use the instruments, as Marius can? Plot and follow a course without a chart-thimble if necessary?"

"Yes, Excellency, if coordinates are available and the flight is within a solar system."

"When Marius takes over his fleet, he'll probably want to keep the *Samnite* as his flagship, but there will be others. Captain Publio of the Black Knife Fleet has been taking pay from Admiral Cato for some time, to supply him with information concerning the joint raids that my fleet and the Black Knives sometimes make. We'll be getting rid of him as soon as the current emergency is over. His ship, the *Evil Dream*, is a fighter-scout with excellent arms and better navigational capabilities than most in the fleets. Now would you like to captain her?"

"Your Excellency can place every trust in me," replied Miles.

"I shall," said Achillia, standing. "Men who betray my trust have an exciting but very brief time in which to contemplate their treachery. Good day, Officer Miklos."

As soon as she was gone, Lame Deer came in.

"You heard?" said Miles.

"I was at the window while I kept lookout. So, our Marius has a fleet to command if he betrays us. A most tempting proposition for such as he."

Miles was thoughtful. "Yes, but he knows the might of the Church. He knows that these pirates would stand no chance in open battle."

"He also knows our weakness. He can betray to his friends here the fact that all they need do is stuff their ships with innocent hostages and the Church will be powerless against them. The days of 'God will know his own' are past. If the Church doesn't strike soon, they'll find out, anyway. It's common knowledge on Charun that we took Cadmus as we did to spare innocent lives."

"That is all too true, but as yet these are nothing but rumors." He was struck by a sudden thought. "How are your men at spreading rumors?"

"Perfection itself, as only soldiers can be." Lame Deer grinned with dawning comprehension. "You have some rumors you want spread?"

"Several. Remember, if asked, they're to say that

they heard this information from traders on Melos, or from refugees from Cadmus, or Charunites, but always second-hand.

"First, the Church forces are religious fanatics who want to kill sinners at any cost in innocent lives."

"But, they already know about Cadmus. Some of them do, anyway."

"Reality has no effect on rumors. Besides, none of them were on Cadmus. That's just rumor to them, too. Next, tell them that the way the Church will try to take them is by direct bombardment of Illyria, that they have ways of finding planets without chart-thimbles. That'll tempt them into a space battle, so we won't have to risk killing people here. Oh, yes, and our ships are as antiquated as theirs; you've talked to experienced spacers who've seen them. The big ship is just a long-distance carrier, to keep the fleet together on flights of extreme duration. It has no fighting capabilities. Spread these rumors for now, and I'll think up some more later."

Miles sat at his ease in one of Port Royal's many dives. This one was the *Skull and Glass*, a known hangout of the Black Knife Fleet. The pirates wore no uniforms or insignia, but men of the different fleets congregated separately in different taverns. Miles knew he was courting danger by showing his face here, but it was the only way he could get in touch with Polycarpio. The young captain was here nearly every evening, to carouse with his friends. Miles had attracted some long and somewhat hostile looks, but no one had said anything to him or taken exception to his presence. There was a truce of sorts between crewmen of usually-feuding ships and fleets, in view of the common emergency.

He was sipping his second glass of bluegreen wine when Polycarpio came in, surrounded by his officers and crew. He glared around him pugnaciously, and most of the men were careful to look in another direction. Clearly, the young man had been having a hard time of it lately. His eyes lit on Miles and began to glow ferociously. His hands clenched and unclenched, grasping and crushing some invisible throat. Obviously, he remembered Miles as a witness of his humiliation. He signalled his men to remain where they were and strode over to Miles' table. The bar tensed in anticipation of entertaining action.

"What are you doing here? Aren't you from the Cimmerian Fleet?" His voice grated on the edge of hysteria.

"First officer of the *Samnite,* to be precise," said Miles calmly. "Why not have a seat?" Polycarpio stiffened, reaching for his pistol, then stopped suddenly. Miles had a small beamer pointed directly between his eyes. He hadn't seen the hand move. He dropped into the chair with a demented change of mood.

"Say, you're fast! Well, that bastard Marius picks good men, I've heard tell. Why are you here?" His voice suddenly went suspicious. The bar had relaxed. There wasn't going to be any killing anytime soon.

"I thought we'd have a few words about our mutual friend Marius, and about his girlfriend, Milla. I take it you've no love for them. Would you like a drink?" Miles beckoned to a waitress. Polycarpio ordered a deadly-looking maroon concoction that shaded to black at the bottom of the glass. He frowned into it.

"Those two! For days after that ball, everywhere I went, it was, 'Still sore, Polycarpio?' and 'what vintage was your bath tonight, Polycarpio?' I killed a few of them, and it stopped, but they're still thinking it." He glared about him, once more causing men to quickly look away. Miles had never seen such a textbook case of criminal psychopathia. The man was a homicidal paranoic of the most dangerous type, with no conscience and very little concept of the future. Such a man lived entirely in the present, and could not be deterred by fears of future consequences or punishment. For him, the future didn't exist.

Miles knew that he would have to tread very carefully, using every bit of his skill as a psychologist and diplomat. This man would kiss him or kill him on a whim. He saw the marks of overweening vanity, and decided to play on that.

"You're like me, Polycarpio, too good a man to be walked on by the likes of Marius. There's no reason why we should feud. Hell, maybe we could help each other." He made his flattery sound genuine, his tones oily and soothing. The man's ruffled vanity and wounded ego had to be handled as delicately as a bag of rocket-starter.

"You're right about that. At least me being too good a man to take any insolence from Marius. You'd like for me to kill him, wouldn't you?" His voice became sly. "What's he done to you? Or would you just like to take over his ship?"

"The *Samnite's* a sweet ship, all right. I captained her for him for five years before he lost everything and decided to go back to being a pirate."

"Well, that's your lookout. I'll kill him, all right, as soon as this big fight's over."

"He may be too big for you to just come out and challenge then. He'll be an admiral, and you'll still be just a captain with a single ship." He made clear his sympathy, and watched as Polycarpio burned with the sheer injustice of it all.

"That's what Hora—" He cut off suddenly and looked away, his mind seemingly having taken one of its shaky jumps into an alternate line of thought and mood. He gulped his drink and stood. "It's good we met — ah, I didn't get your name."

"Miklos."

"Miklos, it is, then. Well, we may be meeting again soon, and we'll discuss this question further." Now he was suave and courteous, smiling slightly. "I'll get word to you soon. I have to go talk to somebody now." He bowed slightly and left. Miles let out his breath in a long, relieved sigh. That had been touch and go. The man was mad as a March hare, and swimming in drugs, to boot. He must, Miles reflected, be one hell of a ship's commander to keep his command despite all these handicaps. Or maybe he just kept everyone terrorized with his reputation as a duelist. Polycarpio was terrifying in that way. No matter what the provocation, a sane, or even moderately sane man will hesitate slightly before taking human life. This man would have no such hesitation. There wouldn't be the slightest gap between the decision to kill and the action. It was a tremendous advantage in a true killer, and this one needed even less motive than most. Miles decided that, should he ever have to fight Polycarpio, he'd bring along plenty of backup, then take the man in the dark with a decided superiority of armament.

The summons came from an unexpected quarter. One of Lame Deer's men, who had been rumor-spreading in a tavern frequented by members of the Dragonship Fleet, among others, was approached by a common crewman of one of the ships of that fleet. The man had given him a sealed note to take to Miles. It read, simply: "Let's continue our conversation. Meet me at the tavern of the Two Dragons, on Shipyard Road. Captain P."

"Lame Deer," asked Miles, "can you and a couple of your men tail me without being seen?"

"We could tail you across a dinner table without being seen." He seemed slightly insulted that Miles should ask.

"Then do so. I'm not sure where I'll be taken, and I may need some backup. Do you remember Captain

Polycarpio?''

"You mean the one Ludmilla dumped in the wine fountain?" He showed big teeth in a shark's grin. "Sure, I remember him. I've been asking around about him. Seems he's some kind of crazy killer; really loves it."

"It's true. I spoke with him early this evening. He's been up to something with Admiral Horatio, all right, and he's burning for revenge, too. He thinks I'm plotting against Marius. Whereas, of course, I'm actually plotting with Achillia, who has a separate plot going with Marius, who, I suspect, is plotting against us all."

"What a nest of lies," spat Lame Deer. "If we live through this, we'll have to spend the rest of our lives in the confessional."

"I'm going to see Polycarpio again tonight. Keep track of me. I think he's going to take me to see Horatio. If you see Polycarpio make a suspicious move, kill him without hesitation."

"Sure. It'll be a venial sin, at worst."

The tavern was nearly identical to the one Miles had been in earlier that evening, a low-ceilinged single room with long tables of fine, inlaid wood, and a bar in the rear. There were plenty of open windows and doors in evidence, for customers here liked to have a number of quick exits handy. Miles stood in the doorway, waiting for his eyes to adjust to the gloom. He and Polycarpio saw each other simultaneously, and the young captain stood quickly and came to join Miles. Two very tough-looking characters came with him.

"Ah, Miklos, good to see you again." Polycarpio was friendliness and joviality personified. "These are my men, Second Officer Timon and Crewman Kurt." Miles acknowledged the introductions briefly.

"I'd like you to meet a friend of mine, Miklos. A very important friend."

"I'm sure you would have no unimportant friends, Captain. Lead on."

"Just so." Polycarpio led the way out of the tavern and across the street to a small transport. Miles hoped that Lame Deer and his men would be able to follow. He was wearing his armor suit and he had a number of weapons secreted about his person, besides those in sight on his belt, but these men would not be easy. Taking pirates was an entirely different proposition from handling a few thugs on Charun.

The transport stopped by one of the city's many parks. They got out and Polycarpio took the lead. Miles walked gingerly, seeming relaxed, but ready for action at any moment. At the far side of the park, they reached a high wall. Polycarpio went to a low door and knocked with a measured cadence. The door opened, and they passed through into a darkened courtyard. The building before them was one of the palatial residences of the pirate chieftains. They crossed the courtyard and entered. The building seemed empty, but Miles assumed that they were being scanned by hidden guards.

They climbed a flight of wide stairs covered with two-inch-deep velvet, passed potted exotic plants, and came to a door of some strange blue wood. It opened before they could knock. Polycarpio and Miles entered, while Polycarpio's henchmen remained outside. Behind a broad desk covered in reptile-hide sat Admiral Horatio.

"Ah, good evening, gentlemen. Please be seated, and tell me what you would like to drink." He waved at a well-stocked bar. Miles spotted at least one bottle of a type manufactured only on a world well within the sphere of the Church. He chose a light green wine, and Polycarpio one of his marroon constructions, laced with yet another drug.

"Now, Officer Miklos," began Horatio, "Captain Polycarpio informs me that you are not overly fond of your own captain. If this is true, perhaps we could be of assistance to one another."

"It's quite true," said Miles. "He has been my employer in the past, which was satisfactory enough. Then, I was captain of the *Samnite*. Now he's decided to play captain himself, and I'm demoted to first officer."

"Marius does have a facility for making enemies. He has made one of Polycarpio, here. Our unfortunate friend was to kill him as a perfectly impersonal business deal, but suffered a great deal of embarrassment instead." He smiled gently at the young captain, who was fuming so badly that he had to take a few pills to calm himself. "Tell me, Miklos, do you think Polycarpio could take Marius in an open duel?"

"The captain certainly has a fearsome reputation," said Miles, "but, if he'll pardon my saying so, so does Marius. He's been an officer of constructs and, for the last few years, a trainer of games-fighters at his own school on Ludus. He's tough and tricky, and I wouldn't care to bet on the outcome of such a fight."

"I can take him!" Polycarpio almost shouted, leaping up from his chair.

"Calm yourself, Captain," commanded Horatio. "Do not force me to take steps." Polycarpio sat down again. "Your pardon, sir," he mumbled.

"Now, Captain Polycarpio, if you will excuse us, I have business with this gentleman which would only bore you. I shall not further detain you from your duties." He pressed a button and the door was opened. A liveried guard stood outside. "Castor, show these gentlemen to the garden door." Polycarpio stalked out, followed by his myrmidons.

"Polycarpio has been a useful agent in the past, but

I fear that he reaches the end of his utility. He's not very stable, you know, and he takes too many drugs." He smiled at Miles. "Now you strike me as the kind of man who would never allow himself to reach such a state."

"I try to restrain my baser impulses. I like to retain complete control of myself."

"I admire a man who is complete master of himself. Marius is such a man, and so am I. Another such is Admiral Achillia. It seems that these two have been conspiring against the rest of us."

"How so?" Miles sounded genuinely puzzled.

"So far, we have stayed balanced by having five great fleets. That way there can't be an even alliance. There's nothing as destructive as an internecine war between evenly-matched forces. There have been such wars, but they always were short and relatively bloodless, with three fleets joining forces against the others.

"Now, Achillia wants to change all that, and allow the formation of a sixth fleet under Marius. To begin with, it would be smaller than the other great fleets, but such a man as Marius would quickly remedy that."

Miles gave a low whistle for effect.

"This must be stopped. You are close to Marius, and you can stop it."

"Marius isn't here."

"He will return soon. Eliminate him for us and you will be well rewarded."

"How well?" Miles summoned up all his greed. These people trusted greedy men.

"When we've taken care of Achillia, you can have the *Samnite* as your own command, with this option: I control the Werewolves, a small fleet of some five armed vessels. The petty-Admiral who commands them is elderly and will retire within the next two years. When he does, you may have that fleet."

"What about his officers? They'll be jealous. I'd have to watch my back all the time. Of course, I do anyway."

"There will be a massive reshuffling after the fight that's coming up. I'll have those officers kicked upstairs into other commands. There'll be no complaint."

"And for this all I have to do is eliminate Marius?"

"That, and keep an eye on Achillia."

"I'm just a humble first officer of the newest of her ships. I'm not exactly privy to her councils. And, as you probably know, my masculine charms would have no effect on her."

"To be sure, Achillia's tastes are well known. But, you can keep track of her doings with Marius."

"You don't wish him eliminated immediately he returns, then?"

"I'll send you word when the time is right. Are we agreed, then?" Miles knew that he would never walk out alive without agreeing.

"Of course. Where else would I get an offer like that?"

"Where else, indeed?" smiled Admiral Horatio.

Achillia was faintly amused as she listened to Miles' report.

"Poor Miklos! If you could just accept everybody's offers, you would have a sizeable command of your own."

"The thought had struck me, Excellency, but it is, alas, impracticable."

"Quite so. Tell me, why did you accept my offer, when Horatio's is so much larger?"

"I am sure that Admiral Horatio has no intention of elevating a mere first officer of someone else's fleet over the heads of many senior officers of his own fleet for a mere assassination. No, he will eliminate me, also, and cover his tracks."

"So he would. Now, at least, we know whom to watch. Besides watching everybody else, of course. You must report to us instantly when Horatio tells you it is time to kill Marius."

"Naturally, Excellency. Will there be anything else?"

"Not just now. I'm very pleased with you, Miklos. I wish all my officers were as loyal and efficient. I see a great future ahead for you."

"I try to do my duty, Excellency." Miles bowed and left.

Marius entered the cardinal's office, ushered in by a gray-robed secretary. The cardinal was seated behind an enormous desk, covered with papers and thimbles, some of which littered the floor. He looked up without love as the lanista approached. Marius noted that the room was excessively long, its dimensions subtly tapered toward the rear to force the perspective, making the cardinal loom gigantic at the end of the room. Anyone who walked toward him was bound to feel tiny, and more and more insecure as he walked the seemingly endless path to the cardinal, exposed like a bug on a plate. Marius was not so intimidated.

"You have a message for us?"

Without a word, Marius handed over the tube. The cardinal pried off the seal, withdrew the rolled-up paper, scanned it for an instant, and tossed it into a trash bin.

"Anything else?" The voice said that there had better be something else, or Marius was going to be a very unhappy man. He grinned, reached inside his doublet, and withdrew the dagger, still sheathed.

"There was this. Father Miles said that this would

signify that the message was from him and no other."
The cardinal looked at it briefly, then handed it to
his secretary.

"Scan this thoroughly and bring me a report." He
turned again to Marius. "What was the situation
when you left Illyria?" His eyes were cold, his face
emotionless. In spite of himself, Marius began to
sweat.

"The council of the pirate chiefs has decided to
fight it out. They fear that you'll ruin their profitable
slave trade. They want to drive you from the system,
but they also want to be able to raid you for ships and
more wealth. There's been a severe attrition of ships
lately, and they want to capture some war vessels
from you in the fighting."

"That's comforting. A close-in space battle with
plenty of boarding action. In the end, it's the least
bloody way."

"Not the way the pirates fight. No prisoners."

"But we do not use their tactics," said the cardinal
in a voice like tungsten. "And they shall not win."
They were interrupted by the returning secretary.
"Well?" asked the cardinal.

"It's a thimble for Illyria, all right. Also, Marius got
into the dagger—his aura's all over it." Marius was
surprised. He wondered what an 'aura' was.

"Of course I looked into it." He grinned. "Nobody
said I shouldn't."

"True enough. Well, how nice." The cardinal took
the blob of sealing wax that had closed the end of the
tube and broke it open. A chart-thimble fell out into
his hand. "Now we have two of them."

XVIII

Ludmilla was, as usual, shopping and sightseeing. With equal predictability, she was accompanied by Parma and Hedulio. Both men were laden with packages. Ludmilla had lived her life in a palace where anything she wanted was available for the asking. Now, she was intrigued by the idea that she could go out and get things for herself. It had never occurred to her that there were so many things in the world to covet.

They stopped in the great central park, where Ludmilla had to admire every fountain they came upon. She was always delighted at the effects the old artists had been able to achieve with stone, air and water. As she turned from the latest of the day's fountains, her smile faded like a snowball struck by a beamer. A man was approaching, and she recognized him as the one she had kicked into the wine fountain the night of the grand ball. Miles had warned her to be especially

careful of this man, and never to go anywhere without
an escort.

She saw that he had two very hard-looking men
with him, but then, she reflected, so did she. She saw
Parma stiffen at the sight of Captain Polycarpio, lean
over and speak a few low words to Hedulio.

"Rejoice, we meet again," said Polycarpio, all
smiles. "I only wished to apologize to you, my dear,
for my boorish behavior of the other night. I trust you
will be so gracious as to forgive me." His teeth shone
pearly white in his dark, handsome face. His manner
was positively courtly.

"As I recall, sir, it was you who endured most of
the suffering. No forgiveness is therefore necessary."
She was wary, but she could not resist digging at this
man who so repelled her. His eyes made her skin
crawl. He colored at her reply, but with a visible
effort forced himself to continue smiling.

"Even so, my dear. Would you honor me by demon-
strating your forgiveness? There is a ball being given
for officers of the Dragonship Fleet. I would be most
pleased if you were to accompany me."

"I regret, Captain, that I am already spoken for."

"Captain Marius is not here. He cannot object if
you spend time with someone else in his absence."

"He can, and will. I, for one, have no intention of
enduring his wrath."

"I'll settle him when he returns!" Polycarpio was
shouting and turning an apoplectic puce.

"The lady has made herself abundantly clear, sir,"
said Parma calmly.

"What?" Polycarpio seemed almost dazed. "Did
you speak to me, boy?"

"I did."

"I am not accustomed to being spoken to without
leave by common crewmen, especially those with the
marks of a slave ring on their necks." He snapped his

fingers at his lackeys, pointing to Parma. They advanced, grinning. Hedulio stepped before them. They stopped dead, looked at each other, then at their captain. He stared at them wildly.

"Are you going to let that ex-slave speak insolently to me?" With a strangled cry, he went for his pistol, but Parma's knife was quicker. When Polycarpio's hand reached where his pistol-butt should have been, his holster had been cut away from his belt. A second cut removed his dagger. Almost casually, Hedulio backhanded the two thugs, dropping them in a heap with a single sweep of his mallet-like hand. A second blow landed behind Polycarpio's ear, dropping him to lie beside his companions.

"This fellow is becoming tiresome," said Hedulio. "Shall I kill him, My Lady?"

"Repugnant as it seems," said Parma, "it is probably the wisest course."

"No, he's an odious man, but we don't want the others checking up on us too thoroughly. Besides, Father Miles has been up to some kind of business with him, and I don't think we should kill him without Miles' approval."

"Best to kill him, anyhow," grumbled Hedulio. It was with uneasy minds that they returned to their house at the villa and reported the incident to Miles.

"Hedulio was right, it would have been best all around to have finished him," said Miles. "Polycarpio is not very stable at best, and two such humiliations in a row will be enough to push him over the edge. He'll be out to kill you now." The priest lapsed into a deep silence. He was a man with a lot on his mind.

Marius returned in less than the thirty-six days he had promised and reported directly to Admiral Cato, who called an immediate meeting of all ship's captains and officers. Once again, Miles went to the great, booty-stuffed hall and heard the pounding of the pistol-butt on the table. This time, there was no drink in sight.

"Order!" shouted Cato, unnecessarily, since everybody was quiet for once. "Marius has returned from his reconnaissance mission, with the following report. The naval forces of the Church of Rome consist of some three hundred warships of the first class and two hundred of the second class, of which less than half are now committed in the Flavian System. The big ship now over Augusta is a mother vessel for transport and supply, not a fighting ship. These priests have been raising trouble among the slave populace on other worlds, giving them their freedom and not reimbursing their owners. Ships carrying slaves and prisoners have been taken over by slave-mutinies and taken to Charun, so the council forbids any ship going into action against these people who have slaves or prisoners aboard.

"Now, the entire combined fleets of Illyria, plus allies and part-timers, will total quite a few more ships than the Church fleet has in this system. If we take along our transports we'll look even bigger. There should be no difficulty in driving this force out and keeping it out. They'll look for easier pickings elsewhere. The decision of the council is as follows: At noon tomorrow, Port Royal time, all the fleets will mass in orbit around Illyria prior to heading out for Charun. We'll hit the Church fleet before it knows we're there, drive it out, then double back and sack Augusta, something we've wanted to do for generations, but up till now they've been our best customers. We'll have the loot of the palace to pay for the expedition and the pick of the shipyards to replace any craft we lose in the fighting." The meeting broke into wild cheering. Cato pounded again on his desk. "All captains report to me after the meeting for your orders and places in formation." The pistol-butt came down again and the meeting broke up amid cheers and jubilation.

"So, you decided not to sell us out, after all." Lame Deer's voice was truly wondering.

"Did you really think I couldn't see who was going to win? Admittedly, I was tempted to ransom the thimble, but it was just a passing fancy. No, you are going to build us all a great, shining new world, where a man like me will be able to do much better for himself than command a paltry pirate fleet, or run a school where slaves learn to fight." He smiled complacently.

"I'm sure that your adaptability will prove equal to the task," said Miles. "Oh, by the way, I got word this evening that I'm supposed to kill you during the battle with the Church fleet."

"Who wants me dead this time—Achillia?" He was not surprised, only interested.

"No, Admiral Horatio. I think Achillia really means well by you."

"As long as it pleases her, no doubt. So, that old fart Horatio is up to his plots again?" He grinned. "I'll have to see about that."

"Do it on your own time. We have to figure a way to identify ourselves to the Church fleet."

"Simplest way would be to just attack a pirate vessel."

"We'd be surrounded by them."

"They'll be too busy to do anything about it, when they see the surprise your compatriots have planned for them. We just lock on to one of the pirate ships, board and take her. That way, we do our bit for the Church fleet, and advertise who we are at the same time."

The combined pirate fleets massed in orbit for the

first time in living memory. They were arranged in
two lines, the first composed of nearly seven hundred
warships of the first and second classes, plus armed
yachts, scouts and merchantmen. The second line,
much larger, was composed of transports with dummy
armaments manned by skeleton crews. The highly
complex battle formations of the great star navies
had long since fallen out of use. The best these rugged
individualists could do was charge in a line, allowing
the battle, once joined, to break up into innumerable
engagements and boarding actions. It was very difficult for one ship to come to the aid of another, so the
outcome of the battle depended entirely upon which
fleet could win a greater number of individual combats. It was a crude method of battle, but then, so
were the pirates.

The *Samnite*, being an armed yacht, was positioned
near the tip of the left wing. The line was crescent-
shaped, with the first and second-class ships massed
in the center. At the very tip of each wing were rein-
forcing heavy warships, to prevent outflanking early
in the battle. Each ship was stuffed with as many men
as it could carry, for extra strength in the boarding
actions.

Marius was disgusted with the whole thing.

"Look at that line! Staggering like a drunk. If they'd
cared to learn, I could've taught them a dozen different classical battle maneuvers that would have increased their effectiveness a hundredfold. But do
they care? No, they have to go up against a strong
enemy fleet like a teenage gang going to a mob-war in
the park. Disgusting!"

"Don't take it so hard, slaver," grunted Lame Deer.
"After all, we do want them to lose, don't we?" Lame
Deer was less inclined to be affable towards Marius
now that, as he saw it, the lanista's usefulness to the
Church was at an end.

"Sure," answered Marius, "but I'd like to see them go out with a little style. Life around here is going to be pretty dull without them."

They had been cruising for nearly fifteen ship-days in hyper, under the guidance of their thimbles. They had shifted into realspace two days earlier off the planet of Colloseo, once a mining world, now long since deserted. There were still thimbles left for it, and it had been decided that the fleet should rendezvous there to reorder their lines. Colloseo was in the same solar system as Charun, but was conveniently remote. They would be unlikely to be spotted so far out. When all was in order, course was set for real-space cruise to Charun.

The intership communicator blared the alarm, jerking every man and woman in the fleet to his or her feet. "Battle stations! Enemy in sight!" This was repeated over and over again until nerves were taut to the snapping point. Within minutes, the Church fleet was in view on the individual screens, without magnification. Both fleets had slowed to a crawl, so as not to overshoot each other. This was to be an old-fashioned boarding-fight, so there was no exchange of beamer fire. Beamers nearly always destroyed a ship.

The Church ships were massed outside the orbit of Charun's small, outer moon. The fleet was even smaller than reported, but they were ominously undemonstrative, spaced to hairsbreadth evenness, their gold finish glinting richly in the unfiltered light of Charun's sun. There was no sign of armament breaking the smooth sides, and the only visible marking was a pair of silver crossed keys.

"Attack!" The order went through the pirate fleet. There was a ragged volley of crippling rockets, then the pirate vessels began to advance at speed. None of the rockets struck home. Thin beams lanced out from

the golden ships and detonated each of them before
they had a chance to strike.

"Miles, there's a ship breaking formation." Marius
was in the pilot's seat of the *Samnite*, Father Miles in
the first officer's seat next to him.

"They're all beginning to break."

"This one's heading for us."

"Do you recognize her?"

"Dragonship Fleet markings. Looks like the *Fire
Dragon*. At least this settles our identification problem."

"Captain Polycarpio, out for revenge. I'd hoped to
go for Horatio's flagship, but this will do almost as
well. Lame Deer, are your men ready for a fight?"

"Are you kidding?" came Lame Deer's voice over
the ship's intercom.

"Sorry I asked. We'll be in action a little sooner
than anticipated. Marius and I will be joining you at
the lock in a few moments."

Admiral Cato took his flagship *Yellow Skull* straight
to the center of the enemy line. He had spotted a very
large vessel, situated dead center, which he took to be
the flagship of the Church fleet. Suddenly, a voice
crackled through the faulty speaker of his intercom:
"Attention. Attention, pirate fleet. This is Admiral
Archbishop Von Stern speaking. Surrender now, un-
conditionally, and you will be allowed to retain your
lives and ships, leaving only your arms with us. Fail to
do so, and you will be destroyed."

"Stuff it, priest," roared Cato. He drove in at the
big ship, locked on, and matched airlocks. With a
final check to see that the fleets were now thoroughly
mixed, he clapped on his helmet and seized his pistol
and mace to take part in the boarding. The others
would have to take care of themselves now. There
was nothing further he could do. At the lock, his men

were having some difficulty in forcing the other ship's
hatch.

"What is it?" demanded Cato.

"Some alloy we've never run into, sir. It won't blow
or burn through." The first officer's voice was worried.

"Well, we can't just sit here and wait for them to
open the door!" He was furious and exasperated. But
open the door they did. With a sudden snap, the hatch
of the enemy ship slid aside, revealing a huge chamber stuffed with hundreds of armed men. They poured
aboard the flagship before the pirates could collect
their wits. Suddenly, Cato found himself fighting not
for victory or plunder, but for his life and the survival
of his ship.

A bulky man in a visored helmet loomed suddenly
before him, bearing a slug pistol and an axe. He fired
twice, but the slugs failed to penetrate Cato's cuirass.
The impact threw the admiral off balance, but he
managed to bring his assailant down with a slug from
his own pistol to the man's knee, finishing him with a
kick in the neck, below the helmet. He looked around
dazedly. He would not have believed it possible for so
many men to come out of one ship. With pistol, feet
and brass knuckles, he fought his way back to his
bridge, leaving the first officer with orders to close
the hatch at all costs. After a dozen fights all the way
back, he stumbled into the control room, dogging the
hatch behind him.

"What's going on?" he shouted into the intercom.
"Achillia, Horatio, Sestos, Josip, answer!"

"There's millions of them!" came Sestos' voice.
"It's like we locked onto a nest of quirtz! Every ship's
stuffed with 'em."

"Look! Here come more!" It was Achillia's voice.
Cato stared at his long-view screen. Sure enough,
there were more ships, hundreds of them, converging

from the far sides of the tiny moon. "Sorry, Cato, but I'm pulling out." Achillia's ships began to break off engagement.

"All ships, break and head for home!" Admiral Cato's voice was a despairing shriek. "Every man for himself."

"Attention, pirate fleet!" Somehow, the Church fleet had taken over his long-distance view screen. A man in a white robe with a red cross on the breast appeared at the screen. "This is Admiral Archbishop Von Stern speaking. Observe the following transmission." The screen flickered to show the main plaza of Port Royal, dominated by the looming presence of the *Gladius Dei.* So immense was the ship that Cato almost didn't notice the hundreds of uniformed church soldiers all over the plaza. The scene flickered again to show the interior of the Great Hall. In Cato's seat was a tiny, wizened man in red robes.

"This is Cardinal Van Horn speaking, by instantaneous transmission from Illyria. I have your home and your fleet at my mercy. Surrender now and be spared. The clemency of Rome is great. That is all." The cardinal broke transmission. The same scene was viewed by all in the pirate fleet who were not otherwise engaged.

"Break off engagement," commanded Cato, in a shaking voice. "Hand over your arms, there's nothing left to go back to." In the confusion, order gradually returned. Cato saw Achillia's ships break away as a unit and flee, pursued by a squadron of Church ships. Illyria wasn't her home, anyway. He hoped she'd make it. Soon all was still along the battle line, except near the tip of the pirates' left wing, where one fight was still raging.

When the *Fire Dragon* was within easy range, she launched a quick volley of rockets. Marius' counterfire accounted for most of them, but he took two hits, not enough to hole the ship, but sufficient to adversely affect the *Samnite's* steering and maneuverability. Marius cursed and tried a few shots with his beamers, but the old light-guns were ineffective, and used up energy at an alarming rate. Polycarpio wasn't using his beamers, weapons like that being far too impersonal for his tastes. He liked to feel his knife go in. A few more disabling rockets, and the *Fire Dragon* closed, locking onto the *Samnite.* Marius set his controls, pulled on his gauntlet and shot down the companionway to join his crew at the airlock.

At the lock, each man was in armor and atmosphere helmet, in case of holes appearing suddenly and embarrassingly in the fabric of their vessel. A space battle could always mean a swim in space. Handguns were out, reserve weapons handy. Hedulio stood beside Ludmilla, a heavy mace in each hand. Lame Deer's team was ready to attack at once when the hatch blew. They would be outnumbered at least two to one by the heavily-manned pirate vessel, so they had to take the initiative.

Miles had his slug pistol and truncheon, and was backed by Parma with his knife. Nearest the hatch stood Lame Deer, with his two tomahawks in his left hand, his pistol in his right. "Ready!" he shouted, then, with a grin, he recited the ancient formula: "Stand by to repel boarders!"

The hatch of the enemy ship slid open and the pirates began to board, but the warrior-monks fired and advanced instantly, taking the fight to the enemy. There was a brief, murderous struggle for control of the hatchway, then the monks were through and carrying the battle into the *Fire Dragon.* A line of pirates went down under a volley fired by the monks, then the fight was too close for projectile weapons.

Miles surveyed the boarding-room, looking for Cap-

tain Polycarpio. He spotted the captain on a stairway
leading from an upper deck to the boarding-room,
shrieking and urging his men on, literally frothing like
a mad dog. He fired into the milling crowd below him,
scoring hits on at least as many of his own men as
enemies. Miles began to fight his way toward the
stair, flanked by Parma on his right and Marius on his
left. Lame Deer was left to direct operations in the
boarding-room. Ludmilla was fighting on the edge of
the mob, seemingly having the time of her life, with
Hedulio plying his maces to see that she came to no
serious harm.

Suddenly, the scene which had been mere confusion turned to pure chaos. The power plant of the antiquated pirate ship failed, and men began floating
about the room, now in zero gravity. This added
whole new dimensions to the struggle. A fired slug
pistol would rocket the shooter backward to smash
against the nearest bulkhead, bowling over anyone
behind him. Nevertheless, several inexperienced
pirates attempted it, and suffered the consequences.
A knife thrust at an enemy merely pushed its wielder
away from his foe, failing to penetrate. Axe and mace
lost effectiveness when they weighed less than the
lightest feather. The only way to fight was to grapple,
seeking to hold an enemy fast while trying to push a
blade into him, or apply strangulation or bone-
breaking leverage. Only a beamer was truly effective
in such fighting, but beamers were far too dangerous
to use in such close quarters.

Miles, Marius and Parma, temporarily disoriented,
lost sight of Polycarpio. Miles was first to recover. He
saw Polycarpio soaring toward the hatch joining the
two ships. Getting his feet against a bulkhead, Miles
launched himself in pursuit, through a tangle of men
who caromed off one another and the bulkheads like
so many billiard balls. Behind him came Marius, like

a bowling ball among ninepins. Miles sailed through
the hatch, to fall with a resounding thud as soon as he
entered the artificial gravity of his own ship. Marius
landed on top of him and added to his miseries.

"Sorry, Miles," said the lanista. "Got to go save my
ship." He disappeared up the companion stair in pursuit of the pirate captain. Miles lurched to his feet
and staggered after Marius. He had to keep Polycarpio from separating the two ships. If he did, the ex-
pulsion of air from the boarding-room would blast
men all over space, certain death for any whose suits
had sustained damage in the fighting.

Marius had Polycarpio cornered in the control
room. He blocked the door as the pirate turned at bay.
His eyes were drugged pinpoints, his reflexes unnaturally quick.

"Marius, you traitor!" he screamed. "You sold us
out! We're being beaten!"

"So?" said Marius. "Nearly everyone of importance on Illyria was plotting against me. What did I
owe them?" He drew his knife and loosed his flail.

"I'll drink your blood!" shrieked Polycarpio de-
mentedly. He slid forward with reptilian grace, a
knife in one hand and a short sword in the other. Marius swung at Polycarpio's head with the flail and
made a simultaneous cut at his right knee-tendon with
the knife. The pirate ducked the flail and leaned over
the knife in a move so fluid that it would have been
beautiful had Marius been in a more aesthetic mood.
He replied with a flick of the short sword that drew
blood from Marius' cheek, where the lanista had
thrown back his visor for the sake of better vision.
Marius leaped back, and the two men circled, obli-
vious to anything else. For several minutes, they
danced, swung, cut, and thrust. Blades rang on
blades, helmets, gauntlet and metal-shod boot. Polycarpio, his strength sustained on drugs, began to tire

quickly. Marius was hardly even sweating.

Without warning, Polycarpio broke from a close exchange of cuts, deftly changed hands with his weapons, and threw his dagger. Marius threw his flail at the exact moment that the dagger left Polycarpio's hand. The dagger glanced from the gauntlet, but the pirate went down, both ankles broken by the flail. As he fell, Polycarpio drew a small beamer from his belt. But before he could squeeze the trigger-button, a small axe landed squarely in his forehead.

Marius looked around and saw a sizeable crowd watching him from the hatchway. Lame Deer came into the control room and retrieved his tomahawk from the late Captain Polycarpio's head. "Had to do that," he muttered. "Idiot would've burned a hole clean through both ships."

"How long have you been there?" asked Marius.

"Since the fight started," replied Miles, smiling. "It was a good one. I wouldn't have missed it for anything."

Parma and Ludmilla had left the grand banquet hall and found themselves some privacy in a small drawing room. Neither wanted to be the first to speak. Ludmilla looked older and strangely content. Parma fumbled nervously with his wine glass, then broke the silence.

"Ludmilla, I can't stay here. Father Miles has declared me eligible to enter the seminary on Loyola, and I have to go." His voice held equal parts of eagerness and despair.

"I know. It was obvious where you were headed from the moment you began taking instruction from him. Well, I have to go to school too, now. I'm going to be learning government and administration from the Benedictine professors the Church will be shipping in here. I've had my fun, playing lady pirate and fighting

ship-battles, but now it's time to go to work. I've a
planet to govern, after all. But I'll be sorry to see you
go."

"I'll be back." He was a bit disturbed at her equa-
nimity.

"Of course. But not any time soon. Not that it matters much, now that we can begin thinking of our lives
in terms of centuries." Nothing seemed very urgent
any more. They sipped their wine in silence.

In the spaceport waiting room Friar Jeremiah sat,
as travellers have done since carriages and vessels
were invented, waiting for his ship to leave. He
wasn't alone. The spaceport had become a very busy
place in the last few months. Many people, mostly in
some Church habit, were pouring in daily, others
leaving for business in parts of the galaxy now open
to citizens of the Flavian System for the first time in
centuries. He saw two men enter the room.

"Father Miles!"

"Ah, Jeremiah, so we're to be travelling companions again. Where are you bound?"

"Someplace called Tauros," replied the friar. "Just
rediscovered and crawling with heresy and black
magic. I'm to go there and have a look around before
they declare it a Restricted World." These were the
peculiar worlds that sometimes turned up, obeying no
rules of conventional physics or religion, where magic
really worked and local gods seemed to hold sway.
They were anathema to Christianity, Islam and
Judaism, and any person who landed on such a world
went at risk of his soul. Miles favored him with a com-
passionate look.

"Your superiors do seem determined upon placing
you out of your depth. I'm bound for Loyola, to enroll
Parma, here, in the seminary. After that, I'll be going
back to my classes on Gravitas." Jeremiah winced at

the memory of the place. "I hope my substitute hasn't fouled things up too badly."

The boarding-bell rang, and they found their seats aboard the shuttle which would take them to the big transport bound for the center of XV Sector. Before they left, another had come to join them.

"Ah, friend Marius," exclaimed Miles. "I thought perhaps you would be leaving."

"It's possible that there may be some hard feelings here among my former comrades, as well as my enemies. I judged it prudent to leave. Besides, your stories of the glories and opportunities available to a man of ambition and abilities in the rediscovered galaxy have given me an urge to travel and try my luck."

"God help us!" whispered Jeremiah. Marius was carrying a large bag, which he set on the floor with an audible clank. Wherever he was going, he would be prepared. Marius sat back in his recliner and closed his eyes. Whole new worlds were opening up for him. There would be businesses, rackets, operations on an unlimited scale, and opportunities of unguessable magnitude available for a man of his talents. A brave new world, indeed.

Cardinal Hilarion was occupying his seat as Supreme Nuncio of the Papal delegation to the UF. His star was ascendant, his success in settling the problem of the Magsaysay System had awed the entire UF and firmly assured his position in the Church hierarchy.

On the floor, the year's Speaker, Judah Ben Sanballat, was welcoming the new representative from the Flavian System. Cardinal Hilarion took notice for the first time that day. He remembered sending some agents to that system a few years before, and dispatching some vessels of the Church Militant when a short campaign was called for. Beyond the yearly reports from Benedictine and Dominican administration specialists, he had heard nothing of the system, which was just one tiny spot among so many big ones in the rediscovered galaxy.

The representative from the Flavians was a tall, stunning blond woman, some kind of consul, from what Hilarion could gather from the Speaker's welcome. It was unusual for a system to send a representative who was not a member of the clergy, but the Flavians were a new system and, Hilarion reflected, they probably preferred to be represented by a native. He signalled for his page. The young man was a Jesuit, doing his year's service at the UF before being sent on his first mission. He carried the cardinal's briefcase in one hand, and in the other the staff of a Cestus Dei initiate.

"You were in the Flavians once, weren't you?" asked the cardinal. "Tell me, Father, do you know who that young woman is down there?" The young priest smiled and fingered the handle of the knife he always wore under his robe.

"I know her quite well, Your Eminence. We were friends once, and, I hope, will be again. She is Ludmilla I, the hereditary consul of the Flavian System."

"So?" said the cardinal, eyeing the young man in a new light. "Well, it's good to know that all your brotherhood aren't cold-blooded ascetics. Go tell Her Holiness that the representative from yet another Papal System has arrived, and see to it that the consul receives her invitation to the banquet tomorrow. As a matter of fact, you'd better deliver it yourself." He sat back with a chuckle.

"With pleasure, Your Eminence." The young priest bowed and left the cardinal's side, grinning. When he was out of the Great Hall and in a deserted corridor, he began twirling his staff. He twirled it all the way to the Pope's office.

Best-Selling Science Fiction from TOR

DAVID DRAKE

●●●●●●●●●●●●●●●●●●●●●●●●●

☐	48-541-7	**Time Safari**	$2.75
☐	48-552-2	**The Dragon Lord**	$2.95
☐	48-544-1	**Skyripper**	$3.50

C.M. Kornbluth

☐	48-512-2	**Not This August** C.M. Kornbluth revised by Frederik Pohl	$2.75
☐	48-543-3	**The Syndic** C.M. Kornbluth revised by Frederik Pohl	$2.75
☐	48-570-0	**Gunner Cade/Takeoff** C.M. Kornbluth and Judith Merril	$2.95

Best-Selling Science Fiction from TOR

☐	48-549-2	**Paradise** Dan Henderson	$2.95
☐	48-531-X	**The Taking of Satcon Station** Barney Cohen and Jim Baen	$2.95
☐	48-555-7	**There Will Be War** J.E. Pournelle	$2.95
☐	48-566-2	**The McAndrew Chronicles** Charles Sheffield	$2.95
☐	48-567-0	**The Varkaus Conspiracy** John Dalmas	$2.95
☐	48-526-3	**The Swordswoman** Jessica Amanda Salmonson	$2.75
☐	48-584-0	**Cestus Dei** John Maddox Roberts	$2.75